Geo. G. (George Gordon) Scott

Clumber Chase, or, Love's Riddle Solved by a Royal Sphinx

A Tale of the Restoration: Vol. III.

Geo. G. (George Gordon) Scott

Clumber Chase, or, Love's Riddle Solved by a Royal Sphinx
A Tale of the Restoration: Vol. III.

ISBN/EAN: 9783337137229

Printed in Europe, USA, Canada, Australia, Japan

Cover: Foto ©Andreas Hilbeck / pixelio.de

More available books at **www.hansebooks.com**

In 2 Vols. Price 21s.

(Second Edition.)

THE MARKED MAN.

By FRANK TROLLOPE.

"'The Marked Man' is by many degrees the best novel we have met with this season."—Bell's Messenger.

"It will be read with avidity."—Liverpool Albion.

"The best novel we have read for years."—Record.

"Mr. Trollope has achieved a great success in the 'Marked Man' which is not alone equal to any novels that have emanated from the pens of the clever family of the Trollopes, but is far superior to the great bulk of fictions that have inundated the libraries for some time past. In the *dramatis personæ* there is a marked individuality. The character of Theodore Hook is so true to nature, that we can scarcely realise the fact that the racy humour, the brilliant witticisms, and the clever sayings, are not his own instead of Mr. Trollope's."—Brighton Examiner.

"Jackson, the Irish man-servant—Lady Bendishe's lady's-maid—old Wilson, the housekeeper—and the pert, but faithful, little Cockney factotum at the cottage, are life-like sketches."—Athenæum.

CLUMBER CHASE,

OR

LOVE'S RIDDLE SOLVED BY A ROYAL SPHINX.

A TALE OF THE RESTORATION.

IN THREE VOLUMES.

BY

GEORGE GORDON SCOTT.

"Acerrima proximorum Odia."
TACITUS.

" I love thee to the level of every day's
   Most quiet need, by sun and candle light,
   I love thee freely, as men strive for right ;
   I love thee purely, as they turn from praise.
   I love thee with a passion put to use
   In my old grief, and with my childhood's faith
   I love thee with a love I seemed to lose
   With my lost Saints, I love thee with the breath,
   Smiles, tears of all my life !—and if God choose
   I shall but love thee ' better after death.' "
                                        E. B. BROWNING.

VOL. III.

LONDON :

T. CAUTLEY NEWBY, PUBLISHER,
30, WELBECK STREET, CAVENDISH SQUARE.
1871.

CLUMBER CHASE.

CHAPTER I.

THE FIRST SIGN.

EIGHT months had passed since Mrs. Phillipa Broderick's death, and nine since her nephew's most mysterious disappearance, and not the slightest tidings had been heard of the latter ; the outside world had even ceased to wonder, or to conjecture on the subject, and so had passed on, as is its wont, to utter oblivion about him ; for it is astonishing, or rather would be so, if the fact were not as old as creation itself, by what easy and pleasant stages the said world travels swiftly away from all the misfortunes and miseries of others, and never loses its time in tarrying by the way, to read the epitaphs of defunct destinies. It has been said that love cannot exist without hope ; but this, like all other rules, has its exceptions ; for Dorothy had long ceased to hope, but she had by no means ceased to love. Even Oliver Hartsfoot, who had so long hoped against hope, now began to gird on his armour of resignation, but it was with a heavy heart, for his own existence seemed to re-wither, as he felt for the poor blighted young life which had twined now for two years round the sapless stem of his, and imparted to him from its own freshness and bloom a sort of fictitious vitality.

It was a bright, warm July morning : the birds were singing as blithely and as sweetly as they could possibly have done at their first concert in Eden, before the dark Triumveri—Sin, Sorrow, and Death—usurped the rule of the world. The glass door, and the two windows in Oliver Harts-foot's dining-room looking upon the Mall, were all open ; the table was laid for breakfast,—and from the profusion of scarlet strawberries, large pouting, bigaroon cherries, and golden apricots that adorned it, looked like an altar raised by some pious pagan to Pomona—these fruits, with the lovely flowers that intersected them, and the large glass jug full of thick cream, had all arrived fresh from The Chestnuts, with a kind little note from Dorothy, about an hour before— and near the window sat Master Hartsfoot, read- ing Plato, and awaiting the arrival of his two guests, Mr. Locke and Dr. Fairbrace. Noah Pump had made several unnecessary entrances into the room, and exits from it ; had even coughed slightly, and cleared his voice, to attract his master's attention ; but all in vain, for that taste- less individual, it appeared, preferred Plato to

Pump, and made no sign ; till at length, fairly
worried by the irritation of Mr. Pump's feeble
imitations of the rumblings of an earthquake,
achieved by dragging chairs along the sides of
the polished oak floor, to which the Turkey carpet
did not extend, and crumpling and rattling "The
Whitehall Gazette," Master Oliver looked up,
and said—

"That will do, Pump ; Barton has put everything, till you bring the breakfast when Mr.
Locke and Dr. Fairbrace come."

"Beg pardon, sir," said Noah, making a stand,
like all persons long in office, against this sort of
summary dismissal, "but it's on my mind, it
raley is."

"What's on your mind ?" said his master, now
closing his book, and looking at him really with
attention.

"Why, sir, this here tremenjus piece of wicked-
ness—the *on* accountable vanishing away, for all
the world like a *Sperr it*, of the poor dear Cappen
—Cappen Broderick in course understood."

"It's on a great many persons' minds for that,
Master Noah,—and on their hearts, too. I'd
give all that I most value of my small posses-
sions, if I could only get the slightest clue to the
mystery."

"You'll ex-cuse me, sir, what I'm a going to
say," and here he twisted a napkin he held in his

hand into a sort of model man-of-war's rope;
" but it strikes me forcible—it do, indeed, sir—
as they has been a trying some of their infarnel
hexperiments upon the poor young gentleman."

" Why, what *do* you mean, Noah? And who
on earth do you mean by ' they ' and ' trying experiments upon him ?' "

" Why *them*, sir."

And Noah nodded his head, winked his right
eye, and jerked his thumb over his right shoulder
in the direction of the cedar parlour, or rather of
the laboratory within it.

" You are enough to drive any one wild with
your nods and winks and riddles ; do, for Heaven's
sake, speak out in plain language, so that your
meaning may be got at, if you have any meaning."

" Well, sir, you'll promise not to be offended,
cause in course it ain't no fault of *yourn*, though
there is summut of a proverb 'bout evil communications corrupting on them as has manners,
which has often made me afeard for you ; least
ways, that you might be 'ticed or snared into
what you had little notion of."

Hartsfoot, who thought by all this beating
about the bush that he had some positive intelligence respecting Gilbert, was now fairly worked
into a passion, and rising from his seat and flinging the book he held to a table at the other end
of the room, exclaimed—

"In the name of all the asses that ever brayed, once for all, will you leave your confounded inuendoes and conundrums, and say in plain English what you are driving at?"

"Well, sir, they *does* do most *on*accountableist things, and that's no news to you; and don't you think but they may, without meaning on it; mind I don't say as they *meant* it, but they may have missed the trick, and done it wrong upon the Cappen?"

"Once for all, who *do* you mean by they? And what trick have they done?"

"Why, them there saveons, to be sure. There, it's out now, and I feel considerable better."

Angry as he was at this solution of Mr. Pump's complex enigmas, Hartsfoot burst into a tremendous fit of laughter.

"Why, surely," said he, as soon as he could speak, "you are not such an arrant donkey as to suppose that scientific gentlemen of high standing, or *saveons*, as you call them, would try murderous experiments upon any one, much less upon a person so universally loved and respected as poor Captain Broderick?"

"I may be a great fool," rejoined Noah, shaking his head solemnly, "and better be that than a knave; and in course the quality is, and ought to be, the best judge of fools, but I can give you a case in *pint*, sir, of the doings of them saveons, and it was done only last week, at White Hall, too, under his Majesty's very nose, and he seed it with his own eyes. True as I stan' here, they had a dead sheep brought into the matted gallery, and if Surgeon Pierce, Sir John Baber, and a lot of these here saveons, didn't bewitch the poor beast in some most *impus* manner; but as sure as your there, sir, it stood up on all fours agin, just as naitrel as if it had been alive. Surgeon Pierce said as there war only one man in the world as know'd how to do this, and he had taught him."*

"Yes, I have heard Mr. Pierce describe this phenomenon, and it certainly is very extraordinary, but it is all produced by electricity and natural causes, which would be too long to describe to you; but I really cannot see that giving momentary motion to a dead body is a case in point to suspecting people to putting to death a living one."

"Naitrel causes!" groaned Noah, "strange naitrel causes to snap their fingers at natur in the most diabolicalist manner. Don't 'ee be lead away by 'em. Now *pray* don't 'ec, my dear good master, for it is contrairy to the natur of things, to 'tice angels into doing on the devil's work."

* An Italian, a Venetian of the name of Salviati, who had, as a matter of scientific experiment, anticipated the discovery of the Bolognese Galvani by nearly a century, but neither practised nor perfectionised it like the latter, but had simply hit upon the fact of the peculiar sort of electricity contained in the body of all animals.

" I thank you, Noah, for your anxiety touching my welfare," smiled Hartsfoot, " but I do assure you that I have not the least intention of doing the devil's work, nor have my friends any of entrapping me into doing it."

" Not knowingly, I knows you haven't; but lor, them saveons, and save alls, they ain't the sort to save souls."

" You have not heard anything, then, about poor Captain Broderick ? I was in hopes when you began that you had."

" Not I; I'd give three years' wages to hear for certain sure that he was alive, and another year's to the back of that to set the Abbey bells a ringing when I had heerd it."

Here Mr. Locke and Dr. Fairbrace arrived together at the glass door ; and while their host welcomed them, Noah withdrew to order up breakfast.

"I fear," said Locke, " we have kept you waiting."

" Not in the least," interposed Hartsfoot.

" But the fact is," resumed Locke, " Dr. Fairbrace was good enough to meet me, by appointment, at poor Mrs. Marvell's, Andrew's niece, to see what could be done to ease her of some of her burden, poor soul ! She is nearly distracted with all the sapient *advice* she gets, but not one grain of help ; each of the intermeddlers having some

pet scheme of their own, and each being Popes
in his estimate of his own wisdom; and if she
does not choose to follow one, or rather all of
these plans, however different, she may starve,
for all they care. Moreover, as she has a rich,
childless uncle, he is the person who *ought* to
help her; and if she is so foolish as not to apply
to him—though they know how infamously he
has behaved to her, and that she would rather die
than do so—why then she may die, and there's
an end on't."

"Ah!" sighed Dr. Fairbrace, as they seated
themselves at table, "if relations in particular,
and everybody else in general, always did, or
could be made to do, exactly what they *ought* to
do, no one would ever be in any sort of distress,
or ever want anything; and if all this A B C
plain sailing routine of doing this, that, or the
other, was practicable, no one in an untoward position, who was not an idiot, would ever want advice,
or even, what is much more valuable, assistance.
But there are mysteries of insurmountable difficulties in all exceptional positions, only known
to the victims themselves. This, we English,
never take into consideration, even in the broad
generalisation of theory, much less by the humane
and conscientious, but troublesome process of
weighing and sifting, and putting ourselves in
others' places. Everything with us—Legisla-

tion, Charity, Sympathy, Religion ! itself, all
seems formed out of a sort of block machinery,
so that we have, nor can have, no individuality
in anything : all is routine. Oh ! yes, of course
it is our duty to help our fellow-creatures, and to
relieve distress ; but, then, it must be done in a
proper orthodox way,—people *must* be happy, re-
spectable, or even miserable in a legitimate
manner. As we have made arrangements for
them, we classify all moral, misery, oppression,
injustice, and distress, under certain categories ;
people *must* range their grievances under one of
these, for out of them there is neither redress nor
salvation, nor, least of all, compassion. Whereas,
if people would allow themselves to be sentient
and responsible beings, instead of a mere working portion of the great general orthodox machinery, and have sufficient identity to look into
individual positions, they would find that there
are no two cases precisely alike, any more than
there are any two faces. And that, consequently,
no one's difficulties, or grievances, can be lumped
in a category, and adjusted by rule. It is this
want of care, and of all consideration for others,
that, in a legislative point of view, ever renders
most things a bungle in this country. Is a
barrack, or any other public building to be
erected, who would ever dream of devoting half
an hour to planning and organising what would

be the most conducive to the health, comfort, and
convenience of those who are to live in them?
No—the only thing thought of is to get a con-
tract for them at the least possible outlay—which
is generally the dearest way in the end—and
never even superintend it, to see that the con-
tract is carried out properly so far as it goes."

" Too true," assented Locke and Hartsfoot.

And then the latter, giving vent to the thought
uppermost in his mind, said—

" Have you been able to glean any intelligence
about poor young Broderick?"

" I am sorry to say," replied Locke, " that I
have not; but I was not a little disgusted yesterday at hearing a conclave of dowagers, with
husband-wanting daughters, at the Duchess of
Newcastle's, pitying—within his hearing, of
course—' poor dear Sir Allen! and lamenting
how ill he was looking from grief at his son's
disappearance and his sister's death, and that
really he must be a man of great sensibility (!)
to take things so much to heart, and how they
wished—no doubt of it!—that he could form
some new ties to prevent his brooding so much
over his losses!'"

" Oh!" said Hartsfoot, "I feel so full of gall
as to be quite wicked, when I look round the
world and see how guilt flourishes—how virtue
suffers; to see how selfishness, injustice, pride,

and cruelty prosper, increase, and luxuriate; while the disinterested, the just, the merciful, the generous, the unassuming, not only fail, suffer, and lose, but are run over and mangled by the gilded chariot wheels of infamy!"

"Aye, truly," said Dr. Fairbrace, "while we only feel and writhe under it, and are not sufficiently cool to reflect upon it, this dark tortuous mystery is the greatest trial and touchstone of our faith; but we must remember that we are specifically told that the wicked *shall* prosper in this world—in fact, that it is *their* world, and all things prove it. So we must not be too hard upon the devil for his one virtue of taking care of his own."

"We must also recollect," said Locke, "that clever bad men—and no man can be successfully bad without being clever—invariably contrive to varnish and conceal their iniquity by false rumours and purchased panegyrics; for they never lose sight of Horace's too true assertion—that the world is invariably less influenced by those things which are *subjecta oculis* than those which are *demissa per aurem.* And thus they find their account in the oblivious eyes and retentive ears of a somewhat asinine and always indifferent public."

"That is quite true; for apathy is naturally the inseparable shadow of our national selfishness."

" Yes, and the worst of it is," said Locke, " that while the raw material remains the same, revolutions only bring us a change of evil, not an extirpation of it."

" That would be difficult," replied the Doctor, " since it appears to me that in all revolutions or political convulsions, the principle—or rather the want of it—upon which the sworn allies of the upsetting party act, is the same upon which Luther and his boon companion Ausdorf, on the one hand, and Melancthon, his disciple, successor, and in every respect superior, acted on the other. Ausdorf going one step beyond his sensual master, and maintaining that *good works are a hindrance to salvation!* in vindication of his fradulent tenet that of ' imputed justice,' to the exclusion of all acts of virtue and good works. Upon this, what I should call rank heresy, here is the Christian humility! with which Doctor Martin Luther vaunts himself. ' This article,' he writes, ' shall remain in spite of all the world. It is I, Martin Luther, Evangelist, who say it; let no one, therefore, attempt to infringe it; neither the Emperor of the Romans, nor the Turks, nor of the Tartars, neither the Pope, nor the Monks, nor the Nuns, nor the kings, nor the princes, nor the devils in hell. If they attempt it, may infernal flames be their recompense. What I say here is to be taken for an inspiration of the Holy Ghost!' "

"Yet, notwithstanding this pretty piece of fiatical blasphemy, and despite the terrible threats and imprecations of their master, Melancthon, with the rest of the Lutherans, immediately after his death abandoned this monstrous article, and went over to the opposite extreme of Semipelagianism—that is, they not only admitted the imperative necessity of good works, but by way of clenching their recantation, they also taught that good works are before the grace of God! And so it is with political reformers; they generally part company to climb the faster, and thus jump from one heretical extreme to the other, troubling their heads as little about their former desperately contested and vehemently maintained opinions as about the apples they stole, and the tarts they eat in childhood; once these have given place to venison and champagne. Neither are they without the means of raising a large auxiliary force of precedents, like one Oliander, a Lutheran, who asserted that for and against good works there were twenty-seven different opinions, all drawn from scripture, and held by different members of the Augsburg or Lutheran Confession, and your mob leader—for all politicians *are* mob leaders—or at least, mob seekers, ' with a difference,' will never be at a loss to find double that number of reasons to prove that the two opposite extremes of his words and deeds were drawn equally from the same (of course) pure! source—to wit, their zeal for the common weal, *Credat Judeas!*"

"Well, may Dryden say," said Hartsfoot, "that—

> 'Luther, Calvin, Zuinglius, holy chiefs,
> Have made a battle royal of beliefs;
> And, like wild horses, several ways have whirled,
> The tortured text about the Christian world !'"

"Aye," rejoined Dr. Fairbrace; "and no wonder that the Roman Catholics say that the staple of Protestant faith seems to be doubt."

"All of which," said Locke, "only proves the truth of Sir Dudley Carleton's dictum—'that there will be mistakes in Divinity while men preach, and errors in government while men govern.'"

"That will there," assented the Doctor and Hartsfoot simultaneously.

"And now," added the latter, "I am going to tell you of a discovery I have made, and although I don't think it will exactly rival any of Lord Worcester's in a scientific point of view, I still think it a very valuable one in a social point of view, and you shall both judge whether I overrate my discovery; it is as to the way of preparing and drinking the new China shrub, which we call tay, but which, I understand, should be tea."

"Horrid stuff!" interrupted Locke. "The best tay—or tea—house, as you say it ought to be called, is at 'The Mulberry Tree;' and yet it appears to me always like a very indifferent sort of physic, which one would get much better, and without so much parade, at the apothecary's."

"Exactly," said Hartsfoot, "because they stew, as it were, the life and soul out of it, by keeping it like some poor wretch in Chancery, so long in hot water, till it becomes flat and bitter, and conveys to one a perfect idea of demented senna; but the sea captain, who told me that it should be called tea, and who has been many voyages to China, tells me that the Celestials, who even drink it with their dinner, make it very quickly. That is, with quite boiling water, taking care the teapot is well warmed first, by being rinced with boiling water first before the tea is put in, and then, instead of at first putting little water, as we do, and then adding more, they pour in all the boiling water at once, and hardly let it stay a minute, but pour out the tea quickly, which from not standing or stewing, has then a delicious aroma, though my friend, the captain, told me also that we never can drink tea in perfection, as in Cathay they gather it fresh from their gardens as they want it, as we do our salads. Well, I tried this plan of making it quickly, and truly found it a wonderful improvement; but *that* is not my grand discovery, but only the sea captain's experience. But here is mine, and judge for yourselves," added he, pouring out two cups full, into which he put not only sugar, but cream.

"Oh! come," cried Locke; "*this* is really delicious. As many more cups of *that* as you please to give me."

"And you, doctor; what say you?"

"I say—that is, I shall say, when you have given me another cup—that it is some superior sort of nectar, reserved exclusively for the goddesses; for it is ten thousand times too good for such an old scamp as that Jupiter, and all his fellow disreputables."

"I'm glad you both so thoroughly appreciate it. Well, the cream was my grand discovery—*mine*, remember, exclusively mine—for in China they have no milk, or at least drink none; and so, *cæteris paribus*, could not have cream."

"I'll tell you what though, Hartsfoot, would be a still *greater* improvement, *sans equivoque*, if one could drink that now really delicious beverage out of larger cups, for these confounded little acorn cups are only fit for Oberon and Titania, though quite large enough, in all conscience, for the demented senna, as you truly call it, that one gets at the taverns," said Locke.

"I thought of that, too," rejoined Hartsfoot, "and think I shall have some made with the still farther improvement of a handle to them, that one may not burn one's fingers, as one does with these egg shell affairs ; I'll have the cups made the size and shape of that chalcidony *tazza* that Mr. Evelyn gave me, with saucers in proportion, and a wreath of the tea shrub itself painted round them, which I think, with its blossom, will look very pretty on the white china."

"Beautiful, I should think," said Dr. Fairbrace.

"Well, gentlemen, you may be as ungrateful as you please, and despatch these delicious strawberries in silence ; but I cannot follow your example," said Locke, "for with the cream they are simply perfection."

"*L'éloge se fait en mangeant,* you know," smiled Hartsfoot. "But I assure you I have no intention of being ungrateful, for they come like all my other good things, from my good fairy, pretty Mistress Dorothy. Tell me, Doctor Fairbrace, how she continues to bear up under her heavy, heavy burden, for one so young and so fragile ?"

"Ah! poor, gentle, little soul," sighed Doctor Fairbrace; "Mrs. Neville told me of her heaviest sorrow and hardest trial—her engagement to young Broderick. She bears up bravely—too bravely—for it is a moral Penelope's web the poor girl is always weaving during the day, by the high strain of endurance and apparent resignation she imposes on herself before her mother, and the unwinding or letting down process at night must be terrible, and is beginning to tell upon her; for her peach-like cheeks are gone, and have left her face not so much pale, in the ordinary sense, as with a sort of delicate fairness, like the colourless bloom of a white flower. But for the happiness she is always in some way or other bestowing upon, or anticipating for others, I don't think she could exist at all under the complete wreck of her own. However, I play the part of Job's comforter to her, and tell her that her trials are a judgment on her, for having reversed the orthodox order of things, and been an angel *before* she became a martyr."

"Poor young thing! poor young thing! so good, so admirable, so loveable in every way; it *is* hard," said Locke.

"Truly is it," sighed Hartsfoot; "the muscular strength and sterner stuff that forms the Hercules of man's resolution, is often almost vanquished in wrestling with that Nemean lion—a tortured and disappointed heart. Then what a fearful odds must there be against a poor weak woman in such a deadly combat?"

"Fearful! indeed," echoed Dr. Fairbrace.

" Yet He who tempers the wind to the shorn lamb, has made their strength in what we call their weakness : we are oaks, and by contending against, are often up-rooted by the storm ; they are reeds, which bend to it, and though it prostrates, still it passes over them."

As the Doctor was still speaking, Noah Pump entered the room, and, bending down, said, in a low voice, to his master—

" If you please, sir, Ferrol, Captain Broderick's servant, have called, and wants to know if you could see him, as he wishes to see you partickler."

" What !" said Hartsfoot, tossing his napkin on the table, pushing back his chair, and turning quite round so as to look up in Noah's face, " has he heard any tidings of his master ?"

" Don't know, sir. I axed him fast enough, but he shook his head—leastways, he wouldn't say nothing to me, but said as he wished to see you immejet."

" You will not mind Captain Broderick's servant coming in here, will you ?" asked Hartsfoot, appealing to his guests.

" Quite the contrary," said they ; " we shall be very glad, for he may have heard some news of him."

" Heaven grant it may be so ! Show him in, Pump," said Hartsfoot.

When Ferrol bowed himself into the room, he was evidently much agitated, and trembled violently; Hartsfoot rose, poured out a glass of wine, and offered it to him.

"I thank you, sir, you are very kind; but I would rather not."

"You may speak freely, Ferrol, before these gentlemen—they are sincerely interested in Captain Broderick—and I do hope you have come to tell me that at last you have had tidings—good tidings of your master."

"Well, sir," said Ferrol, " I would rather have your judgment on the matter than my own; my wishes set too strong that way for me not to dread the chance of being fooled into drifting into hope, and I know it was a rule with the Captain always to treat every anonymous communication with contempt, however plausible or friendly it might appear. But here, sir, is a letter that was thrown down into Mrs. Swinburn's area this morning, when, or by whom, I have no idea; but she, poor woman, in spite of all I can say to put her off of it, so thoroughly believes in the vague good tidings of this letter, that she has actually ordered new furniture for the Captain's drawing-room."

Hartsfoot eagerly took the letter; it was clean, and written upon good paper, and sealed with a figure of Hope, leaning upon an anchor, but there was no guessing at character, or tracing the author from the handwriting, inasmuch as the whole letter was written in an imitation of printed characters. It was, moreover, well spelt, as spelling went in those days. These were the contents :—

"To Mistress Swinburn,
     "97, In the Pell Mell,
              "London,
"over against 'The Young Man's Club House.'

"GOOD MRS. SWINBURN,—

          "What ever else you do, don't lett Cap^n. Broderick's lodgings, as you don't know the moment he may return—though not like a thief in the night ;—but it won't bee just yett, nor for many months to come. The Cap^n. is quite safe, and well ; ditto, the dogs. 'And all's well that ends well,' as you who go to the Playhouse know. So don't go, and make 'Much ado about nothing,' by blabbing this news about the town, but keep your own Council, and, like his Majesty's, lett it bee a Privy Council, except to friend Ferrol, and those whom it may concern.

     "No more at present, from your
          "Humble Servant,
              "NEMO.
          "July 20th, 1670."

Hartsfoot read this letter over twice, apparently weighing every word; his two companions in their turn did the same, Ferrol watching their three countenances as they read, as if his life had depended upon their verdict.

" Well ?" asked Hartsfoot, as soon as Locke had laid down the letter.

" Well," said Locke, " I am of Dame Swinburn's opinion, that this is an authentic—I mean a *bonâ fide* document."

" So am I," said Hartsfoot ; " but your reasons for so believing ?"

" In the first place there is no sympton of extortion, and evidently no motive for extorting, and no attempt at beguiling, or betraying, or leading into, or on to anything. Had it been from an impostor, or a person with any nefarious design, it would have been conceived in a very different vein ; it would have said, if a certain sum of money were sent to, or left at such a place, &c., &c., or if Mrs. Swinburn on such a day and such an hour, would be at some particular spot, she would hear tidings of Captain Broderick. Again, an impostor in his or her anxiety to appear plausible and authentic, would have, as the lawyers say, ' proved too much ;' he would, either by hints or round assertions, have attempted to account for the young man's disappearance, or invented some pretext for his not writing, or for his not being able to write, but there is nothing of the kind. Again, the writer is evidently well and correctly acquainted with the *carte du pays* of the Captain's household, and calls his servant ' friend Ferrol,' allowing him to be informed of his master's safety and well-being, but prohibiting this much news of him being made a matter of town talk. Lastly, we must recollect that with the exception of his own father, the young man was so well beloved, that he had not an enemy in the world ; and the absence of all motive for fraud or imposition is in my mind the best guarantee for the genuineness of this letter. And although the mystery of Captain Broderick's disappearance remains as dark, or indeed, darker than ever, I think we may fairly conclude, without any fear of future disappointment, that he really *is* safe and well."

"And your opinion, Dr. Fairbrace?" asked Hartsfoot.

"You have just heard it verbatim; only so much better expressed in Mr. Locke's words."

"There! My good fellow," said Hartsfoot, turning to Ferrol, "we all three believe this letter to be true and genuine, and that you will, as it states, in some few months see your master again, safe and well."

"Oh! God Almighty bless you, gentlemen," exclaimed poor Ferrol, the tears gushing from his eyes as he was about to fall upon his knees, had not Hartsfoot prevented him, and insisted upon his taking the wine to drink Captain Broderick's health and safe return.

" Now, Ferrol, will you trust this letter with me till to-morrow ?"

" Oh ! for ever, sir, if you wish."

" Nay," smiled Hartsfoot, " curb your generosity, for we might both be indicted for felony ; you for stealing Mrs. Swinburn's letter, and I for accepting it, knowing it to be stolen.   But come to me the day after to-morrow, and you shall have it safely back ; and now take my advice, go home, try and get out of your bad habit of not eating, which Mrs. Swinburn makes such sad complaints about, or your master won't know you when he comes back, and will insist upon looking out for a more comely servant, more like what his much valued Ferrol was.   And as idleness is the root of all evil, employ your hands and amuse your mind by helping Mrs. Swinburn to arrange the new furniture in Captain Broderick's drawing-room.   There, off with you," said Master Hartsfoot, opening the dining-room door for him, and giving him a slight push, which, gentle as it was, acted as such an impetus, that it sent him straight into the arms of Mr. Pump, who was hovering about in the hall, and Ferrol, " improving the occasion," as itinerant preachers say, in the exuberance of his delight, nearly squeezed the Pump dry, or at least, all the breath out of his body, as he said—

"Oh! Pump, I begin now to hope that I really shall see him again!'"

"Who? the Cappen? Hooray! Well, Ferrol, you always was a sober chap; so when the Cappen *does* come back mind it's to the Pump you comes to drink his health."

"Now," said Hartsfoot, so soon as the door had closed upon Ferrol, "I'm sure Mr. Locke will excuse us; and I think the sooner you and I, Dr. Fairbrace, take water at Westminster Stairs and reach The Chestnuts with this letter, the better."

"So say I," said Locke; "and I'll walk with you as far as Westminster Hall."

Hartsfoot rang; Mr. Pump appeared somewhat compressed from his late squeeze.

"My hat and gloves, Pump, and tell Barton to get ready directly to come with me; I am going to Richmond, and he can take the opportunity of seeing his mother and sister."

CHAPTER II.

THE SUREST AND SHORTEST ROAD TO HAPPINESS IS TO MAKE OTHERS HAPPY.

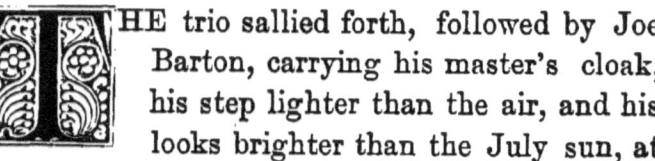HE trio sallied forth, followed by Joe Barton, carrying his master's cloak, his step lighter than the air, and his looks brighter than the July sun, at the prospect of seeing his mother and sister, to say nothing of a row up the river and another row back in the cool of the evening. They hurried on, as kind-hearted people do when they are the bearers of good news to those who have long waited for it, but waited in vain. Locke had just left them to go into Westminster Hall, to call at Gillyflower and Heanman's for *Hobb's Three Discourses on Humane Nature,* which they had just published, wishing them God speed, when Master Hartsfoot saw approaching, at a somewhat slow and dignified-pace what, upon the first casual view, appeared like a small meadow completely overrun with buttercups, so that the indigenous green only appeared here and there with a few poppies or

some other scarlet field flowers cropping up at
rare intervals; but upon closer inspection it
turned out to be Mr. Pepys' bright yellow coach,
with his green fustian liveries, green reins, and
the horses' manes and tails platted with scarlet
ribbons, the tails afterwards done up in a club,
for all the world like an ancestral chignon, and
altogether as gorgeous an affair, barring the
Lord Mayor's coach,* as could be seen on a summer's day. Very erect and very forward on the
front seat sat Mr. Pepys'; for what is the use,
or at least the pleasure, of having a coach
—and such a coach!—if one does not let the
groundlings see to whom it belongs; and know,
whose are the horses and wheels that be-

* This was the coach that Pepys built, of which we hear so
much in his "Diary," and the most amusing thing we *do* hear
about it is, not that Mrs. Pepys "was ready to jump out of her
skin"—which would have been a pity, since it was such a fine
one—when she heard she was really going to jump into her own
coach, but Mr. Pepys' lamentations the very *next day after he had
this coach*, of "the way hack vehicles jostled gentlem coaches
in the Park, which really should not be allowed!" Now, verily,
this is a little too oligarchical, considering that Mr. Pepys himself
had all his life been one of these hackney coach nuisances till
within four-and-twenty hours of that aristocratic protest of his.
There seems to have been as great a discrepancy in the prices of
things in those days as there was between the mixture of ranks
in society, for this very coach, we are told, despite all its splen-
dours, cost new £53; while upon one of the many occasions upon
which Mrs. Pepys was stowed away in the country Mr. Pepys in-
forms us that he "did pay two shillings for a pound of cherries
for Knipp." And he mentions on another occasion, giving six
shillings for two Thames eels. House rent and coal appear to
have been always dear, while on the other hand servants' wages,
including those of cooks, were £3 and £4 a year; but even with
regard to this, there occurs another anomaly, for Mrs. Pepys'
maid, Mercer, and all her own maids that she had in succession
had £20 a year, which are the average wages of *femmes de chambre*
in the present day.

spatter their plebeian feet with their native mire.
But all this splendour was confined to his equip-
age, for Mr. Pepys himself was attired in solemn
black, his very wig having gone into mourning,
and being perfect jet instead of the flowing
chestnut locks that used to float over his shoulders
of yore.   The fact was, that for the last ten
months Mr. Pepys had been a widower; he had
been a tour through France and Holland, or as
he himself said " in foreign parts," with his wife,
who had returned from thence quite well; but a
few days after her arrival in England had gone
out of her way to catch a fever, of which she
died.   And Mr. Pepys, having done everything
in " the genteelest " and most orthodox manner
with regard to her obsequies, had, so far as the
Knipps, and Kates, and " Barbarys " went, become quite a reformed character; for he did find
that they did expect him, now he was free, to
spend too much upon them, and not any longer
having his wife's door to lay the limits of his
expenditure upon these ladies at, he did find that
the only way was to lay it upon his grief, and so
forbear playhouses, taverns, valentines, and fair-
ings, and more especially presents of sacques,
whisks, trinkets, and fruit; and indeed he did
find the benefit of keeping to this vow at the end
of six months, for in making up his accounts he
did find he was £82 7s. 9d. richer than at that

time last year; and though of course he was very
sorry for his poor wife, and the funeral had been
a great expense—not that he did grudge it—and
Mr. Hewer did advise him to exchange his wife's
jewels for plate, which he did think he should do,
so that on the whole everything was for the best,
and God be praised that he did see himself in a
position to eat off plate, and to continue to keep
his coach.

Master Hartsfoot having held up his hand to
the " green fustian" coachman to stop, thought
he would try and find out if Mr. Pepys, through
his official sources, had heard anything of Gilbert
Broderick. So now advancing to the coach door,
he said—

" Good-day, Mr. Pepys; I'm glad to see you
abroad taking the air."

"Good Lord! Master Hartsfoot, to see what
changes may come to us when we do least expect them. I do try to bear up, but for all many
may envy me. I do feel very lonely in my coach
now all by myself, for my poor wife used to take
such delight in it. And I am often sorry now,
that I did check her in the telling of her long
stories from Grand Cyrus—for ah! Master Hartsfoot, death is a longer story than any in Grand
Cyrus!"

"A more natural one, at all events," said
Hartsfoot; "and one that I sincerely hope poor

Mrs. Pepys has found has a more glorious ending. Pray have you heard any news of 'The
Surprise'?"

"I did hear that Mr. Sheres had arrived quite
safe in Tangiers; for that matter," murmured
Mr. Pepys, "he might, as it has turned out, as
well have remained in England."

Now *àpropos de bottes*, as this ending of Mr.
Pepy's reply might have appeared to Hartsfoot,
it was perfectly *àpropos* to his own train of
thought about "his poor wife's" delight in the
coach, and in Grand Cyrus, and in Mr. Sheres!

"I'm glad Mr. Sheres has arrived safely, but I
was not exactly thinking of him at the moment;
in fact, I wished to ask, if you had heard anything of poor young Broderick?"

"Not a word, except that he did NOT sail in
'The Surprise' for Tangiers; and that Sir Allen
did offer a thousand pounds reward for any
tidings of him, which I must say was mighty
handsome on the part of Sir Allen."

"Mighty handsome! with a very ugly lining,
like most of Sir Allen Broderick's handsome
deeds," said Hartsfoot, with unwonted bitterness.
"But that thousand pound reward is a very old
story;—I was in hopes you might have heard
some more recent intelligence."

"No—nothing. I do frequent the coffee-
houses, and the Exchange, and even Heaven, so

little now, that all the news I hear has ceased to
be news—nay, is old, and even decrepid, before
it do reach me."

" Well, I won't detain you, Mr. Pepys, from
prolonging your airing, as I hope you will do this
lovely day ; it seems like ingratitude to God,
either to stay in the house, or be unhappy in such
weather."

And Hartsfoot shook hands with Mr. Pepys,
and hurried back to Dr. Fairbrace, telling him he
had failed in gaining any additional tidings of
young Broderick.

" Oh ! well," said the latter, " too much at
once would be bad for our moral digestion ; and
I really think," added he, as they made the best
of their way to Westminster Stairs, " that dear
pretty Mistress Dorothy will now have a sufficient
supply of very genuine hope, to tide her over
several months—and the very vagueness of the
hope is, perhaps, all the better, for anything more
definite and substantial would be too over-
powering for her, after such long absolute starvation."

It so happened that on this particular bright
July morning, the King and all the Court had
gone to Hampton Court, with, in those days, the
obligato accompaniment of music, and French
horns, following in other barges ; so that the
water of the river was almost hidden by the

dense crowd of private and public pleasure boats, and to those who looked down upon the scene from their windows, or garden terraces, it had, from the innumerable bright-coloured pennants and flags, more the look of a gay parterre of flowers than of a river.   It was so far fortunate for the three travellers bound to The Chestnuts, that even all the crafts for hire were in their gala trim, with coloured awnings—either crimson, purple, or green—some being further sheltered by large branches of oak, partially inclosing the sides, for the sun was almost vertical.   So, selecting a barge called "The Boscobel," with the royal arms on a bright red standard floating from the prow, and being a perfect bower of greenery, Hartsfoot engaged it for the day, telling the waterman he should want it to return in the evening.

"What a delicious day," said Doctor Fairbrace, taking off his hat, and leaning back under the well-shaded awning and leafy bower of the boat; "it is one of the few days we have in our English summer that makes one feel that the mere consciousness of existence is almost a plethora of enjoyment!"

"And so it is," rejoined Hartsfoot; "because we *do* live at every pore, and the mere balm of the gentle caressing air as we enhale it, actually steeps us in happiness."

" Oh ! the pity of it—the pity of it ! that there
should be such a terrible and mysterious discrepancy between the beautiful inanimate and the
erring animate half of God's creation ! Para-
doxical as it may sound," continued the Doctor,
" I suppose it is all owing to man having been
fettered with free will, which enables *him* to
infringe the laws, and run counter to the designs
of Omnipotence."

" Partly that, no doubt," said Hartsfoot, " and
still more the insolent pride of intellect, and the
arrogant supremacy which man's vanity has
always awarded to it, no matter how low, or how
immund its possessor's moral nature may be, for
both the contemporaries of intellectual *vaux rien*
and posterity, while incapable of emulating their
genius, or even of individually appreciating it,
are quite capable of, and not only capable, but
apt, in imitating their rascality and want of principle, and there it is that all the mischief is
done. To take a ' modern instance' for a case in
point, every schoolboy in this and succeeding
ages, will be duly impressed with the stupend-
ousness and brilliancy of my Lord Verulam's
Pharos-like intellect; and being so, will naturally wish to learn the history of his life, and in
learning it, must be incessantly staggering and
stumbling at its infinitesimal meannesses—its
ghastly want of principle, and its black and

Colossal ingratitude! But we'll turn from these as if they were mere specks in the sun of such an intellect! MORAL. No matter how infamous a man's life and conduct may be, so long as his intellectual powers are cultivated to the uttermost."

" Of course, that *is* the wicked, all-demoralising moral of the thing ; and men who make all laws down to those of custom, to suit their own lawlessness, have clenched this evil inference into an established fact, by having placed a great gulf between their private and their public lives, holding the former, or rather the vices and frauds of the former, to be sacred and unassailable. And to show that this rule is wholly and solely for the safeguard, impunity, and protection of infamy. When by accident a great man happens by rare chance to be also a good man, what a pother! they do make about it, and what tremendous capital his Biographers, Historians, or Panegyrists make out of his domestic virtues ! and the purity of his private life! as in the case of Sir Thomas More, for instance. Private life is never sacred when it will bear daylight ; oh ! dear, no."

" Too true, my good sir; but neither you nor I will alter it, any more than we could have prevented my Lady Castlemaine's receiving another £30,000 yesterday, for her ten months' debts, while the poor King's wardrobe enables him to *collect his rents*, certainly, so far as his linen goes, but that's all."

"Gad so! as the Duke of Monmouth says, it almost makes one wish for such a royal miser as Louis the Eleventh was, with his anything but royal accounts, of two sols for a new pair of sleeves to an old doublet, and half a denier for a box of grease for greasing his boots! and even the domiciliary *chasses aux souries*, would be better, at least less sinful and less costly than this eternal *chasse aux sourires* of all these wantons."

"Forgive the pun," smiled Hartsfoot, "and don't toss me into the river for it: but it certainly is *wanton* waste, both of money and time."

"I won't throw you into the river this time, not only because it is your first offence, and I don't anticipate a punic war! but because here we are arrived. I will go a little lower down, which will land me at a lane leading up to the Rectory ; and I'll take Joe Barton with me and show him the way to the Lodge. And you had better get out here at the steps leading up to the plaisaunce, and go through the lawn, or rather through that delightful umbrageous charmille, to 'do your spiriting,' and I envy you your mission, or I should envy you, if you did not so

richly deserve to have so great a pleasure. Therefore, should I not see you again before you return to town, I will now say *vale.*"

And the rector and Master Hartsfoot shook
hands as the latter sprang on shore, and telling
the bargeman when he had rowed Dr. Fairbrace
to where he should direct him, to return and
moor the boat, he might then do what " he
pleased till six in the evening, that is, with the
exception of drinking the King's health too
often," which was Master Hartsfoot's delicate
way of forbidding him to get half-seas over.
He then ran up the broad steps leading to the
plaisaunce, and down another flight that ended
exactly opposite the charmille, with only the
broad gravel walk dividing them. Entering into
the profound shade and coolness of that verdant
gallery out of that tropical sun, was really like
making a sudden transit from the infernal regions
into paradise. Master Hartsfoot stood still for
one moment to take off his hat, breathe, and in
fact, *juir de son bien être,* when, as he looked
through the long vista, he saw a slight figure in
deep mourning sitting, but with her limbs and
feet reclining at full length on one of the green
couches near one of the window openings, and
as her back lent against the arm of the couch, he
did not see her face, but knew it was Dorothy,
as indeed it was, sitting on the very seat where

she had last sat with Gilbert, her eyes fixed on
Cooper's miniature of him, which Hartsfoot had
so kindly given her, or rather her mother for her.
Having recovered his breath and become somewhat cooler, he now advanced up the gallery, and
not trusting to the sound of his footsteps on the
gravel walk, as he never made much noise in
walking, he coughed slightly before he came
quite up to the couch upon which Dorothy was
sitting, not only that he might not frighten her
by his sudden appearance, but also that he might
give her time to replace her treasure in her bosom,
as he knew very well that these were a sort of de-
votions that she would not like to be surprised at,
for what was there in the way of deep, or gentle,
or refined feeling that Master Hartsfoot did not
know ? and with such a heart to teach him by
precept and example, ever since he had slain his
first dragon in the shape of A B C, he would
indeed have been an inveterate dunce had his
knowledge been only half a sigh less in these
" Humanities."

Dorothy started when she heard the cough,
and hastily concealed the picture, and putting
her feet to the ground turned round to see from
whence, or rather from whom, the cough had
come.

" Ah ! dear, good Master Hartsfoot at last !"
said she, holding out both hands to him as was

her wont. " It was only yesterday I was abusing you, and saying that after all, you were like the rest of the world, out of sight out of mind, and that with all your promises to come and see us— no, to come and see The Chestnuts—you never came."

" Well, but, Mistress Dorothy," said he, seating himself beside her, without relinquishing the two little hands she had placed in his, " listen to reason for once, if you can, by way of a change, you who are always depriving everyone of our unfortunate sex of that invaluable attribute. What was the use of my coming to this charming place—a place which seems to me only fit for fawns and fairies—what was the use, I say, of coming to it merely for my own selfish pleasure, unless I could be the bearer of any good news ?"

" My God !" exclaimed she, flushing to her very temples; " can it be possible that you have heard anything of—"

She could not finish the sentence, nor was there any necessity that she should do so.

" Well, yes, I *have* heard some good tidings; not *from, mind,* but of him."

" You are in earnest ? Oh! yes—yes—you would not be so cruel unless it were a certainty."

" It *is* a certainty in *one* way, yet not exactly in the way you, and all of us would wish, and

you must not let your thoughts fly too far, or
they will go beyond the bounds of the reality."

Dorothy did not utter another word ; she could
not, had her life depended upon it, but now became deadly pale again.   She withdrew her
hands from Master Hartsfoot's, clasped them together, and looked into his face with such a painful and imploring intensity, that she brought the
tears into his eyes, as he put his hand into his
pocket and brought forth the letter to Mrs. Swinburn.

" Now, my dear soul," said he, before he gave
it to her, " believe me, this *is* very good news ;
but don't expect too much—that is, don't be disappointed because it is not still better ; our hopes,
you know, are   such   terrible braggarts, that
reality can seldom come up with them."

She took the letter, and without staying to look
at the superscription, or seal, tore it open, her
heart beating so violently, and her pulse throb-
bing so painfully, that the paper shook like an
aspen tree in her hands as she read.   When she
came to where it stated that Captain Broderick
was safe, and well—

" Safe, and well, and not let me know it !   I
can't believe *that*," said she, as her hands, with
the letter in them, fell upon her lap.

" Depend upon it, that he *cannot* let you know
it, and that is the mystery of the thing ;—in

common humanity, he would also have let his
poor faithful, heart-broken servant Ferrol know
it from himself *if he could.* But I am as certain
as that I am now sitting here speaking to you,
that he *is* both safe and well.''

Dorothy caught at the words.

'' You think so ?—you really think so ?''

'' I most solemnly assure you that I do.''

'' But—but—see,'' said she, the next minute,
with a face of blank and utter despair, as she
turned the letter over in all directions, and scrutinised its every comma, '' this is only an anonymous letter written to a lodginghouse-keeper ;
surely, *if* he were safe and well, he would not
leave it to the shadow of a chance that I might
hear of it through such a vague and unsatisfactory channel ?''

'' Given the impossibility—that is, his being
stringently forbidden, or, rather, *prevented* from
holding any communication with his friends for
the present, I do think he would be glad to
avail himself of such a chance, if, indeed, he is
cognisant of it ; for after all, it may be only the
humanity of his jailors to let his friends know
that he *is* safe and well. Surely an immense
boon to their anxiety ! as this unfathomable
mystery now stands. And if you think that I
am a sanguine and romantic young fellow ! too
easily led away by my hopes, you will not, surely,

include Mr. Locke and Dr. Fairbrace in that category? And they were breakfasting with me when Ferrol brought that letter this morning, and I'll tell you how Locke weighed and analysed every word of it, and his reasons for believing, with Dr. Fairbrace and myself, that it *is* genuine and *bonâ fide*, and means exactly what it says." And looking steadily into Dorothy's inquisitorial eyes the while, he repeated verbatim what Locke had said.

She listened to his every word with that almost painful analytic intensity, with which those do listen whose whole heart and soul are in their ears, making alternate pulses of hope and fear. But hope at length predominated—

"And you, and Mr. Locke, and Dr. Fairbrace *really do* believe that this letter tells the truth, and is not either some premeditatedly cruel, or some thoughtlessly idle hoax?" said she, at length, after having made him repeat over and over again every syllable of Locke's argument for its being a *bonâ fide* communication, and almost his every look in delivering that judgment.

" I do, indeed," replied Hartsfoot, " believe it as firmly as one can believe anything of which one has not been an eye and ear witness; it creates in my mind perfect faith, according to the best definition of faith—' the evidence of things not seen.' "

" Oh! dear—dear, kind Master Hartsfoot, how
happy you make me always ; always the angel
or messenger of glad tidings to me."

And she burst into a passion of tears and hid
her face on his shoulder, while he held one of her
hands.   At this juncture, Mrs. Neville, who
thought she had been long absent, came to look
for her, and entered the *charmille* from the upper
or lawn end, opposite to the river entrance, by
which Hartsfoot had come.   At the tableau
before her, of Dorothy hiding her face on his
shoulder, her hand in his, and he looking down,
of course, tenderly at her, for his back was towards Mrs. Neville—the latter stood transfixed,
and almost breathless from conflicting feelings.
Anger and surprise at Dorothy.   Was this her
eternal love for Gilbert ?   Then the horrible
duplicity and hypocrisy of the thing in one so
young, and of such seeming crystaline candour
to be always urging *that man's* suit with her
mother, while she was carrying on such a game
with him ! Oh ! it was too—too horrible ! As
for Master Hartsfoot— but what was *he* to her,
that she should waste even disgust and contempt
upon him ?   Of course, *he* was welcome to make
love to any and every woman, from the baggages
at Whitehall to the blacks of Carolina—to every
woman except *her* daughter ; *that* was rather too
much ! too insulting—too—too utterly ridicu-

lous! Oh! men—men; they were *all* alike : all
hollow, vicious, vain, selfish, and more unstable
than the wind; but so far as *that man* was concerned, what was that to her? Nothing, less
than nothing, if there was anything to that pre-
cise amount in creation ; but that a child of *hers*
should be capable of such duplicity ! that was,
indeed, horrible !—most horrible ! However, she
should see that her hypocrisy was discovered, and
with this resolve, Mrs. Neville advanced, with
that sort of solemn determined step which persons adopt when they are marching, as it were,
upon their fate. The black silk or padusay that
composed her dress was too rich, thick, and soft
to rustle; neither were her light step, and the
little silken slippers in which her feet were in-
cased, calculated to sound any note of alarm to
the *guilty pair !* for such they had become in her
estimation as she approached them through the
long vista of the charmille; but she was armed
with a very large green fan, almost like a small
punka, which sent forth the very audible sound
of a sort of sail-like flapping when it was agitated, and agitated it was when she neared the
culprits, till even the polyglot fan of an Andalu-
sian, could not have proclaimed her ineffable scorn
more plainly.

Dorothy, who had had her cry out, was in the
act of raising her head from *that man's* shoulder

as she approached, and consequently was the first to perceive her.

"Oh! darling mother," cried that hardened young sinner, totally unabashed, "thank God you have come, for now I shall know what *you* think of it!"

"I should think it was very easy to know what I think of it!" said Mrs. Neville, as her eyes flashed a sort of covert fire, which the undulations of the fan appeared to blow into flames. If Dorothy had looked, and still looked as innocent, and certainly as beautiful as Eve before the fall, not so poor Master Hartsfoot! who, at the sound of Mrs. Neville's voice, had started to his feet, and extended his hand to her, but which she quite failed to see, and stood rigidly, but slowly fanning herself. The light, it is true, was subdued in that umbrageous gallery; the garish meridian glare being deliciously filtered through its greenery. Still, there was quite sufficient light to see that Master Hartsfoot was "Redder, if not exactly ruddier, than the cherry." Was it that the poor man, like Adam, *after* the fall, had tasted of the knowledge of good and evil? Well, of course he had, for is not such the fruit of all experience? and Oliver Hartsfoot would be forty-nine in ten days more.

What an obstinate, disobliging mule the earth is, that it *never will* yield to people's wishes, and "open and swallow them up" when they desire it ; and such was Master Hartsfoot's most fervent and clearly defined wish at that moment ; but, no ! it seemed like his own peculiarly uncomfortable position to grow harder and harder every moment.   Poor Master Hartsfoot ! to be so—

> ' Gentle, but unfortunate !
> Dishonestly afflicted, and yet honest.'

Ah ! he is not the only one ;—it is the old, old story, which began with the world, and will only end with it.   For truly says that great Apostle of human nature, Victor Hugo—

> ' Nous avons beau tailler de notre mieux, le bloc mystérieux dont notre vie est faite, la veine noire de la destinée y reparaît toujours.' "

But dauntless Dorothy threw herself into the breach, and came to the rescue.   She put her arms round her mother's neck, despite that mother's resistance ; and then showing her the letter to Mrs. Swinburne, she said—

"Read this, dear mother ;—dear, good Master Hartsfoot is really my deputy-Providence—every gleam of sunshine I have he collects for me— who but he would have set off with it instantly this broiling day ?"

Mrs. Neville began to have an uncomfortable vague idea that she had made a mistake, and had not "judged righteous judgment"—as those seldom do, who judge from appearances—but she felt it was due to both herself and her sex, to show that even if she had put the saddle on the wrong horse, there still *was* a horse to be saddled, otherwise *she* should not have bridled as she did when she came up to them. So, before reading the letter, she said, with a gravity that was almost stern—

" Well, my dear, whatever good news Master Hartsfoot may have been kind enough to bring you, young women should not be so demonstrative ; it is very unseemly."

Then feeling that it would never do to let him know, or see, that she cared one straw what *he* did,—at the same time, that it would be just as well to let him know that if Dorothy was so foolish and impulsive, *he*, at least, was old enough to know better, and not aid and abet such nonsense, —she turned to him, and putting out her hand, which he could not have taken more gingerly had it been a red-hot iron, said—

" I beg your pardon, Master Hartsfoot, I had no idea you were here ; and seeing Dorothy lying with her face hidden upon a man's shoulder ! I really was so taken aback at so extraordinary ! and, I must say, so indecorous a proceeding, that, displeased as I was with her, I did not even look at you (!)."

Oh ! Mrs. Neville ! did you mean this as a practical illustration of Falstaff's axiom of " How this world is given to— ?"

Though we did do Master Hartsfoot the in-

justice of likening him to Adam, he was far, very
far from having any of the dastardly meanness
of that prototype of all masculine moral cowardice,
for he did not transfer the blame from his own
shoulders to those of poor little Dorothy; he
merely said—

" I think you will be glad to hear the news I
have brought, and will agree with Mr. Locke,
Dr. Fairbrace, and myself—that it *is* very good,
that is, very satisfactory news."

" Now sit down here between us, dear, while
you read that letter," said Dorothy, taking her
mother by both hands, and seating her in the
centre of the couch, with its elastic, velvety,
green moss squabs.

" Well, really," said she, when she had read it,
" if this were not an anonymous letter, it would
give me great hope—but—"

" Oh !" interrupted Dorothy, "just listen to
the explanation Master Hartsfoot has been giving
me. I no longer have any doubts about it—I
cannot, I *will not* doubt—for it would kill me if I
doubted now."

Hartsfoot recapitulated all that Locke, Dr.
Fairbrace, and himself had said, and thought,
upon weighing the *pros* and *cons* of that letter
when he had received it that morning ; and he
ended by impressing Mrs. Neville with as firm a
conviction of its sincerity and genuineness as he
had done Dorothy.

A revolution then took place in her mother's
heart, and she also burst into tears; but it was
on Dorothy's bosom that she wept, and not upon
Master Hartsfoot's shoulder ; but still, thinking
that it was only common gratitude—which, by-
the-bye, is an erroneous expression, as *the* most
*un*common thing in the whole world is gratitude;
—but at all events, thinking that it was only fair
that one who ever studied their welfare and happiness in all things, should at least share in that
which he had now brought them, she turned her
streaming eyes full upon him, and holding out
her hand to him pressed his in a way that seemed
to indicate that her daughter's unseemly demon-
strativeness had produced the usual effect of evil
communications, as she said—

" You are, indeed, our good genius, Master
Hartsfoot, for you never come but with kindness
and comfort in your wake."

And as she spoke one of her tears fell upon
his hand; he raised her hand to his lips, but in
reality kissed that tear off of his own. It was
fortunate for him that none of the Anti-Popery
spies were lurking in those sylvan shades, or it
would have gone hard with him, for his evident
idolatry of this drop of holy water. And now
they re-seated themselves, and began castle-
building, and wondering—and wondering if after
all Sir Allen *was* at the bottom of Gilbert's
disappearance; and if not, who and what could

be the cause of it? and what power could constrain him to silence? And so they talked the sultry hours away, till they heard the dinner bell, followed by a tremendous barking of dogs.

" Where on earth have those dogs been that they've actually deserted me for the last two hours? I must go and hunt them up, if you'll give my mother your arm, Master Hartsfoot; and in the cool of the evening I'll introduce you to all my flowers and birds, and indeed the whole of my dominions," said Dorothy as they emerged from the charmille.

" Oh! what a charming place," said Hartsfoot, shading his eyes with his glove from the sun, as he looked round; " and what a perfect palace of a kennel," he added, as he saw Diamond and Finette, followed by Clove the turnspit, now tearing down its broad steps to greet their mistress.

" Ah!" whispered Mrs. Neville, " that was a present of poor Gilbert's; he had it copied from one he saw at Bocobel, and the dogs delight in it, and seem to know that it is their especial property."

" Hey-day, Master Clove, how came you here at this hour, sir? Does that mean that we are to have no dinner?" asked Dorothy, shaking Clove's proffered paw. " Allow me, Master Hartsfoot to present to you our *chef*—Mr. Clove,

Master Hartsfoot. He's the gentleman who rules the roast here, so you must not attempt to supplant him."

As they approached the house the two pea-cocks were strutting, followed by their beautiful long trains; but seeing Dorothy, and thinking that as usual she had some pound cake for them, they made them into magnificent fans, which is a peacock's mode of salaam.

" By-and-bye, Gloriano; by-and-bye, Belli-occhi," said she, as they passed them to enter the house, where Upton and Jessop stood at the hall door, for since her father's death Mrs. Neville had taken the former into her service.

" I hope I see you quite well, sir ?" said Jessop, bowing low to Hartsfoot, and taking his hat, for though it was the fashion in those days for men always to keep on their hats at dinner, the weather was now so sultry that Hartsfoot re-quested permission on this occasion not to do so, as they did not dine in the large hall, cold as a vault, even in summer, but in the large certainly, but very comfortable dining-room.

" Now, Master Hartsfoot," said the Châtelaine, as they seated themselves at table, and she helped him to some of that delicious *potage aux coquillage*, made of crabs, lobsters, oysters, scallops, cockles, prawns, and cream, which one only gets in perfection in Edinburgh, " eating is a very secondary consideration this weather ; but drinking is all-important. Jessop knows your taste in wines, but for other beverages there are cucumber cup, megthelen, golden pippin cup, cider, and prestonpans beer."

"Thank you, I never drink anything but claret and water this weather."

"I suppose the river is thronged like a New-market race to-day, on account of the King's going to Hampton Court?" said Dorothy.

"So thronged that it took us an hour and a half to get here, and it's impossible to say, so far as colours go, which is the finest, the barges or the city madams."

"Chicken à la daube, sir?" said Jessop, offer-ing him a plate.

"Thank you, no."

"Ducks and green peas, sir?" said Upton, offering another plate.

"Not any, thank you."

"There is a cold neck of lamb and salad on the sideboard, sir," said Jessop, returning to the charge, for it was never from any inhospitable oversight on his part, if his mistress's guests did not eat.

"Salad—and more especially your salad—*is* a temptation certainly, Jessop," said Hartsfoot; "so I think I must have some cold lamb and salad."

" Give Master Hartsfoot a china plate for his lamb and salad, Jessop," said Mrs. Neville; " they are cooler than silver ones. My dear Thea, you are eating nothing."

" And yet I have dined better than any of you ; *car çe n'est pas tous les jours qu'on dine d'un plat de bonnes nouvelles !"* said she.

" *Surtout en suprême d'espérance,*" smiled Hartsfoot.

" As you say ; and here's to the health of the newsman."

" I'll drink that with all my heart," said Mrs. Neville.

Strange power of sympathy that the wine they drank should have so flushed Master Hartsfoot, for he took none, and " Drank to them only with his eyes."

Jessop did not like people to speak French, which was much spoken since the restoration, the King having set the fashion, for it came more naturally to him ; but Jessop did not like it because he did not understand it ; but, as he observed to Ruffle afterwards, it was " a way the quality had of always jabbering French at table before the servants when they had any secrets ; however he did not care as it was easy to see that both madam and Mistress Dorothy were in much better spirits than they had been for months and months, whatever good news Master Hartsfoot had brought them; for that there *was* some good news he was certain."

At length the dinner was over, and then came the dessert in the good old legitimate style, before the bloom of peaches and the aroma of pines were insulted by the fumes of viands, fish, and soup, as they are now in *diners à la Russe*; and when the dessert came in, the servants went out, and people could talk without restraint.

" Those cherries," said Hartsfoot, covering his face with his hands, "remind me of my black ingratitude; not because they are black, but I have never had the grace to thank you, Mistress Dorothy, for your magnificent cherries and strawberries, and above all, your delicious cream, upon which Locke, Dr. Fairbrace, and I feasted this morning."

" That cream you owe to my own cow, pretty Daisy, and she shall give you a syllabub this evening; that is, if you do not stand too much upon your masculine dignity! and will promise to kiss her, for that is always her charge for a syllabub."

" The weather is quite too hot now," laughed Hartsfoot; "but if she will give me credit till the autumn, then I will faithfully discharge my debts."

" Oh! well, I'm sure Daisy will wait; for with those fine large black Italian eyes of hers, I daresay she knows that *un bacio dato, non e mai perduto.*"

"By-the-bye," said Hartsfoot, taking a paper out of his pocket, " those cherries—not the black but the red ones—remind me to show you some lines I copied out of the book they keep in Heaven. I don't allude to the Recording Angel's vast volume, but to the scribbling book they keep at the Club, which our mad gallants have profanely christened Heaven. These lines are so like Herricks, or his are so like them, that either he must have stolen his 'Cherry Ripe' from them, or they have stolen it from him, for there is no end either to the plagiaries of authors, or the wits jumping of geniuses; these lines were simply signed with the initials R. L."

"Perhaps," said Dorothy, " they are poor Colonel Richard Lovelace's?"

"Aye, may be so. I did not think of him; but here they are—

> "'There is a garden in her face,
>   Where roses and white lilies grow ;
> A Heavenly Paradise is that place,
>   Where all pleasant fruits do flow ;
> There cherries grow that none may buy,
>   Till cherry ripe themselves do cry.
>
> Those cherries fairly do inclose,
>   Of Orient pearl a double row,
> Which, when her lovely laughter shows,
>   They look like rosebuds filled with snow ;
> Yet these no peer or prince may buy,
>   Till cherry ripe themselves do cry.

> Her eyes like angels watch them still,
>   Her brows like bended bows do stand,
> Threatening with piercing frowns to kill,
>   All that approach with eye or hand,
> Those sacred cherries to come nigh,
>   Till cherry ripe themselves do cry.' "

" They are very like Herrick," said Dorothy. " Dr. Fairbrace was a great friend of poor Herrick's ; I'll show them to him if I may, and ask him if he knows anything about them."

" Oh ! certainly," assented Hartsfoot; " only poor Herrick was so little in London latterly before his death, I should think that perhaps he had written them in that book, and signed them with the initials of the lady in whose praise they were written."

The day wore on, as even the happiest days will do, and the happier, alas ! the more quickly. In order to make the most, as he said himself, of his little *talens de societé*, Master Hartsfoot not only told them of his wonderful discovery about the capabilities of tea, but he showed them how to make it, and they declared that it was such perfect nectar, that they would have it daily for breakfast instead of chocolate or coffee. And Dorothy laughingly declared, that henceforth Columbus must hide his diminished head ! as he had only discovered a great country, but Master Hartsfoot had discovered a great comfort !

When the cool of the evening came, they ad-

journed to the meadow; Daisy was duly patted
and admired, and furnished the promised syllabub.   And as it is impossible to leave people
better than in clover, whether cows, or merely
cowed lovers, we will leave Master Hartsfoot to
enjoy all the beatitudes of " The Chestnuts,"
till it is time for him to return to town, and go
and see how Joe Barton passed his day.

CHAPTER III.

HEN upon landing from the boat in the morning, Dr. Fairbrace had accompanied Joe Barton as far as the high road, and pointed out the Lodge of The Chestnuts to him, he left him, and Joe walked on briskly till he came to it, but instead of entering in at the door at once, which he might have done, for it stood, as well as each lattice, wide open, on account of the heat, he crouched down under one of the windows, amid the roses and woodbine that so thickly surrounded both windows, and as his eyes were on a level with the sill of the window, and the foliage at once sheltered and concealed his head, he could look into the cottage and reconnoitre the interior. But a fine blackbird that hung in a wicker cage above the door which divided the two windows, being himself a bird of great probity, who never stole anything, even when given his liberty, and allowed to range about, did not approve of such stealthy proceedings, and mistaking Joe for a thief, began flapping his wings, jumping down from his perch, whistling at the top of his voice, and in short, in ornithological language, crying as loudly as he could " Fire ! murder ! thieves !"

"What on earth ails the bird ?" asked Mrs. Barton. "Tinker, poor fellow, what is it ? You hav'n't forgotten to put his water, Bridget, have you ?"

"Oh! no, mother; nor his seed, nor his groundsel, and even a bunch of cherries."

" Dear me," said Mrs. Barton, rising and going to the door with a chair to take down the bird, "I hope he's not been stung by a wasp, poor fellow?"

And even after she took him in, and examined him, and ascertained that he had not met with any bodily injury, he continued for some minutes in a state of excitement, evidently showing that he had something on his mind. This, however, did not prevent Joe using his eyes, and learning the interior of the lodge by heart: in an arm-chair, with a good cushion covered with a red and white check, sat his mother; at the other open window, knitting a stocking at a table in the centre of the room—could he believe his eyes !— stood Bridget,—her hair smoothly rolled up under a snow-white cap, a brown stuff gown made to fit her really nice trig little figure, a clean linen kerchief pinned over the body of her dress in

front and in a point in the back, short sleeves,
finished with clean linen bands, above her elbow.
The dress pinned up behind, which displayed a
green-quilted serge petticoat, and, also, her clean
white stockings drawn up smoothly over her
ankles, and her clean, thick, black leather shoes,
with their large, square, silver buckles ; the latter
a present from Dr. Fairbrace, to commemorate
her improvement in Psalm singing.   She was
ironing her mother's caps and lawn kerchiefs ;
folding, sprinkling, and doing them deftly and
neatly enough altogether, not only as if she had
the perfect use of her hands, but of her intelligence too, without which no one can have the
proper use of their hands.   On one side of the
room was a small dresser, replete with every
cottage convenience ; a few bright pewter plates
and dishes, mugs, and flagons hung upon hooks
before them.   On one side of this dresser stood a
large, tall, oak clock case, the clock of which
ticked loudly and distinctly, as if it felt that it
had a right to be heard from never telling anything but the exact truth, and strikingly enforcing
it every hour ; on the other side of the dresser
hung a bright brass warming-pan, which, only to
look at, was to make one wish oneself in bed of a
cold winter's night after it had acted as *avant
courier.*   Over the mantel-piece were smoothing-
irons, a couple of pairs of bright brass candle-

sticks, and a few strings of birds' eggs festooned against the wall ; the grate—like all grates at that time—was enormously large, with oak benches within it at each side, iron dogs for burning wood, and an iron pot suspended from a hook, in which their mid-day meal of bacon and beans was boiling. On one side of the room— one opposite to the window—was a walnut-wood chest of drawers, with 'a slanting top to it, like the side of a house, which let down and served as an escretoire; while above it, was a book-case, with glass doors, which Dorothy had well stocked with books, as books went in those days, and which were a great source of delight to Mrs. Barton, for having, as she herself said, been brought up amongst them, she always looked upon books as old and sure friends that she had an affection for. Within the grate sat a big tortoise-shell cat—a sort of Alexander Selkirk of a cat—who seemed to think he *was* " monarch of all he surveyed," and was evidently used to be minded by everyone, and to mind no one; it was sitting with its tail curled round its fore-paws, indulging in one of those perpendicular naps of which cats and dogs alone have the secret. Upon the uproar that Tinker the blackbird had made, the cat had opened one eye, but closed it the next moment, as much as to say " There is no use in a cat wasting its time in looking after such a cowardly sybarite as you, with cages, and bipeds, and every other sort of unnatural protection, instead of taking your chance upon a tree as other birds do."

"Well, Bridget," said Mrs. Barton, resuming the conversation with her knitting, as soon as Tinker had calmed his nerves, and once more subsided into silence, "so you really can write without lines now, and will be able to write madam a letter by next Christmas? only there are no letters unfortunately or no words that can ever express to her and that young angel Mistress Dorothy all we owe to them, and all we feel for them, or to Master Hartsfoot either, for being the saviour of my poor Joe."

"That is true, mother; but we can at least tell them that we *do* feel it."

"You are right, my poor girl, and as for re-paying; it is only God who can repay either for good or for evil, and He would never have let us incur such a debt if He did not mean to repay it for us."

Joe had seen and heard quite enough; like all boys of his age he was ashamed to cry, and yet in spite of himself he was crying; and he thought that as many hands make light work surely many hearts must make it easier to bear such a great weight of gratitude, and that it was his bounden duty to go and help his mother and

sister to bear it, by sharing it with them. So,
drying his eyes, he said in a feigned voice—

" Pray, dame, does one Mrs. Barton live
here ?"

" I am Mrs. Barton at your service, sir," said
she, rising, and coming to the door to see who
the person was who was inquiring for her, when
Joe caught her in his arms and nearly stifled
her with a perfect bear's hug. She screamed,
not seeing at first who it was.

" My dear boy, how you frightened me; but
how you are grown, and how well you look in
those nice clothes. If I had met you in the road
I really don't think I should have known you."

" Oh! yes you would, mother, though fine
feathers make fine birds all the world over."

" Why surely," said Bridget, who quickly put
down her iron, and came and threw her arms
round his neck, " this can't be my poor Joe ?"

" And surely," said Joe, pushing her back and
eyeing her from head to foot with as much surprise as delight, " this can't be my poor half
daft Bridget ? That's what you may call a pair of
wrong-side-out compliments. But you don't
mean to say it was *you* I saw doing mother's
ironing ?"

" But I mean to say," said Mrs. Barton, "that
she does not only do my ironing, but all the work
of the house, thanks to that angel, Mistress

Dorothy, who in the midst of all her own grief and trouble, has persevered with her till she has taught her to do everything, and everything well, too."

"That means the other," said Joe, sententiously, "for nothing is *really* done that is not well done. That Mrs. Merrypin is always dinning into me till I see she is right."

"Oh! Joe, I'm sorry you have come to-day, too."

"Well, that's a nice affectionate way of receiving a brother that you have not seen for a whole year, Madam Bridget."

"Oh! I don't mean it in *that* way, that I am sorry to see you, Joe, for you know that is not true ; I was only sorry that it happened you came to-day, for I was to have written to-night to ask Master Hartsfoot's leave to let you come next Saturday, when I was to have dressed such a fine dinner for you all by myself."

"Oh! hang the fine dinner, I get a good dinner every day now; and all I care for is to see mother and you, which I can't do every day."

"It's very unlucky," said Bridget; "we've only beans and bacon for dinner to-day, and Mistress Dorothy told me that Mrs. Merrypin was such a fine cook that if I did not dress the dinner I asked you to, to perfection, you would not be able to touch it."

" It was very kind of Mistress Dorothy, like
all she does," said Mrs. Barton, " to tell you
that, Bridget, to put you on your mettle to do
your best; but I should hope Joe had both too
much good feeling and too much good sense to
be so wanting in gratitude to God, and to dear
Mistress Dorothy as ever to forget, much less so
soon, how short a time it is ago that he had not
even dry bread enough to eat."

" Never fear, mother," said the poor lad;
" they say eaten bread is soon forgotten, but I
don't think the bread one had *not* to eat is ever
forgotten."

And Joe again kissed his mother, made her
sit down in her arm-chair, while he sat on the
floor at her feet, and said—

" Now, Bridget, for the beans and bacon; for
I can tell you I'm almost as hungry as I used to
be in old times."

" God forbid !" said Audrey Barton, passing
one hand through the boy's thick curly hair,
while she dried her eyes with the other; " hunger
that has food waiting for it is only a luxury; but
the other !—the real gaunt hunger !—that knows
no food.   Oh! Joe, how can we ever be sufficiently grateful to those who rescued us from
that ?"

Bridget quickly removed her ironing things,
carrying them into a sort of little back kitchen,
which adjoined the room they were in, and served

them also as a laundry; after which, she busied herself in laying the table, Joe watching her all the time with a sort of open-mouthed astonishment.

"And how is Alice Merrypin?" said Mrs. Barton, "for she was a good friend to me when I had no other friend."

"She is very well, thank you, mother; and she *is* a good old soul as ever was. You don't know how good she is to me, and what trouble she takes with me. At first I was, as I needn't tell you, mother, very ignorant, very awkward, and very stupid, for it was all so new and so strange to me; and I'm ashamed to say, that instead of being grateful to her for taking so much pains with me, I used sometimes turn sulky, when she used to make me do things over and over again, till I did them properly. But when, instead of being angry with me, she told me so seriously that I never could in any other way prove my gratitude to God, to Master Hartsfoot, and to Mistress Dorothy, but by *not* being stupid, awkward, and forgetful; and she also impressed upon me of what great value all master's china, glass, and plate were, and that breaking and spoiling things all arose from a *habit of not being careful*, for that one thing that was either broken or spoilt by *accident*, a dozen were from carelessness. Well then, I turned to in good earnest, and determined I *would* do well, and I *did;* and goodness knows, I have been more than rewarded by master's praises and all his kindness, and through him by the kindness of all the gentlemen that come to the house, and even Noah Pump is very good to me in his way; but as for Mrs. Merrypin, she *is* so kind to me, and reads to me, and even what I like better of an evening, tells me such nice long stories about great people —real people that she or her family have known, for she has seen a deal of the world, has Mrs. Merrypin, and as she says herself, she's sorted the people she's known as she sorts her fruit, picked out the best and preserved them in her memory, and thrown away the rest. And when we read a chapter of the Bible morning and evening, it does me good to hear her explain it; she makes it all as clear as noonday to me."

" God bless her for her goodness to you," said Audrey Barton, as they seated themselves at the table, upon which the bacon and beans now smoked.

" Well," said Joe, by way of commentary upon the first mouthful, " I call this a dinner fit for a king."

" Ah! but if I had known you were coming, you should have had a cherry pie with it," said Bridget.

" Well, he must only eat the cherries by themselves," said his mother; "but bring one of those six bottles of perry that Mistress Dorothy gave me the last day I was up at the house. I can't open them on a better occasion, for it's not every day you can have an opportunity of drinking an angel's health; so you shall drink Mistress Dorothy's."

"With all my heart, mother; but as I keep an angel, too, you must also drink the health of mine."

"You mean Master Hartsfoot?"

"Of course I do; and I think he ought to come first, as a he angel, is a deal rarer than a she one."

"That's true, Joe; and the longer you live and the more you see of the world, the truer you'll find it. And poor Mr. Hollar, that I nursed—that first happy week that the tide turned for us all—how is he getting on?"

"Oh! he's bravely now, thanks to his and my angel. Master Hartsfoot's good health," said Joe, standing up and holding the foaming glass of perry in his hand which his sister had filled for him, and waiting till she had helped her mother and herself.

"Master Hartsfoot's good health, and may God bless and reward him, and all like him, if there are any like him," said Mrs. Barton.

And then Mrs. Neville's and Dorothy's health were duly honoured.

" Well, that is capital stuff !" cried Joe, putting down his empty glass. " I never tasted perry before; I really think it ought to be kept on purpose for drinking angels' healths. Do you know, mother, Mr. Hollar always asks so kindly after you whenever I see him, which I did last Sunday. More betoken, I was too late for church, looking over all his beautiful drawings and engravings, which he was so good as to show me when I brought him a book from master."

" You should not have stayed away from church, my boy, to look at drawings, however beautiful, or engravings, however choice; it was almost breaking the commandment of ' Thou shalt not make to thyself a graven image of anything in Heaven or earth, nor of the waters under the earth.' "

" Ah ! but, mother, I did not go without my prayers, for all that."

" What ! I suppose you went to some conventicle, then ?"

" No, I didn't ; I went to a place of worship where you, and Bridget, and I, have often prayed."

" Oh ! to St. Martin's-in-the Fields ?"

" No ; to Saint Famishes-in-the-Mud."

" Dear me ! what extraordinary names those Puritans do give their places of worship ; but I wonder they don't think it too Popish to tack Saint before it."

" Perhaps *they* might," said Joe ; " but the christening was mine. In fact, mother, I had never been in Catchpole Lane since the happy day the Lord sent his angel to lead us out of it ; so I thought I'd go and take a look at our poor shed. There it was, mother, with its bare walls, and the ricketty old wooden bedstead, with the withered fern leaves in one corner, where poor Bridget used to lie all day long, learning how to bear hunger without working to increase it, which was good common sense, at all events ; there the poor terrible old place was, just as we had left it, for it seems, thank God, that no one since us has been poor enough to live—or rather to starve in it. When I had made sure that every bit of the misery was there, not a stone of the walls, nor an inch of the damp mud floor missing, I knelt down in the very midst, and didn't I pray, that's all ? I didn't want any more sermons that day, for the poor old ' abomination of desolation' preached me a sermon that will last me my life."

" I should hope it would, my poor boy," said his mother, bursting into tears as she threw her arms round his neck.

The tears were streaming down Bridget's cheeks, too, as she said—

" Oh! Joe, if ever I go to London again, take me with you, and I'll go and pray there too ; for I think God must expect it from us."

"Now, Bridget," said Joe, "take away the dinner things, for I want the table."

"Oh! but there are the cherries to bring," and Bridget cleared the table, and when she had taken the dinner things into the back kitchen to be washed up in the evening, she took from the larder the basket of cherries, and getting a large round cracked china dish, that Ruffle had given her, she went out to gather some roses, wherewith to decorate the dish, as she had seen the dessert done "up at the house," placing an enormous fresh cabbage leaf on the dish first before she put the cherries into it; *this*, she was aware was an anachronism, and to show that she knew what was what, she said, as she placed the dish on the table, apologetically addressing the superior refinement of her brother—

"I know, Joe, that the cabbage ought to have been with the bacon, and vine leaves under the cherries; but we have no vine leaves down here, unless I had gone up to the garden, and asked Mr. McPherson for some, and that would have kept you too long."

"Never mind, Bridget, I never eat vine leaves; but I always eat cherries whenever I come in their way, or they in mine," said he, helping himself to some; and after having eaten them, and said they were the best he ever had eaten— very different to the poor London dwindles, he put his hand into his pocket and brought out a small, heart-shaped, dark slate coloured leaf or purse.

"Oh! what a pretty, soft innocent thing," said Bridget, smoothing it with her hand; "do feel it, mother. It's ten times softer than the cat's ears."

"What is it?" asked Mrs. Barton.

"It's a purse," said Joe, "that Mrs. Merrypin made me out of the velvet jackets of two poor little moles, that died of cold last winter."

And undrawing the strings as he spoke Joe emptied it on the table, displaying four angels and several shillings.

"There, dear mother," said he, pushing over to her first the four angels, "there are my first year's wages, £2; and there, Bridget, are fifteen shillings that the gentlemen who come to our house have given me at different times; buy yourself a gown with it. I would have done so, but I did not know what you would like."

"But indeed, dear Joe, thanking you all the same, I will not take your money, for I am given so many things here, that I really don't want it."

"But indeed, dear Bridget, you MUST have something for my sake; but a gown, not a Joseph mind. And I am given *every*thing, so that I literally want nothing."

"My dear boy," said his mother, "provided

for so amply and comfortably as I now am, you
cannot suppose I would take your wages?"

"Oh! but you really must, mother; at all
events you must keep them for me, till I ask you
for them, as they will be much safer with you
than with me."

· "Well, that I'll do," said Mrs. Barton, rising
and unlocking the wallnut escritoire, and placing
the four angels in a secret drawer within it."

"Now," said Joe, "I want to see the rest of
your palace; the bedrooms upstairs."

"That you shall, for you never saw nicer, or
more comfortable ones."

"Well, mother, you are well off indeed," said
Joe, as soon as they came downstairs again, and
were seated at the open window; "and well may
you say Mistress Dorothy is an angel, for doesn't
it seem to you every day as if you had got into
heaven out of the other place? I know it does
to me where I am, particularly when I look at
master's kind heavenly face; for, to my taste,
he's the handsomest man I ever saw in my life;
and such a beautiful hand, as white as a lady's.
Did you remark it when you were at Mr.
Hollar's?"

"Yes; no one could help remarking it."

"Mrs. Merrypin says she thinks it must be
bleached and beautified with blessings, for as he
has been giving and holding out a helping hand

to others all his life, she thinks blessings must have been left in it in exchange."

" I shouldn't wonder if it was so," said Audrey Barton.

" How I should like to walk through all these beautiful grounds and go all over this fine place," said Joe, stretching his head out of the window, and looking up the long vista of the avenue of Spanish chestnuts, from which the place took its name.

" And so you shall some day that the ladies are in town, if your master can spare you."

" You and Bridget will walk down to the river side with me in the evening, when I go down to the boat to wait for master; won't you, mother ?"

" Bridget shall ; but I cannot leave the Lodge."

" What's that you say I'm to do, mother ?" Bridget called out from the back kitchen, where she was washing the plates and putting the things away.

" Why, walk with Joe down to the boat in the cool of the evening."

" Oh ! thank you ; that will be nice, for they say that the river is for all the world like a fair to-day ; it's so thronged."

" Poor fellow !" said Joe, trying to ingratiate himself with Tinker. " Do you know he took

me for a thief, mother, when I stooped down to
hide among the leaves to have a peep at you
before I came in, and it was that that made him
kick up such a row.   I'll hang up his cage again
outside, shall I ? and then he'll know me another
time."

"Yes ; do put him out, for it's a great deal
too hot for him in here."

And having hung up the wicker cage over the
door, to Tinker's no small delight, Joe returned
to his seat, and he and his mother sat talking
till about five o'clock, when Lancelot appeared
outside the window.

"Mrs. Barton," he began, but seeing Joe, he
thrust in his hand, and said, "Joe, my boy, how
are you?   How's old Pump?—in great request,
no doubt, this hot weather. Mrs. Barton, I came
to tell you, in case of any visitors, you are to say
Madam and Mistress Dorothy have gone for a
long walk, and I must go back to carry some
hoods and things into the meadow after them.
So good-bye, Joe; come and see us when you
can get a day, and let us know what you think
of Madam's audit ale ?   It's better than the
Pump, I can tell you," he added, as he turned
upon his heel and retraced his steps up the
avenue.

"What is audit ale, mother ?" asked Joe, who
had the sense never to be above confessing his
ignorance when in quest of knowledge.

" Why, the strong ale that is given to the tenants when they pay Madam's rents, and when the steward audits their accounts."

" Then why should Lancelot offer me any of this ale, since I am not one of madam's tenants, and have no accounts to settle."

" Why, indeed, Joe; only servants always *are* so hospitable at their masters' and mistress's expense."

" Well, that I can't understand."

" And I hope you never will understand it in a way to practice it, for those who are not faithful over little are seldom so over much."

Lancelot had scarcely been gone half-an-hour when the rumbling of wheels and the trampling of many horses was heard, and in due course a coach and six, with two running footmen, stopped before the large iron gates. Mrs. Barton rose, smoothed her pinners, and prepared to issue forth.

" Shall I open the large gates for you, mother?" said Joe.

" There is no necessity for that, dear, as the coach won't come in."

And she issued through the small iron side gate, and curtseying very low to two very stately looking ladies of a very certain age, and a young gentleman dressed in the ultra extreme of the mode, his flowing hay-coloured curls assorting only too

well with the firmament of freckles that studded
his face above the two red love apples of his very
high cheek bones, informed them that the ladies
were gone for a long walk.

" Dear me, how unlucky," said the nearest of
the two ladies, who acted as spokeswoman. "My
good woman," said she, " do you think you can
remember names, and deliver a message correctly ?"

" I will endeavour to do so, madam," replied
Audrey Barton, with another low curtsey.

Now in those days visiting cards were unknown, and indeed, so late as the time of George
the Second, all the arduous duties of visiting and
invitations, were transacted by autographs on the
back of the Knave of Clubs, or the Ace of
Hearts.

" Well then," resumed the lady, " will you
give Mrs. Bridget Mauleverer's and Mrs. Alice
Throckmorton's kind love to Mrs. Neville and
Mistress Dorothy, and say that our nephew, Sir
Angus Tullibardin, *this* gentleman here," leaning back with much relative pride, so that the
" good woman " might have a full view of that
charming object; " our nephew, Sir Angus
Tullibardin, being again staying with us, we took
advantage of his coach to come over and see
them, and are so sorry to have missed them. We
are quite aware, say, that they do not yet frequent

assemblies, therefore we should not think of inviting them to one; but if they would come and dine with us to-morrow—all in the family way—we should be so very glad. Now do you think you can remember all that ?"

Mrs. Barton's only answer was to repeat the message word for word.

" A very intelligent person, upon my word," said Mrs. Alice Throckmorton, fumbling in her pocket, from whence she excavated half-a-crown, which she presented to Audrey Barton.

" Thank you, madam, but there is no necessity for that, and Mrs. Neville never allows any of her servants to receive gratuities."

" A prodigious well-spoken person, I protest," said Mrs. Alice, receiving back, with a sort of fatted calf jubilance of expression, the prodigal half-crown, as she returned it to the place from whence it came.

" Ahem ! ahem !" came sharply from Sir Angus Tullibardin's throat, like a paraphrase on the command, " Attention."

Mrs. Alice turned quickly round, but it was only to receive a rapid succession of telegraphic winks. Still she was dull of apprehension, so that Sir Angus was driven into adopting extreme measures, and knocking the funny bone of her elbow with the hilt of his sword, the result was a sound exactly such as it would have been had he

knocked the weapon against his own very pro-
minent teeth, and a slight wincing on the part
of Mrs. Alice, as she rubbed her assaulted elbow,
and nodding her head like a Chinese joss, said—

" Oh ! yes—yes—yes—I understand," and then
turning suddenly round again, she cried out, at
the same time beckoning her to approach, " Oh !
and, good woman, we are particularly anxious to
know if Mistress Dorothy has recovered her
spirits yet ? And we should be so delighted if
she would come and stay a week or two with us ;
and now that we have the convenience of my
nephew's coach we could make so many nice excursions, and he plays so charmingly, both on
the theorbo and the French horn, that I am sure
she would find much diversion in listening to
him."

" I shall not fail to deliver the message,
madam," re-curtseyed Audrey.

" Gad so ! where air those demmed vairlets of
mine ?" said Sir Angus, putting his head out of
the coach window, so as at one and the same
time to display what he conceived to be his
Whitehall air, and perfect English accent, though
it was ungenerous to do so in maledictions upon
the unhappy running footmen, who were perfectly
visible to the naked eye; as though evidently
melting away, they had not the slightest idea of
running away till they were compelled to do so

ex-officio by their master's giving the word of command.

"Hom! back to the leddies, at Twick-en-ham."

The "demmed vairlets" stepped out briskly, flourishing each his long gold-headed cane before him, like a *Tambour Major*. They were dressed like all running footmen in light silk, not coats, but round jackets. Those of Sir Angus Tulli-bardin were of salmon colour, with sky blue breeches, silver garters, white silk stockings, with gold clocks, and gold shoe buckles large and square, covering the whole fore part of the foot. Instead of hats, like all running footmen, they wore jockey's caps for lightness and coolness; theirs were composed of alternate quarters of salmon-coloured and sky-blue silk, with a narrow silver lace band round the cap.* While the coach was in the slow, but by no means sure, process of turning, Mrs. Alice Throckmorton put her head out of the window, and called out—

" Now, be sure, good woman, and don't forget to tell Mistress Dorothy that I am sure my nephew's playing on the theorbo and the French horn will divert her; he does wonders, too, on the fiddle, only he has left his fiddle in Scot-land."

---

* This barbarous fashion of running footmen, even for long journeys, continued till 1770. The poor wretched men, so hunted by " coaches and six," seldom lived beyond the age of thirty.

" And a good thing, too," said Joe, who was within earshot, as the coach at length succeeded in turning and drove away, " for the Scotch fiddle is not an agreeable instrument by any means."

And they re-entered the lodge, and resumed their seats and their chat, till Joe was startled by the clock striking six.

" Fancy! six o'clock already," said he, starting to his feet, " and it don't seem to be more than an hour since I have been here, instead of six hours. I was to have been down at the boat by six, waiting for master. Make haste, Bridget; get your hood quickly."

" I tell you what," said Mrs. Barton, " as the ladies are gone out walking, and Master Hartsfoot with them, I have no doubt he won't be at the waterside just yet. So I'll just write Madam Throckmorton's message on a sheet of paper, and you shall leave it up at the house, and go that way to the river, which is a much shorter one than round by the road, and you will then see that much of the house and grounds, and mind you don't rumple or soil the paper, and ask Mr. Jessop, or whoever opens the door, to be so good as to lay it on the hall table for madam to see when she comes in."

" Oh! thank you, mother; that will be famous, for I should so like to see the house and the grounds, for Lancelot told me there was a beautiful green covered walk in the garden, at least, in the front garden, longer than the matted gallery at White Hall, and the quality called it by some French name—a Charnel, I think—an odd name for anything in a pleasure garden."

"Charmille," corrected his mother, as she opened the walnut escritoire, and seated herself before it to write her message, which, when written, she handed to her son.

"Now, Bridget," said he, "give me down one of those bright pewter plates of yours; I'll lay the paper upon it, with a penny piece, to prevent its blowing away, though I hope you haven't forgotten the gentleman's fiddle, mother? as the French horn alone might blow the paper away; however, the fiddle might scratch the plate, and Bridget would not like that."

And before taking up the plate, he took an affectionate leave of his mother, who stood at the door watching him till he and his sister were out of sight, the latter not a little proud of being his cicerone, and doing the honours of "The Chestnuts." As for Joe, he was in extacies at all he saw; and no wonder, for even those who had seen all the fine places in England were always charmed with the air of luxurious comfort there was about this carefully kept up, quaint old place. What then must have been its effect

upon the unsophisticated taste and eyes of Joseph
Barton, who had never seen anything of the kind
before, or indeed, anything greener than the not
over verdant grass of the London Parks? With
the Charmille he was lost in alternate wonder
and admiration, and said he should like to sleep
there on one of those mossy couches every night
while the hot weather lasted. But, "Duty first
and Pleasure after," was one of Mrs. Merrypin's
maxims, that had been well kneaded into him.
So he cast one last, long wistful look at it, and
hurried on to the waterside, down the broad steps
of the Plaisaunce, where he found the boat and
his master's cloak, and the boatman asleep within
the impromptu oak bower of the barge, which
leafy *retiro* was still wonderfully fresh and green,
the bargeman having kept it constantly deluged
with water during the day, which had enabled it
effectually to resist the scorching rays of the
sun.

But Master Hartsfoot had not arrived, nor did
he arrive till a quarter to ten, when a fresh
breeze had sprung up, and the moonbeams were
dancing on the waters, which gave their ripple
the appearance of diamond beads, playing bo-
peep, and running after each other. As for
Master Hartsfoot, although he had neither been
at an election, nor at a public dinner, this really
had been " the happiest day of his life." And as

even an averagely happy day always gives the
fortunate mortal to whose lot it has fallen quite
enough to think over, we will not be such bores
as to obtrude ourselves upon Master Hartsfoot's
unusually pleasant cogitations, but leave him
tête-à-tête with them, to return to town.

CHAPTER IV.

T may be somewhat late in the day, or rather, night, since it was past ten p.m., to attend upon his Majesty at Hampton Court; unpardonably so, indeed, only it is not exactly with him that our business lies, but with one of the personages included in his suite upon the occasion of the King and the Court having had " an outing " on that particular 20th of July to Hampton Court;—and that is the proper word, as those who have " outings " there in the nineteenth century, or to Greenwich and Fairlop Fairs, scarcely indulge in more *sans géne,* coarseness, and vulgarity, with sundry other things, than did royalty, and the satellites of royalty, in those days. The Queen always, or nearly always, formed one of these parties, for appearances must be kept up ; and John Bull, whatever *striking* instances of affection he may bestow upon Mrs. Bull, would not in *those days—car nous avons changé tout çela*—have thought it right to " go a pleasuring " without

his " missus," consequently it was not deemed
polite that the King should do so either.   And
as Charles the Second had at least the justice and
the gratitude to own that Katharine of Braganza
was the best woman in the world, and bore with
a great deal, because he took care to supply her
sans relâche with a great deal to bear with, she
never was the least in his way—let the reader
twist that phrase into whatever sense he pleases—
so she was always quite welcome to come as a
make weight in these excursions ; and as for the
poor Queen, all she saw and did not like, which
amounted pretty nearly to all she did see, why
she had only to grin and bear it *comme çela se
pratique parmis mesdames les épouses,*—who have
not even the compensation of being queens, or,
being treated like Katharine, with princely good
breeding by their lords and masters.   On this
particular day, the Queen had wisely kept out of
his Majesty's way ; for the Duke of York, always

> " Pleased to ruin other's wooing,
> Never happy in his own,"

had told her that the King was *dans un chien
d'humeur*, Lady Castlemaine having disappeared
with young Jermyn some hours before, and
neither of them having re-appeared since.   When
the time came that they were to return to town,
the absentees put in an appearance ; the lady,
with a little giggle, declaring that they had got

into the maze, and could not find their way out,—
and then she was with perfect *sang froid* proceeding to enter the royal barge, when the King in-
tervened, and swore a great oath that she should
not. This was followed, some months later, by
a disgraceful scene at Whitehall, which Mr.
Pepys and other contemporary writers give *in
extenso*, but which is not—as the newspaper re-
porters sometimes say, though not half often
enough, in police reports—" fit for our pages."
For although to do us justice, vice never was so
rife, or more flagrant, than in the upper and lower
classes at the present day; yet are we finically
fastidious as to the propriety of our language—
never calling a spade a spade for the world, but
always an agricultural implement, for rendering
the argil more productive. Then, there is nothing
for varnishing, concealing, and protecting vice,
like the *suppressio veri* and *suggestio falsi*, or
fabricating fames, and tinkering up characters ;
and public life and public character, being the
only things needful in our enlightened age, we
have, what our poor blundering ancestors had not
for that purpose, the invaluable institution of
public dinners, conducted on the strictly Caledo-
nian co-operative system of "scratch me, and
I'll scratch you ;" where one (so far as the con-
veniently ignored myth of private life goes), notoriously unprincipled *vaurien*, be-plasters, with

the most fulsome flattery, some other notoriously
unprincipled *vaurien,* or *vauxrien,* — and the
Press disseminates the mendacious juggle, and
perpetuates the puff from pole to pole, till poor
Truth is effectually hustled back into her well by
this rabble rout of *charlatanrie* and clap-trap,
there to be hidden *sine die.*   But although we do
so carefully call a spade an agricultural implement, for rendering argil more productive, *de
facto,* it remains a spade, for all the fine words in
which we can disguise it to tickle the ears of the
public, and ineffectually, try to cheat the devil.
But despite this sesquipedalian epidemic, the real
will occasionally crop up in the midst of this
Brummagem verbal ideal, or rather, because of
it; as, for instance, when the penny-a-liners, in
describing a marriage, always speak of it as " the
imposing ceremony," which it most unquestionably is, and not only imposing, but a most
terrible imposition to at least nine women out of
ten.   As for us Athletes of the might is right
sex, the very worst blank we can draw in the
Matrimonial State Lottery, has no more disad-
vantages, or permanent influence upon the " pro-
cession of our lives," than a pebble—or say even
the heaviest stone when flung, were it with giant
force, into a river ;—the waters are divided for a
moment, an abnormal circle widens round the
division for another moment, then the waters

close, and are free and smooth as before, and the
current flows on in the same course. But with our
victims it is very different; if Fate decides against
them, in their one venture, their lives are torn up
root and branch in a present, that becomes an
Eternity without a future! for what after sunshine *can*

    " Raise the flowers that droop from a blighted bough?"

And as all our laws are made in the sole aim
of crushing the weak still farther, and giving
more brute force to the strong, where is there
hope for them? For what is ONE John Stuart
Mill, profoundest of thinkers, most honest,
and large hearted of men!—and ONE Russell
Gurney, noble, political Leonidas! as he is,
or ONE Jacob Bright, against so many?
Then, God only helps those who help themselves; and, what between silliness, selfishness, and the Procrustes bed of stultification
and nullity, upon which Custom has stretched
them, women alas! do *not* help themselves; so
they must e'en remain, what Mr. Mill so truly
calls them, " THE SUPPRESSED SEX." And we
must return to the only class of women, who,
upon the homœopathic principle of like to like,
divide, and govern, and share the world with
men—the profligate and the worthless;—so that
from this equitable plan of going halves, this

sort of women in our days are very properly called the *demi monde*.

Lady Castlemaine, when the King insisted that she should *not* enter the royal barge, and, moreover, made a parade of holding out his hand and announcing that he was waiting to hand the Queen in, tried to brazen it out, and endeavoured to push past and get into the barge, as if she had not heard the royal veto, or affected to think it was not addressed to her ; but Jermyn pulled her back, and said, in a whisper—

" For goodness sake, don't ; for don't you see the state he is in ?—besides the devil's own passion, he's not very sober ; and, as *in vino veritas*, he might say things for the benefit of the boatmen that you would not like."

" Oh ! then I'll go with the Duke of York."

" That's all in the succession," said Lord Rochester ; " for, of course, the Duke of York comes after the King. But since when, belle Barbara, have you been such a stickler for legitimacy ?"

" Ever since I have thought it the most natural thing in the world to box the ears of such an impertinent jackanapes."

And, suiting the action to the word, she gave John Wilmot, Earl of Rochester, a swinging box on the ear.

" I thank your ladyship, in my wife's name, for so kindly taking so much trouble off of her hands," said he, removing his hat, and making her a low bow.

" Ho ! Killigrew," he cried, turning round and clutching his cloak, " which barge are you for ?"

" I was thinking of going with the Duke of York."

" Oh ! then, if you are going with the King— "

" Going with the King ?" interrupted Killigrew. " What are you thinking of man ? don't you know that figuratively, or literally, the Duke of York and the King never row in the same boat ?"

" Yes—yes—I know that as a rule; but all rules have their exceptions, and anon I saw the Queen hanging on the Duke of York's arm, and just after, I heard the King calling for his cloak —that is to say, his Queen—and so I thought we were to return in state, all the royalties under one consignment. For to tell you the truth—I know you like novelty—I want to go in the same boat with that charming Madame de la Tour de Pin, that friend of the queen mother, who, by-the-bye, seems quite horrified at our *laisser aller.* I suppose, like the rest of her deluded compatriots, she thought we were a nation of *Guindées* and *collets montés;* at all events I have not been able to make any way with her all day."

" Ho ! I say, Rochester," said Lord Berkeley,

coming up, and taking him by the arm, "I wish you would go in the Duchess of York's barge; she wants me to go to trim the boat, as she candidly told me ; but Titus has promised me some fun with four more fellows, in a boat he has chartered, the butt being that pompous ass Broderick, who is as surly as a bear, and as drunk as Bacchus."

" *À tout seigneur, tout honneur !* Not for the world, my dear Berkeley, would I deprive *you* of the honour of escorting her royal highness. Ahem ! first, because I don't think that a plump white hand, is sufficient compensation in any woman for such a face. *Suprême de Gorgon à l'imbécile,* I should call it, and next, because we have been playing hide and seek all day. I leave you the Hyde, while I seek my French inhuman. By all that's graceful, and charming, and provoking, there she goes, and by herself, too."

And he darted after Madame de Latour de Pin, as she was walking down to the waterside.

" Permettez, Madame ?" said Rochester, offering her his arm.

" *Merçi, monsieur, mais me voila arrivée.*"

" *Ah ! Madame,*" said he, clasping his hands, and sighing profoundly; " *par pitié ? par charité ?*"

" *Impossible, monsieur ; j'ai mais pauvres.*"

And she walked on, without even looking at

him, when at that moment the Queen called to
her from the royal barge, and invited her into it,
the King extending his hand to help her into the
boat.

Lord Rochester turned upon his heel, exclaiming—

"*Ah! mais elle est charmante, du moins elle
vous pique avec des bons mots; au lien de vous
assomer de soufflets, comme une cuisinière, à la
Castlemaine.*"

"Make haste," cried Colonel Titus, nearly upsetting him as he ran past him to stop Killigrew;
"I've got the boat all ready, the only thing is to
get Sir Allen in, which won't be so easy, for he
vows he'll go with the King."

"I say, Rochester," said Killigrew, "you may
as well go with us, as we mean to get some fun
out of Pomposo, if we can only manage to secure
him."

"What's the matter with him?" asked
Rochester; "I heard he was very ill."

"Pooh! only ill-looking; *au reste*, he is like
Monsieur de Pourçaugnac, '*il mange bien, et boit
encore mieux,*' as we shall see just now."

"There, thank goodness the King's off," cried
Titus, "so Sir Allen *must* fall to our lot now, if
we can only get him by fair means or foul off of
that bench, which he has evidently mistaken for
his bed.   Come, Rochester, you've 'a tongue can

wheedle with the devil ;' come and help us to get this living cask of Rhenish into the boat."

And the trio, headed by Lord Rochester, marched forward to the bench, where Sir Allen was snoring in so uproarious a manner that he must greatly have disturbed and alarmed the poor birds.

" Odds so ! Sir Allen," said Killigrew, poking him with his sword sheath, " are you driving a hard bargain with the night air for a long lease of lumbago ?"

" Ugh !" grunted Sir Allen.

" The King is waiting for you," put in Titus.

" Le—Le—let him wait," hiccoughed Sir Allen, waiving his hand as majestically as his then state would allow him to do.

" Come, come, Sir Allen," said Rochester, " rouse yourself, or you'll lose the last boat, and have to stay here all night."

" Go to the devil," growled Sir Allen, not quite awake.

" *Mille grâces, mais il me faut des renseigne-ments,* I should not like to venture so far, till I have talked the matter over with *you,* knowing that *there,* you are *en pays de connaissance.*"

" Ha ! ha ! ha ! well hit, Rochester," roared Killigrew and Titus.

" What the plague are the fools laughing at ?" said Sir Allen, now opening one eye, and looking up at them.

" We are laughing to think," said Titus, " how we three—Rochester Killigrew, and I— shall have all that hamper of choice Steinberg, sent down expressly for the King, to ourselves going home, since you don't mean to come with us, Sir Allen."

" Oh !" grunted Sir Allen, now putting his feet to the ground, and trying to stand up by clutching the arm of the garden seat. " Oh ! Steinberg—hopeshking don't shink I'm drunk—ish dam damp Irish cimeate, when wash over there, gave rheumacschism in limsh—never walk shrait since."

" But even supposing such an improbable thing as that you *were* drunk, or even an habitual drunkard, my dear Sir Allen," said Rochester, " don't you know that Tacitus, in Siberio, says that men have reformed inveterate habits more by yielding to them, than by warring against them, though a man must so yield as not to encourage, while he so counteracts as not to exasperate—whatever that means ?"

" Tashitush shay that ?—clever fellow ! Ashk him to dinner ;—come and meet him ?—fixsh your own day."

" Yes—but you had better have t'other bottle first, Sir Allen, to show that you have followed his advice."

" Easty shay have t'other bottle ; but where am I to get it ? parch with thirst all day, and not a drop sho drink. T'other bottle! where am I sho get it?"

" Why, in the boat, I tell you; there's a whole hamper full, if you'll only come with us?"

" Yesh, yesh, I'll come," said Sir Allen, trying to rise; "but you mush help me;—can't walk, for thish confounded rheumashism."

" Never mind; if you can't walk, you can talk when you are labouring under an attack of rheumatism, for don't you remember that magnificent (!) speech in the House of Commons that night you were in a rheumatic fever? Gad, sir, the speaker said he never heard anything like it!" said Killigrew.

" Ah! but that dog Apshley wash jealous of me, and tried to talk me down; but I pershevered, though the shpeaker wash drunk, and all the Houshe drunk, for they shaid they could not hear two Shir Allen's at once; shaw double the dogs—shaw double!"

" Well, now, let us have double and quits," said Rochester; " for if you don't quit directly, Sir Allen, we shall have to stay here all night."

" Ah! before I can catch the shpeaker's eye—"

" Or catch anything but our death of cold," rejoined Killigrew; " so you had better let your motion be carried by a majority, Sir Allen."

And so saying, he and Titus seized his shoulders, while Lord Rochester took possession of his feet, and so bore him to the boat, without any resistance on his part, for he was too far gone to make any. Having reached the boat, they lifted this fragment of the collective wisdom of the nation into it, placed him in one corner, Titus sitting beside him to prevent his falling overboard.

" Now for 'tother bottle," said Sir Allen.

" In one moment," rejoined Killigrew, " only —excepting yourself, Sir Allen—we have not a screw on board."

" For mercy's sake," said Rochester, " unless you want to have us all indicted for manslaughter, don't give him any more."

" Never fear," said Titus. " If he wants more drink, there's the Thames for him, and what he likes in his potations, no stint."

" Come now, Sir Allen," said Killigrew, " open confession is good for the soul—*do* tell us what you have done with your son ?"

" Cuff him off with a shilli," spluttered that affectionate father.

" It must be a good sharp shilling to do *that*, when the estate is entailed," rejoined the other.

" 'Twasn't tails, 'twas heads," said Sir Allen.

" Well, heads or tails, no one can make head or tail of what you have done with him."

" Yes, I've done with him—quite done with him—but where's t'other bottle ? Kingsh wine, you shay, sho you needn't shpare it."

" T'other bottle, with plenty of other bottles, you'll find in your cellar at home."

" Thath's the way the king's cheated," hiccoughed Sir Allen; " the peoplesh about him promish to give away hish wine, and never give it."

" Ah !" said Killigrew, " a little more of that very peculiar sort of cheating might set the poor man on his legs again."

" D—n legsh, there no ushe when one's gosh the rheumachism."

The night, which had been as light as day, from the brilliant moon, became gradually clouded; large drops, either of rain or heat, began to fall, and presently the boat was shaken by a terrific clap of thunder.

" There ! see what you have brought down upon us, Sir Allen," said Killigrew. " I shall have to read the act against profane swearing."

And as he spoke there was another still louder peal, which was answered by shrill screams from many of the women in the innumerable boats, which were now trying to row as fast as possible out of the storm.

" Trust the City madams," said Rochester;

"not content with outdoing the duchesses in dress, they must outdo the thunder in noise."

"I tell you we're invaded!" said Sir Allen, a shade more sober from the panic; "itsh either the Dutch or the French; which ish it, the French or the Dutch? for I will fight 'em," trying to draw his sword.

"The Dutch, I should say," said Rochester, "judging from your courage."

"Have at 'em! I don't mind cheese and red herrings," and Sir Allen made a desperate effort to jump into the water.

"In the name of all the devils, be quiet, man, or you'll capsize the boat, and furnish the Thames with more flounders than its lawful quantity," said Titus, holding him down by main force.

Now the rain came down in such torrents, that it returned almost a metalic sound as the myriad drops bubbled and rebounded from the bottom of the boat.

"Let me go!" vociferated Sir Allen; "don't you hear, they are riddling us with shot? It shall never be said that I was afraid to be under fire!"

"Under fire! it's under water you'll be, if you don't sit still," said Colonel Titus, making another desperate effort to hold him down—but being by the skirts of his coat that he held him, the velvet tore off, and remained in the hands of

Titus—and the next moment one tremendous
plash! announced that Sir Allen was in the
water.

"Man in the water!" they shouted as loud as
they could.

"Take hold, Sir Allen?" cried one of the boatmen, holding out his oar; but it was now so
dark they could hardly, in the *mêlée*, distinguish
any object, for there was a sort of general *sauve
qui peut* on the river.

"For God's sake," said Rochester, "is there
no means of striking a light?"

"Bill," said the boatman, who was still holding the oar out over the boat to his comrade,
"there's a tinder-box in the hold, and my
lantern."

And Bill proceeded to grope for them; at last
he succeeded in baffling the rain, and striking a
light, with which he ignited the two inches of
candle in the lantern.

"Give it to me, my man?" said Rochester,
holding out his hand for it, and then holding it
up over the side of the boat. "There he is! I see
him!" cried he, as the little track of light from
the lantern fell athwart the rain on the river.
"Sir Allen!" shouted he, "just turn, and catch
hold of the oar."

But there was another boat still nearer to Sir
Allen, in which were ʼtwo dark figures—one of

very stalwart dimensions—so near, indeed, that
with no greater effort than leaning forward a
little way over the side of the boat; and making
a vigorous grasp at Sir Allen's arm with both
his hands, he drew him close alongside of the
boat, when the other man helped him to draw in
the now perfectly sobered, but insensible baronet.

"Thank God!" said Rochester, re-seating
himself, and still holding the lantern, "he is safe
now, and that is all I care for; for a frolic that
costs a life, however worthless that life may be,
is paying rather too dearly for one's fun."

"Amen!" said the other two.

"It would have gone hard with us," said
Titus, " had he been drowned, because we made
no secret of our intention of making a *plastron*
of him."

"No doubt," said Killigrew, " it would have
been supposed that we had had some hand—
whether in jest or in earnest—in pushing him
overboard."

" Yes, *et gare les apparences!*" said Rochester,
"and you may *do* what you please ; that was the
pivot of old Nol's policy, and see how well it
worked—the winning machine for him ;—whereas,
we fellows, including our royal master, are always
disregarding appearances, and don't they take
their revenge ! in the actions they bring against
us, *via* their attorneys of the firm of Rumour,

Gossip, and Fibs,—and the terrible accounts we
have to settle treble our real debt "

" Aye, very true," said Killigrew. " Yet were
I a saint, and qualified to preach—which I need
not inform you I am not—this is the text I should
take—' My brethren—' "

" Oh—come, none of that," interrupted Titus,
" as a wet Quaker would be the only piece of
sanctification qualified to hold forth under our
present circumstances."

" Don't be alarmed ; I'm not going to discharge the sermon, only to snap the text at you,
which should be ' My brethren, sin is quite bad
enough, for it makes us risk the loss of Heaven ;
but hypocrisy is ten times worse, for it entitles
us to take high degrees in hell.' "

" Bravo ! Kil. You shall have the living of
Porridge-Cum-Pence the very moment it falls
vacant."

" I wonder," said Rochester, " who the fortunate mortals were who fished up Sir Allen ?"

" Two thoroughly unlucky poor devils, that's
evident," said Killigrew ; " practical illustrations
in fact, of that eel and serpent hypothesis of the
basket of eels, containing *one* serpent, which the
typical unlucky wight is sure to draw forth when
he goes fishing for eels. That is, taking it for
granted that the Thames is so far on a par with
the sea, as that there are as good fish in it as

ever were caught, these poor wretches, you perceive, whomsoever they may be, missed all the
good fish and caught the ONE Broderick !"

Here they arrived at Whitehall stairs, drenched
to the skin, and as there were plenty of lanterns
and flambeaux at the landing, they looked about
to see if they could perceive anything of Sir
Allen ; but he, like that other luminary, the
moon, was not visible to the naked eye just
then.

CHAPTER V.

WHEN Sir Allen Broderick, after having had too much wine, was likely to suffer still more from the other extreme, of having a great deal too much water, and was hauled up into the boat of the two strangers, he was perfectly insensible, a circumstance to which, in all probability, he owed his life; for, from being so, he floated passively on his back, instead of struggling against and buffeting the waters, which would infallibly have mastered him, for, unlike his son, he was no swimmer. It so happened that the man who had caught his arm and pulled him to the boat, was a medical practitioner; in short—for we hate having secrets from the reader when there is no absolute necessity for it—it was Doctor Erasmus Everhard and his man, Sampson Golightly, who had also been "a pleasuring" upon that treacherous July day, which had began so fairly and ended so foully.

It was too dark to distinguish the features of

the person they had rescued, but Dr. Everhard laid him at full length at the bottom of the boat, on his face first, so as to let any water run out of his mouth.

"Lord save us! I fear, Doctor, we have been meddling with the sexton's business, and have over-hampered ourselves with a corpse," said Sampson.

"No," rejoined the Doctor, turning round the body on its back, and passing his hand inside the clothes, "there is a slight pulsation in the region of the heart. Put your hand in my right coat pocket, and give me the brandy flask; now don't make a mistake, for the sack is in the left hand pocket, and I'll rub the chest and abdomen well with it."

"Eh!" groaned Sampson, " what people take inside there is, at all events, some comfort in return for it, even if the liquor is given away; but those outside drams always seem to me like throwing it away,—pearls before swine sort of work. However, it's to be hoped you'll bring him to, sir, for he is a sprig of quality, as I heerd the gentry in the boat, out of which he fell, call him 'Sir Allen,' several times, though, to be sure, he may be only a city knight."

"He'll soon be nothing at all," said the doctor, " if we can't manage to revive him. You take off his wet shoes and stockings Sampson, and rub the soles of his feet well with brandy; I'll give you the flask when you have got his stockings off."

" Law ! said Sampson, " no doubt he's a quality, I feel diamonds, or leastways jewels of some sort in the rosettes of his shoes."

" Here's the brandy ; now rub it into the soles of his feet as hard as ever you can."

" Well, there can be no doubt," said Sampson, as he rubbed away with all his might, " that this is the soberest way of taking *sperrits*, for brandy at the feet is not likely to get into the head."

" I say, my men," said the doctor, addressing the boatmen, " as soon as we land have the goodness, one of you, to go and get me a hackney coach. You shall have a shilling for your trouble."

" Very good, sir; I only hope as I shall be able to find one, for these sort of storms we call hack harvests."

" I feel an increased action of the heart," said the doctor to Sampson, as they both continued their frictions. " I think he'll do now, though I doubt his coming quite to himself till we have got him into a warm bed."

When they at length arrived they had to wait full half an hour, before the boatman could succeed in finding a hackney coach, but at last he stopped one with miserably jaded horses, that had

been plying all night, but their owner, for the
bribe of a double fare—there being no Society for
the Prevention of Cruelty to Animals in those
days—at length consented, instead of letting the
poor animals continue their way to the stable, to
make them undergo another martyrdom as far as
the Barbican.   So slow and funereal was their
pace, that despite the deep ruts and otherwise
abominable state of the streets, the jolts, though
by no means few, were yet so far between, that
they did not seriously incommode the living,
while Sir Allen, who was in a very good imitation of death, did not feel them at all.

Arrived before Dr. Everhard's fortified looking
house, the coachman got down, and was about to
tamper with the detonating knocker, when Sampson called out to him to desist, and his master
giving him the key of the hall door, he got out,
opened it, and in the hall struck a light, when he
returned, and paying the coachman, assisted his
master in carrying in Sir Allen, and laying him
on a couch in the " consulting room," till Dorcas
Fairfax, the sum total of the doctor's female
establishment, could be knocked up to make and
warm the bed in " the best bedroom."

" Sir ! Sir !" cried Sampson, holding the candle
to Sir Allen's face, as soon as they had laid him
down—the doctor having walked to the other
side of the room to take off his wet coat and hat

—" Sir ! may I be strait waistcoated if this isn't the very lord that called so mysterious some months ago, and gave me a Jacobus ; leastways, of course he ain't a lord if he's a sir ; still, them as pays like lords may fairly be called lords, as it don't cost no more."

Dr. Everhard rapidly retraced his steps at this announcement, foreseeing vague but golden vistas to his exchequer from it.

" By St. Luke ! you are right, Sampson. Go, for goodness sake, wake up Dorcas, and make all possible haste with the bed ; but it must be warmed, quite hot, hot sheets, hot blankets, and I'll continue rubbing the gentleman till you return."

The doctor did so, occasionally slapping Sir Allen's hands, when he perceived on his little finger a very large sapphire signet ring. He slipped it off and examined it at the light ; there were arms with many quarterings and supporters, a cap of maintenance, but no coronet, only a bloody hand.

" Oh ! then," thought Dr. Everhard, " he *is* a sir, and not a lord after all."

Having ascertained this fact, he carefully replaced the ring on its owner's finger.

Dr. Everhard rubbed and watched, and watched and rubbed, till at length Sampson returned, and announced that the bed was ready ; and Dorcas was continuing to pass the warming-pan through the blankets till the gentleman was ready to be put into them. So they carried him upstairs ; the doctor acting as valet, and, carefully removing his purse, watch, and a pocket-book from the pocket of the wet clothes—which though, of course, completely spoilt, he gave to Sampson to have dried—and slipping one of his own shirts over " the patient," as he called Sir Allen to Dorcas, ordered her to get his linen washed and done up by noon the next day, as he certainly would not be sufficiently recovered to leave before that hour. Once carefully enveloped in the hot blankets, the doctor sat beside the bed, ordering Dorcas to keep ready a hot sack posset all night, and as soon as the bricks that Sampson had put in the fire were heated, to bring them up to apply to " the patient's " feet.   Dr. Everhard, as soon as his servants had withdrawn, felt an almost irresistible curiosity to examine the pocket-book—to try and discover from its contents some clue, if possible, to " the style and title " of his patient ; but prudence, that frequent deputy for honour, restrained him, for the pocket-book, which was a purple velvet one, clasped with a gold clasp, was saturated ;—the papers might be in a pulp, and if so, would not gratify his curiosity, but would certainly compromise him by leaving it evident that they had been tampered with.   The shoes he next looked at ; in the centre of each of the large, crimson ribbon rosettes were, as Sampson had announced, " jewels "—that is, a large diamond button, set in a *pavé* in each of them. These Dr. Everhard now took out of the wet ribbon, and laid carefully on the table beside the watch, purse, and pocket-book—to show the gentleman when he awoke, that even if Dr. Everhard had enacted the good Samaritan, he, the gentleman, had not " fallen among thieves."

The night wore on, or rather morning, for it had been two a.m. before the rumbling old hackney coach had deposited its freight in Barbican. The " patient," at about six, when the bright summer sun was piercing through the interstices of the heavy, black, oak shutters, breathed a profound sigh, like a person suddenly relieved of a great weight; the doctor felt his pulse—there was nothing feeble or uncertain about it.

" If your Majesty chooses, I'll ask Prince Rupert ; he ought to know," murmured Sir Allen, and then called, in a louder voice, " Charlton ! my boots ;—we ride to Hampton Court."

Charlton was his valet, and Hampton Court was evidently still uppermost in his mind.

" Ah ! that's better, and safer, than going by water, sir," responded the doctor.

" Who the devil asked your opinion ?" said Sir

Allen, not quite awake, and thinking it was
Charlton who had the impertinence to obtrude his
opinion; but though not quite awake, it is easy
to perceive by this reply that " The Honourable
Gentleman," as they say in a certain House where
they have a great many " Honourable Gentle-
tlemen," without having too many gentlemen of
honour,—it is easy to perceive, we say, by this
reply, that " The Honourable Gentleman " was
quite himself.

" Well," said the doctor, again feeling his
pulse, " I should not have obtruded my opinion,
sir, had I not seen how nearly the water had been
the means of depriving you of life."

Sir Allen now opened his eyes with the intention of selecting some missile to fling at Charlton's head; for which purpose, he raised himself
by leaning on his right elbow, and with a look
of half-rage, half-bewilderment, stared fixedly in
Dr. Erasmus Everhard's face ; and at length, removing his eyes from it, and looking round the
strange, unfamiliar room, upon a chair of which,
opposite the foot of the bed, reposed the neatly
folded ticking of a quite new strait waistcoat,
surmounted, by way of crest, with a pair of handcuffs laid on the top of it. Sir Allen now sat
quite upright in bed, as he exclaimed—

" Why ! where on earth am I ?"

" No doubt, sir," replied the Doctor : " you

neither remember me, nor the visit you honoured
me with on a matter of very private business,
some eight or nine months ago.   I am Dr.
Erasmus Everhard ; and, with my servant, had
the pleasure of rescuing you from a watery grave
during a terrific storm, about midnight, yesterday,
when you were returning with some other gentlemen in a boat from Hampton Court, having,
perhaps, taken a little too much wine,—as gentlemen are wont to do in these excursions of his
Majesty's—when, unfortunately, you lost your
balance, and fell into the water.   Not having the
honour of knowing your exact name—though the
gentlemen called after you as ' Sir Allen,'—nor
your address, I could not convey you to your own
house ; so had no alternative but to bring you to
mine, and use every possible means of resuscita-
ting you, which has happily succeeded."

" The devil !" murmured Sir Allen, while the
remainder of his unuttered thought was—" to
think that a fellow cannot escape from the jaws
of death without being hurled into the harpy
clutches of danger !"   But he felt that his policy
—that Pole Star of bad men's lives—was to con-
ciliate, and, alas ! to gag—for that is always an
expensive process—the doctor by all possible
means.   So, clasping his hands under similar
obligations, he said—

" So, in fact, Dr. Everhard, I am indebted to

your courage and humanity for my life ; it is not for words to repay such an obligation."

" Don't mention it, my dear sir," said the Doctor, acting upon that peculiar species of commercial generosity, always exercised by tradesmen to customers about to pay them a bill, when it invariably happens that they never do want it, unless *quite* convenient; while to those customers, to whom payment is *not* convenient, their necessity for money is so urgent as to be rather unpleasantly enforced. " Don't mention it. I rescued you in the dark as A should always rescue B, no matter who, or what he may be ; and it was not till I had brought you here that I recognized the gentleman to whom I had been so fortunate as to render this little timely assistance. Your clothes, I regret to say, are of course, quite spoilt ; but your property—that is the valuables you had about you—are, I believe, all safe," added he, bringing them off the table and laying them on the bed ; and then opening one leaf of the window shutter that Sir Allen might have more light to examine the things by. " When I said all your valuables were safe," resumed the Doctor, " I forgot to state that you had no hat on when we drew you up into my boat, so I can only hope that there were no jewels in it ?"

" Only a jewelled hand, worth about eighteen hundred pounds," said Sir Allen, with more resignation, feigned or real, than the mother of the Gracchi could have had recourse to, had she lost *her* jewels.

" Tut, tut, tut, tut !" murmured the Doctor, throwing up his hands and eyes.

" Oh !" said Sir Allen, who, between the external scrubbings of the blankets, which, like many other things, now their services were no longer needed, were very troublesome, and the internal thistles and branches of *contretemps* and dilemmas, was beginning to realise what St. Lawrence must have suffered on his gridiron. " Oh! thanks to your care and kindness, Doctor, I am fortunate in having saved so much."

" I hope," said the sympathising doctor, " that they were not gems of the first water ?"

" Well, they *were*, but now they are of the second water !" rejoined their quondam owner, with a laugh, so crackling and shrivelled, that it really sounded as if it had been grilled to a cinder on the aforesaid gridiron.

" I must go and order you some breakfast, for after rescuing you from drowning I must not let you die of starvation," said the doctor, preparing to leave the room.

" Stay," said Sir Allen, taking up his purse, " I must trespass still further on your kindness, doctor, to let your servant bring for me a horseman's cloak, a plain, slouched, felt hat, without feathers, and a pair of common black riding boots. One of my shoes will show him the size, and if you will extend your hospitality to me till the dusk of the evening I will then trouble your servant to get me a hackney coach ?"

" By all means, my dear sir; but could I not send to your house and tell your servant to bring your own things here for you to dress ?"

" Not for the world," cried Sir Allen, looking rather blacker than the cloud which had ushered in the thunder storm on the preceding night; but adding, in the blandest voice of his *répertoire,* " It would alarm my family too much. Ha! ha! ha! you know what vapourish creatures wives are; but I will talk to you presently of a matter of importance to us *both.*"

And the doctor, scenting more money in his guest's evident reluctance to discover his name and abode, philosophically pocketed this disappointment to his baffled curiosity, and merely said,

" Of course, my dear sir, whatever you wish shall be strictly attended to," as he left the room to order breakfast, and to despatch Sampson for the long horseman's camlet cloak, felt hat, and boots, that Sir Allen had ordered.

Meanwhile, the latter remained for a few minutes in a brown—or rather in a black—study, unmercifully pulling his under lip.

" Humph!" thought he, " that wife scarecrow

was a good blind of mine to throw him off the
scent, and it's quite evident he does *not* know my
name, and only knows that I am a Sir Allen
somebody. Well, thank goodness, there are
other Sir Allen's in the world, though only *one*
Sir Allen Broderick."

And here he involuntarily placed his hand upon
his right hip, and drew up, with that air of ram-
pant self consequence which he called dignity,
and the world—pomposity. Had any one been
there to witness it, the effect was altogether
ludicrous, considering the bathos of the *mise en
scène*, viz., the blankets, a red woollen night-cap
of the doctor's, tightly bound round the head with
a yellow silk kerchief for the sake of heat, and
the charming little *échappée* from the foot of the
bed of the strait waistcoat and the handcuffs on
the distant chair, though in this case, " distance"
by no means "lent enchantment to the view."
But the eye cannot see itself, neither did Sir
Allen, hand on hip and head thrown back with a
fine Roman air, see how superlatively ridiculous he
looked. On the contrary, he was as usual wrapped
up in that great problem—himself; therefore
blankets could not smother, nor red nightcaps
could not extinguish his infinite importance.
At length he exclaimed with an Eureka air, removing his hand from his hip and slapping it
down on the blanket—

" I have it ! Apsley *has* a wife. Blind number two.''

And then seizing the still damp pocket book which Dr. Everhard had left with the other things on the bed, he opened it, and carefully looked over the papers, which were all there, and amongst them a note he had written the day before, all ready sealed, to Sir Allen Apsley. The address—

" To

" SIR ALLEN APSLEY,

" 8, SPRING GARDEN,

" LONDON."

—though the water had caused the ink to run a little, was perfectly, or perhaps on that account, more legible, as it made the writing broader. Sir Allen now carefully broke the seal, crumbling up his own arms, the *débris* of which he put in his pocket-book ; he then carefully abstracted the note he had written from the envelope, putting the former also back into the pocket-book, while the envelope he resolved on his departure from Dr. Everhard's stronghold in the evening, to leave accidentally on purpose on the toilet table, so that the doctor or his man finding it, would naturally conclude that they had discovered his carefully concealed identity, and that they had saved Sir Allen Apsley's life.

Now in this supposition, *per se*, there would have been no great harm ; but, taken in conjunction with Sir Allen Broderick's first visit to Doctor Everhard, with the endeavour to get a certificate of lunacy against his dead sister, in order to invalidate her will, ordinary mortals may consider this—as what it unquestionably was—a most iniquitous and rascally proceeding. But Sir Allen Broderick was not an ordinary mortal ; he was a shrewd, sharp, pre-eminently selfish, and unscrupulous man, which the world condenses into what the said world always worships—as " a monstrous clever man." And your " monstrous clever men," or women either, in the mundane acceptation of the term, are far too clever ever to care by what means they gain their ends, or by what hecatombs of broken hearts and ruined names they secure *their* safety.

When Doctor Everhard returned, followed by Sampson with the breakfast tray, Sir Allen was in the act of rubbing his hands, from satisfaction at having now clearly and thoroughly concocted his whole plot ; for to those who, like Sir Allen Broderick, are in the habit of plotting, scheming, and manœuvring about everything, they naturally become adepts in their craft, and it does not take them long to weave the most complex webs in the service of the poor flies whom they intend to destroy.

" So, my *friend,*" said the great man, with
mingled dignity and condescension, addressing
Sampson ;—the dignity being rather too much in
the ascendant, considering the red woollen night-
cap,—only Sir Allen forgot, or, rather, ignored
that scarlet sin.   "So, my friend, I have much
to thank you for, as well as your worthy master,
and I assure you I shall not forget it."

" Oh ! sir," said Sampson, bowing almost to
the very ground, while his arms and hands hung
in a sort of neutral position beside him, as if he
was going to practice a little amateur carpet
swimming, "both master and I was most proud
and happy to be instruments in the Lord's hands
to save you from the fate of Jonah—or wus—as
there ain't no whales handy in the Thames.   But
I hope, sir," added he, like all his class, losing
no opportunity of *se faisant valoir,* "as you
found all your jewellery correct ? for, as soon as
we had got you safe out of the water, and I felt
—for it was too pitch dark to see—but I felt as
there was jewels in your shoe ribbons, I was
terrible concerned to take care on 'em ; and when
we did land at last, I was sadly afeared—as in
that bad weather, and at that late hour—we
should never get a coach ;—and master, he
rubbed away at your chest, and I at your feet,
till I began to think as we should make holes in
your skin !"

" In my purse, at all events," thought Sir Allen, who perfectly understood the drift of this " abstract and brief chronicle " of all the trouble he had given to master and man.

But thoughts are one thing, and words are another, and as nobody better understood the difference that *clever* people always place between them than Sir Allen Broderick, he said—

" Yes, I am quite aware of all the horrible trouble I must have given you, and I can only repeat, friend, that I shall never forget it."

Sampson bowed in silence; but he had his thoughts, too, which put into words ran thus—

" That's twice he's said he'll never *forget it*, but I wonder if that means that he'll *remember me* as a gentleman ought?"

" Oh!—about the cloak, and things; were you good enough to order them ?"

" They will be here by noon, sir, when your own linen will be ready for you to put on, and when I bring up the water for you to wash and dress."

And Sampson, having placed the breakfast tray on a table by the bedside, and Sir Allen having affably requested the pleasure of Dr. Everhard's company to breakfast, the Doctor inquired what his guest generally took for his morning draught—" a cool kankard? or a flask of Rhenish ?"

" Why, generally Rhenish," said Sir Allen;

" but I suppose, having got into the way of it last night, I'd rather have nothing but cold water this morning; at all events, no wine."

" Oh! well," laughed the Doctor, " as far as *vin de pompe* goes, my cellar is always well supplied. Now mind, Sampson, take the stone pitcher and pump till the water is as bright as hope and as cold as charity, or faith we'll none of it."

" Pray," said Sir Allen, as if the thought had only just struck him, " did those fellows in the boat with me make any effort to save me when I fell overboard ?"

" Oh! yes, they held out an oar to you; lit a lantern, and called out several times—' Sir Allen ! Sir Allen! just turn round and take hold of the oar;' but you did not heed or hear them, being, I suppose, insensible at the time."

" Humph!" said Sir Allen, and remained in silent cogitation till Sampson returned with the water, of which the Doctor poured him out a large glass, with a degree of sympathetic alacrity, that did credit to his memory; and his doing unto others as he would they should do unto him, as the Doctor had suffered from similar causes too often himself, to press any other beverage on his guest, after having " made a night of it."

Breakfast over, the things removed, and Sampson withdrawn,

" Now, my dear Dr. Everhard," said Sir Allen,

in his most cajoling tone, " I must endeavour—
though I feel I never can do so adequately—to
express my deep gratitude for all your kindness
and humanity."

" Oh! my dear sir," interrupted the Doctor.

But Sir Allen waived his hand to bespeak attention, and continued—

" Yet, although I cannot do so adequately, I
will do so to the best of my ability, the more so,
that for certain family reasons, I cannot continue an intercourse with one for whom I have
conceived so high an esteem ; but, unfortunately,
so far as appearances go, we must be as perfect
strangers to each other in the event of our ever
meeting in future, in the many shifting scenes of
life. I only regret, that for your sake, I am not
a rich man, and that I am hampered with a large
and expensive family (!) but, if you will meet
me to-morrow night, at ten o'clock, outside
Hercules' Pillars—for it would not be prudent of
me to return here—I will bring you five hundred
pounds ; only wishing I could make it treble the
sum—but you fully understand, doctor, that in
appearance, in case of any casual meeting between us, we are ever to continue strangers to
each other."

The Doctor *understood* everything, and was
overwhelmed with gratitude, putting in a well-
acted protest against receiving so large a sum ;

but Sir Allen's generosity and gratitude were in-exorable, and so the Doctor yielded, for there are very few in the world who do not yield to golden arguments.

The day wore on, Sir Allen had great difficulty in inducting himself into his shrunken garments ; yet was determined he would not leave them after him, as records, and the long horseman's cloak effectually concealed all their deficiencies and dilapidations.

Dr. Everhard, too, glad of any excuse for so doing, provided an ample and luxurious dinner ; but although he had too much tact and considera-tion to press his guest to drink much wine, that did not prevent him in his *rôle d'Amphytrion,* drinking Sir Allen's health in reiterated bumpers. At length, to the great relief of the latter, evening came, and with it a hackney coach, into which Sir Allen sprang, having first *sown* " golden opinions " of himself throughout the doctor's household, by presenting Dorcas Fairfax, for her services in the warming pan and blanket depart-ment, with a couple of Jacobuses, and Sampson Golightly with twenty.

Upon getting into the coach he ordered the man to set him down at the " Mulberry Tree Tavern," Charing Cross, but immediately after, as if it escaped him inadvertently, in a fit of ab-sence, he cried out—

" No, stop ; I may as well go home at once ; take me to No. 8, Spring Garden."

At which counterorder Sampson winked at his master, and tossing up his cap as the coach rumbled off, and the hall door shut it from their view, he said—

" Well, sir, I think we went a pleasuring to some purpose yesterday ; I also think," added he, chinking the twenty Jacobuses in his hand, " as I ought to change my name from Go-Lightly to *Come*-Lightly."

But we must not leave Sir Allen till we have seen him safely to his own house, for we will not call it home, for there is no home within walls, however splendid, where no affection dwells to greet those who return to them, or to feel anxious at their absence. The hackney coachman drove him as directed, to 8, Spring Garden. Sir Allen got out, paid the coachman, and gave a loud knock at the door. Sir Allen Apsley was out. Sir Allen Broderick, in words, was " very sorry," in reality, very glad. He left a message for him, and then, under cover of his slouched felt hat and his long horseman's cloak, he walked on to Whitehall Gardens, and rang his peculiar, unmistakable peal at his own door. It was answered by Desmond.

" How came you to answer the door ?" growled

Sir Allen.   " Where are all the other d——d
varlets."

" Be jabbers ! den, it's just as I said," replied
that d——d varlet, eyeing, with no little astonishment, his master's novel costume.   " Sure and I
toult 'em, no fear but yez 'ud come back ; not
like the poor Captain."

" Hold your infernal tongue.   Where are all
the other rascals ?"

" Why, den, be dad ! dere all out on a wild
goose chase, looking for you, Sur Allen ; and
shure de King sent to know if yez was found,
and my Lord Rochester, Colonel Titus, and
Mishter Killigrew, have been in and out like
Tantony pigs to ax about yez all day, fearing you
wash dhrownded.   ' Och ! niver fear, gentlemen,'
I says to them, ' Sur Allen 'll be shure to come
back. Shure, it's like Fader O' Flaherty's masely
pig, dat wash for ever straying, but it always
cum back ; so dat his riverence niver got shut
o' de baste afther all."

It was quite true that Rochester, Killigrew, and
Silas Titus had evinced the most feverish anxiety
touching the welfare of Sir Allen, which incul-
pated their own, for although they had seen
him taken into a boat, they were by no means
sure whether, when rescued, he had been dead
or alive.

Sir Allen walked straight to his dressing room,

and as well as he could, with only Desmond's very awkward assistance, dressed himself *point de vice,* and put in an appearance at Whitehall just as the King had sat down to cards, who greeted him by turning round and exclaiming—

" Oddsfish ! Rochester, here's the Thames flounder quite safe, and never did Casanove dress water souchy so well."

But the next night Sir Allen once more donned the long camlet cloak and slouched hat, and with the bag of gold, repaired to the appointed trysting place at Hercules' Pillars, where Doctor Erasmus Everhard was awaiting him with lover-like impatience and punctuality. The baronet placed the bulky leathern bag in the doctor's hand with a silent pressure, but as, " out of the fullness of the heart," or in this instance of the bag, " the mouth speaketh," Dr. Everhard exclaimed—

" Oh ! Sir Allen Apsley, I can never—"

" Hush !" said the personage so addressed, placing his finger on his lip, but inwardly delighted to think how effectually the bait had been swallowed.

Then, with another cordial pressure of the doctor's hand, he turned on his heel, and retraced his steps to Whitehall, grieved at heart at this sad parting with his money !—but what cannot be cured must be endured,—and Sir Allen got off more cheaply than if he had lived in the present day, when he must have disbursed not only hush money, but puff money, for paragraphs would have had to appear in every paper about " the distinguished Baronet's good feeling ! and munificent generosity ! in remunerating the poor man who had saved his life," with plenty more of the puff mendacious *suppressio veri* and *suggestio falsi*. Then again, considering the value Sir Allen set upon himself, he could hardly think £500 a disproportionate sum.

CHAPTER VI.

T is strange,—indeed, there are so many passing strange things in this world, that there would not be room even to name, much less to analyse them, had one as many books as there are in the British Museum, to write down the mere catalogue in,—but it *is* strange, the great distinction that is made in the estimate of things in which, in reality, there is no difference, except the grammatical one of singular and plural—the singular being always the scapegoat, and the plural the hero, suffocated under laurels and honours. For instance, as we all know, to kill one person is murder, and is punished accordingly; whereas, to slaughter our fellow-creatures wholesale—though they have never done us any harm, or we have never seen their faces till we are called upon to " do them to death "—this is called " glory." Just as shooting a man dead in a duel for some slight, real, or even imaginary

offence used to be, and still is, in many places
called honor ! Again, if a chemist sells a penny-
worth of arsenic, or strychnine, and it has been
purchased to commit a solitary murder, or suicide,
said chemist is severely reprimanded, if not
punished ; whereas, had he sold the same poison
by the ton, he would only have been " a whole-
sale druggist." And the same ratio in the estimate of things is extended to the bad passions,
vices, and crimes of mankind ;—when these said
bad passions, vices, and crimes, are exercised by
individuals against individuals, the person so exer-
cising them does so under great difficulties,
having, as the ticket-of-leave gentlemen phrase
it, to " keep it dark," in order to prevent their
incurring the execration of society. Yet the very
same treachery, falsehood, and utter unscru-
pulousness in princes, and, still more, in usurpers
—exercised not against ONE, but against millions
—are precisely the qualities which constitute the
world's " great men." Now, the difference between Sir Allen Broderick and Oliver Cromwell
was merely the world's usual guage of quantity.
Cromwell, it is true, even in the historical estimate of him, is said to " have dug a trench
round the country with crime," but it was quickly
added that " he filled it up with glory "—and
that, of course, is a sort of quick lime that neu-
tralises all corruption. Now, the worst men, and

their very worst deeds, will always not only have plenty of defenders, but even of partisans, more especially in the present day, when the " hero-worship" of great authors for bad men and women of the past, and their mania, in the teeth of facts, for white-washing and gilding them, can only be compared to the ancient Egyptian worship of monsters ; but, without having recourse to modern " cleaners and decorators," it is curious to compare the different estimates of Cromwell nearer his own times.

" He was a tyrant," was the brief but concrete summing up of Algernon Sydney. " The greatest personage and instrument of happiness, not only our own, but indeed any age ever produced," according to Lord Fauconberg. One of the nine worthies, *vide* Maidstone. " A man miraculously raised up by God, and endowed with extraordinary wisdom and courage," says Morland. " A dexterous villain, an intrepid commander, a bloody usurper, and a sovereign that knew the art of governing," incises Voltaire. Next Bossuet gives us a more full-length and more accurately finished portrait as to detail. " A man," says he, " arose of a depth of mind truly incredible, as subtile and refined a hypocrite, as he was an able and transcendent politician ; capable of enterprising everything, and of concealing every enterprise.

In peace and in war, equally active and indefatig-
able, he left to fortune nothing of which he could
deprive her by wisdom and by foresight, and yet,
vigilant and prompt, he never lost an opportunity which she offered to him.   In fine, he was
one of those bold and restless spirits that seem
created to change the destinies of the world."
Then comes Wicquefort's " brief chronicle." " If
ever," are his words, " there appeared in any
state a chief who was at the same time both
tyrant and usurper, Oliver Cromwell was such."
" His method of treating his enemies was mild
and generous, for Cromwell by nature was
generous and humane, kind and compassionate,"
says Harris.   (I wonder what Mrs. Harris said ?)
" A fortunate fool,"· quoth Cardinal Mazarine.
(Was his egotistical eminence thinking of himself ?) " He was a coward," slanders Lord Holles.
—N.B. Does Mr. Eöthen Kinglake, author of
" The Crimean War," happen to be a descendant
of my Lord Holles ? for as experts of cowardice,
they seem both to have derived their knowledge
from the same peculiar source.   Then one John
Milton, late of Barbican, now of the Temple of
Fame, who had a patent for creating devils of
great calibre, asserts that Cromwell was—

> " A person raised
> With strength sufficient, and command from Heaven,
> To free his country."

But there are lords, and lords, and like doctors, they occasionally differ.   So Lord Clarendon, differing from " his noble friend," Lord Holles, calls the Protector " a brave, wicked man ;" and Brandenburgh, following suit, describes him as " a bold, cunning, ambitious man, but unjust, violent, and void of virtue ; a man, in short, who had great qualities, but never a good one."   Then Sir Roger Manley splits the difference with Lord Holles, and says of Cromwell that " with all his faults, although he was a coward at first, he was of great courage and vastness of mind after, since he raised himself up from a private gentleman to the supreme height of the empire ; not altogether unworthy of the degree he attained to, if he had not acquired it by ill means."

Then last, and perhaps least, comes the cartoon of " Hudibras in Prose, 1682 "—

" His face was natural buff, and his skin may furnish him with a coat of mail.   You would think he had been christened in a lime pit, and tanned alive, but that his countenance still continues mangy.   We may cry out against superstition, and yet worship a piece of wainscoat and idolise a blanched almond.   Certainly 'tis no human visage, but the emblem of a mandrake, one scarcely handsome enough to have been the progeny of Hecuba, had she whelped him when she was a dog.   His soul, too, was as ugly as

his body, for who can expect a jewel in the head
of a toad ?"

And now for his parting knell, rang out by
Captain Gwynn—

> "He's a sort of devil, whose pride's so vast,
> As he were thrown beyond Lucifer's cast,
> With greater curse, that his plagues may excel
> In killing torments and a blacker hell."

Which, no doubt, were thought pretty, pious
lines at the time. But so long as the world
lasts, echo can never cease repeating, that "The
evil men do lives after them." And the very
worst of Cromwell's legacy of evils that survived
him, was unquestionably the passiveness of the
nation—from sheer political exhaustion—under
the scandalous influence of the profligate, care-
less, and bankrupt court of Charles the Second,
which can only be accounted for, by the striking
contrast of its dead and stagnant calm being
considered perfectly halcyon, after the devasta-
ting hurricanes and ceaseless hurley-burleys of
the Protectorate. On this account, perhaps, all
might be condoned, but for the atrocious Rye
House plot—*sham* trials—"Damned to everlast-
ing fame"—by being indelibly written in the pure,
untainted blood of William Lord Russell and
Algernon Sidney. Charles's relentless injustice
on this occasion, indeed, brought forth, in a way
never to be forgotten, the hereditary sanguinary

hardness of heart, which has rendered the archives of the Stuarts so infamous. We must likewise remember that we also owe to Cromwell the glorious Revolution of 1688, as but for the vivid recollection of the horrors that desecrated the first pages of the history of the Commonwealth, we never should have had it. And one's sense of outraged justice, in the Second Charles having escaped the penalties of his misdeeds, is very satisfactorily healed by the knowledge that his brother James smarted for them. And yet, detestable and contemptible as James the Second was, upon every score, still there are certain phases in his fate which make one pity him, not exactly with the pity that is akin to love; or if it is, it is only a very distant relation, indeed—say a mother-in-law. But one really does pity him, when one thinks of his horrible wife – that trafficker in human beings, who, in return for the height to which he had raised her, and the rod of iron with which she ruled him, had never, from a very early stage of their marriage, been even faithful to him. Then worse than all, was his horrible and unnatural daughter, Mary, wife of William the Third, who, to increase her own and her husband's power, did all she could to ruin and destroy her father. However, given—a scion of a thoroughly worldly self-seeking climbing race, and what crime is there before which they will

recoil in their avocation of "rising in the world,"
short of those of which the law takes cognizance,
which are by no means the worst; for what is the
murder of a body, whose pangs are ended in a
few minutes, compared to one of those subtle,
occult, moral murders, including the wreck of all
that rightly constituted human beings value, and
extending over the dreary arid waste of a whole
existence? Yet these cruel and dastardly moral
murders, intangible to the law, are what our
"more than kin and less than kind," so often
perpetrate, as did James the Second's, perhaps
very queenly—for her mother had play'd at
royalty before her—but certainly unwomanly
daughter committed upon him? Then, again,
we must contemplate the poor old royal pauper,
shivering over the cold charity of the "Grand
Monarque," at St. Germain en Laye, where he
was so cruelly stinted in fire wood; your very
great people, when they set about it, being able
to achieve such very great meannesses, which
humble mortals would not even be able to conceive. Now in this freezing phase of James the
Second's punishment, there was evidently no
retributive justice ; as everyone knows, he would
freely have supplied the greater portion of his
former subjects with an *ad libitum quantum* of fire
and faggot.

Before concluding this chapter, I have one

protest to make, and that is against its being supposed that, by placing Sir Allen Broderick in juxtaposition with " The Lord Protector," I mean either to whitewash the moral crooked lanes and blind alleys of the former, or to defend the lesser rascal by the example of the greater. Nothing of the kind, and be it understood, that I merely use the relative term of lesser and greater with reference to Sir Allen's lesser career, and his having a more circumscribed sphere for his equally unscrupulous talents, which after all, is the real stuff that goes to the manufacture of your " great men," ancient or modern—at least, what are called such, which is very different from the genuine article, according to the Cornelius Nepos pattern, those who have pride in belonging to that very small minority, whose maxim is " *Magnos homines virtute, metimur non fortunâ.*" Indeed, as the world is at present constituted, knowing by what means success is generally achieved, I have not only no worship and no admiration for the successful, but on the contrary, a strong suspicion of them, closely allied to contempt.

CHAPTER VII.

T was the very end of October; the year had arrived, not only at " the last rose," but at the last leaf of summer. Mrs. Neville and Dorothy had left The Chestnuts, and were again domiciled in the house on the Mall; for the latter had let the house in St. James's Street, which her grandfather had left her, and her tenant was no less a personage than Sir Angus Tullibardin, whose object in taking it for a term of seven years, we are bound to confess, was a firm conviction, duly fostered by his aunt Mrs. Alice Throckmorton, that in hiring the house he should be able to win the owner; and in this hope, or rather certainty! he had taken care to *monté* it in all the taste of the newest fashion, and to keep a large establishment of " demmed vairlets," both in livery and out. Yet, alas! for the bad taste of Mistress Dorothy, since September he had actually been refused twice; nathless, Sir Augus *ne se tenait pas pour battu*, for, as he observed to his aunt—

who had never been molested in her long course
of virginity by even one offer, and who, consequently, must have been a good judge of such
matters—" He knew that those bonnie lassies
that all men were looking after, took a deal ' o'
wooing, and cud nae be brought down at the first
shot, like grouse.'"

As for Dorothy, she really was looking re-
markably well, considering she had subsisted
ever since July upon such very meagre fare as
a vaguely worded anonymous letter; but she was
now becoming ravenous for more substantial
news, and consequently beginning to get nervously impatient, as was indeed, Master Hartsfoot, though he would not own it to her; so that
they were both silently miserable and anxious
in their own way.

As for Master Oliver, with his usual retiring,
sensitive delicacy of nature, he had been far
from " improving the occasion," and taking advantage of the immense advance he had made in
Mrs. Neville's good graces in July; for there
was no room for him to advance more in those of
her daughter, where already he reigned paramount.
He thought it would be presuming! and en-
croaching! so to do; besides which, he had been
so terribly, so supremely happy on that memo-
rable July day that he passed at The Chestnuts,
that he felt that nothing could go beyond it, and,

consequently, anything different must be a loss. So he wished to preserve that happy memory sacred and intact, as Fate itself could not deprive him of *that!* For which reason, he rather kept away from the house on the Mall; and when he did go, either for Dorothy's business or pleasure, he carefully avoided any *tête-à-tête* with its mistress. So that he took refuge more than ever in his books;—those ever ready and never *exigeant* friends, who are never either sullen or offended at, our inattention—no, not even if we fling them from us with impatience, and prefer our own dull thoughts to their most profound ones, or most brilliant sallies. Even his scientific friends he convened less often than formerly; for there was that haunted chamber in his own heart, which he did not want them to pry into, and which he was not always willing to quit for their society. This new state of things was anything but displeasing to Mr. Pump, who had remarked to Mrs. Merrypin more than once—

"Well, I do hope, and believe, as them ere *saveons* noses is out of jint at last—leastways, the house ain't by no means so much infested with them as formerly."

But as Mrs. Merrypin was far from being equally pleased that her light should be hid under a bushel—that is, that her culinary talents should be so long in abeyance—she sharply replied—

" You ought to be ashamed of yourself, Noah Pump, to say such things ; and if you respected Master Hartsfoot as you ought, seeing the solitary life he leads, you'd be only too glad when these gentlemen came, who were sufficiently clever and instructed to be able to interest and amuse him."

" So I think, Mrs. Merrypin," said Barton. " And I know I, for one, am very sorry master don't have his supper parties as often as he used ; for it was as good as a book to hear them talk— they seemed to know everything, and as for My Lord Worcester, he just beats all the conjurers I ever saw, or ever heard tell of."

But in consequence of the cessation of Master Hartsfoot's parties, Barton had his evenings a great deal more to himself, and passed them very agreeably, either in reading out to Mrs. Merrypin, or hearing her inexhaustible store of anecdotes about the places and persons with whom, in her early days, she, and her father before her, had lived ; while he, Barton, improved himself in wood carving, for which he had a very remarkable talent, and, in pear tree, had already carved her a very pretty frame for a looking-glass, in leaves, fruits, and birds,—and was now busy upon another on a much more magnificent and artistic scale, which, if worthy of such an honour when finished, he intended to present to Mistress Dorothy, having got Mr. Hollar to draw him some Cupids, doves, and wreaths of flowers for the design.

It was one evening late in October that he was, as usual, sitting in the housekeeper's room cutting away at his frame, while Mrs. Merrypin sat at the same table—her tambour frame before her—tambouring one of her own elaborately worked muslin aprons. This room, being next the dining-room, though without any door of communication, looked out upon, and was on a level with, the Mall ;—it had, what was rare in those days, a sash window, put up expressly at Mrs. Merrypin's desire, that she might ventilate the room from the top—which it is impossible to do with casement windows—and, on this particular evening in question, the chimney having slightly smoked, the window had been opened about nine inches at the top.

Mr. Pump, who never stood upon the ceremony of an invitation, had ensconsed himself in an arm-chair against the wall, and fallen fast asleep, which was his usual way of enjoying improving conversation.

"Your flowers beat mine hollow, Joe," said Mrs. Merrypin ; " I declare, that double carnation you have just finished looks as if it was just tumbling to pieces, and that a breath would blow all the leaves away. I never saw anything so natural in my life."

" Well, I'm glad you think so," he replied, " for I shall be proud if my frame is good enough to offer to Mistress Dorothy when it is done."

" If you finish it as well as you've begun it, it will be fit for the Queen, and consequently just suitable for Mistress Dorothy."

Here, whether in assent or dissent, is not on record, Mr. Pump gave one such tremendous snore that Mrs. Merrypin put both hands up to her ears, as she exclaimed—

" There you are, on the east of Eden again, in the land of Nod, Noah Pump. I do wish you'd go into the kitchen ; Martha and Betty, perhaps, don't dislike snoring, but I do beyond everything."

But Mr. Pump, being equally impervious to the critique and to the command, she got up and shook him violently, screaming in his ear at the same time—

" Do, for pity's sake, take your pigs to some other market, for it is enough to deafen one."

" Ugh !" grunted he, opening one eye.

" Ugh ! I want you to ugh ! into the kitchen," said Mrs. Merrypin, again shaking him, and this time so effectually, that he was now completely awake. " Do go into the kitchen," she repeated,

" for there is no hearing oneself speak for your snoring."

" Oh !" said he, rising and shaking himself, and not in the best of humours, as sleepers thus rudely awakened seldom are, " I know I ain't never wanted *here ;* haven't book larning enough to suit such great folks.   You and Joe ! Joe and you ! that's the bill of fare.   My belief is, that you are just a ruining on the boy, trying to make a *saveon* of him, which is a perwiding him with starvation for his stomach, and addled brains for his head."

And flinging, *viâ* the impetus of a very savage look, this generous draft on the future at Joe, Mr. Pump left them his room, which they certainly did prefer to his company.

" Well, now he's gone and has shut the door, do, Mrs. Merrypin, if you please, be so good as to tell me one of your nice stories."

" One of my nice stories !   Why, I'm afraid, Joe, I've come pretty nearly to the end of my bag of odds and ends."

" Oh ! no, I'm sure you have not ; if you'll dive down into it once more I'm sure you'll find another."

" Well, what is it to be ? A make-belief story, book story, or a real story ?"

" Oh ! a real story.   I do like hearing about real people, high or low, rich or poor, good or bad; it seems like learning in the horn book of life what one is to hope, fear, expect, do, or not do, and not feel exactly as if one was the only person in the world, and that the things that happen to us had never happened to any one else."

" Well, there's a good deal of truth in that, Joe, for when we come to hear and to know about a good many different sorts of people, we begin to find out that things are much more evenly and equally divided than we thought; and seeing only the outsides of people's fates is very like picking all the plums out of a pudding, and judging the whole compound by them, and not considering all the other ingredients that went to the making of it. Did I ever tell you about Squire Hastings? At least, that's what the country people used to call him, for he was really the Honourable Frank Hastings, my Lord Huntingdon's uncle. If I have? don't let me tell it you again, for there is nothing so bad 'as a twice-told tale; it's even worse than a stale muffin."

" No, you never told me anything about Mr. Hastings; you told me about the red worsted bed that Lord Huntingdon's grandmother worked for Lady Hunsdon, with the royal arms all in gold, and real diamonds in the lion and the unicorn's eyes, that Queen Elizabeth slept in; but you never told me anything about Mr. Hastings.'

" Well, in the year 1638—Lord, how time
flies—that is just thirty-two years ago, and I
remember it as if it was only yesterday. Well,
in the year 1638, when the Honourable Frank
Hastings lived in Dorsetshire, my father lived
with him as steward. Mr. Hastings' place was
called Woodlands; he was very old and strange
in all his ways, was Mr. Hastings—at least he
seemed so to the generation then living; but I
have often heard my father say that he was only
just like what the rest of the nobility and gentry
had been in King James's time. I see him
now, in my memory, as plain as I see you in
reality, Joe; he was short and thick-set, but very
strong and active; nothing personable about him,
for he had reddish flaxen hair, and always dressed
in a sort of homely green cloth, his clothes
never costing five pounds when new, which was
more remarkable at a time when the gentry—as
they do now—spent often several hundred pounds
upon one suit, and were all velvet, jewels,
feathers, and embroidery. His house was quite
in the old-fashion, in the midst of a large park,
well stocked with deer. Near the house was a
rabbit warren; but that was only for the use of
the kitchen; the domain was full of fish ponds,
and abounded in fine timber—some magnificent
oaks, fifteen and eighteen hundred years old!
There was a bowling-green too, but that was

long and narrow, and full of high ridges, it never having been levelled after it was ploughed; it had a banquetting house, like a stand, and also a larger one, built in a tree. He kept packs upon packs of sporting dogs, deer hounds, fox hounds, harriers, and dogs for otter and badger-hunting. Ger falcons and hawks, long and short-winged, of course, and all sorts of nets and tackle for fish. He had, too, a walk in the New Forest, in the parish of Christ Church, which supplied him with red deer, sea and river fish; and, indeed, all his neighbours' grounds and royalties were free to him, and he bestowed nearly all his time on these sports, except that which he passed in a much more reprehensible way; for I am sorry to say, Joe, that Mr. Hastings was terribly like King David, in the matter of sinning, though not sufficiently like him on the score of repentance. But being rude to the yeomen's wives and daughters made him prodigiously civil to their husbands and brothers, so that, more shame for them, the men liked him, even better than the women, for they were always welcome at the squire's house, where they found abundance of ale, beef, and pudding; and next to money, it is astonishing how many gaps *they* can stop. The house, as you may suppose, was not over neatly kept; the great hall being full of hawks' perches, and strewed with marrow bones, which must have been very pleasant to the hounds, spaniels, and terriers lying about it in all directions. The upper part of the hall was hung with the skins of all the foxes killed in the current and preceding year, with here and there, a pole-cat intermixed by way of ornament, besides gamekeepers' and hunting poles in great abundance. The dining-room was a large long room, properly furnished ; on a great large hearth, paved with brick, were generally lying Mr. Hastings' small pet terriers and choicest of his fox-hounds and spaniels ; and it was seldom that one or two of the great chairs had not litters of pups in them, or of kittens, which were not on any account to be disturbed. Three or four of his dogs constantly dined with him, and he kept a little white, round stick, fourteen inches long, beside his trencher, that he might defend such bits of meat as he had no mind to let them help themselves to. The windows, which were unusually large Mullion windows, served as receptacles for his arrows, sling-bows, and cross-bows. The corners of the room were full of the choicest hunting and hawking poles. And at the lower end of the room stood a large oyster-table, which was in constant use twice a day, all the year round, for he never failed to eat oysters before dinner and supper, in season or out ; the neighbouring town of Poole supplied him with them. The upper part of this

dining-room had two small tables and a desk, on
the one side of which was a church Bible, on the
other the Book of Martyrs; on the tables were
hawking bells, and hawks' heads, and hoods, and
several old green hats, with their crowns thrust
in, so as to hold a dozen or more eggs of a particular kind of poultry, which he took great care
of, and fed himself. There were also plenty of
other tables, with cards, dice, and other games
and in a hole, in the reading desk, were heaps
of tobacco pipes that had been used. On one
side, at this end of the room, was the door of
the closet, wherein stood the strong beer and
wine, which never came out, but in single
glasses, that being the rule of the house, strictly
observed, for he never exceeded in his potations
himself, nor allowed anyone else to do so. On
the other side was a door opening into the old
chapel, no longer used for devotion, and the pulpit
being considered the safest place, never wanted a
cold chine and a venison pasty, gammon of
bacon, and a huge apple-pie, with an immensely
thick crust, extremely hard-baked, which I am
sure would make Master Hartsfoot faint, if I
could so far forget what is due to him as to send
him up anything like it. The Honourable
Frank's table, though it was good and more than
plentiful, cost him next to nothing, as his hunting and fishing supplied him with almost every-

thing, except beef and mutton, and he had rare good gardens, orchards, and dairies. On Fridays he always had a dinner of the best salt fish that was to be got, and that was the day upon which he always invited his neighbours of the greatest quality to dinner. One good old custom, too, he never omitted, which was at his meals, always to pour syrup of gilly-flowers into his sack. Besides this, he always had a large glass of beer standing beside his plate, which he often stirred with a branch of rosemary against the vapours. He was good-natured, but very passionate, and in his passion he often called his servants by oppro-brious names, which he knew better than they did, that they were fully entitled to."

"What a funny gentleman!" said Joe. "Where is he now?"

"In heaven, I hope; he lived to be a hundred and one; never lost his eyesight, and always read and wrote without spectacles, and got on horseback without help till he was eighty-five, and rode to the death of a stag when he was ninety years of age. He, himself, did not die till 1650."

"Thank you, Mrs. Merrypin," said Joe; "though I should have liked the hounds, and the spaniels, and the terriers, and the deer, and the falcons, and even the foxes, and the fine park, gardens, and orchards amazingly, yet I don't think I should have liked to live with Squire Hastings after living with Master Hartsfoot."

" Oh ! for that matter, Joe, you may go from one end of the world to the other, without finding the fellow of Master Hartsfoot. I always think, when Nature was moulding the clay for her two batches of human beings at the time *he* was made, after having blent everything to make a brave and noble man, a good, kind woman fell by accident into the dough, and she kneaded them both well together, and Master Hartsfoot was the result. But as nature is given no authority to make angels—that being God's province, she stopped there, and never ventured upon that experiment again."

" Like enough," said Joe ; " yet it's a pity, too, seeing how well the experiment succeeded, for a few more of the same sort would have greatly improved the world. I wonder—" But whatever was the occasion of his wonder, it was still farther increased by the interruption of a deep, sepulchral voice, crying out in the direction of the window, with a distinctness and solemnity that made him and Mrs. Merrypin jump from their seats :—

" Joe Barton ! Joe Barton ! if you are alive, look alive ; and take that, before you are two minutes older, to Mistress Dorothy Neville."

The " *that* " alluded to in this mysterious mandate, being a letter which had been flung down into the room through the window left open at the top.

Joe Barton, though by no means of a cowardly nature, turned very pale ;—for anything trenching on the supernatural asserts its unseen but felt power even over the lower animals, for dogs and horses often tremble, and recoil, before some invisible influence.

" Good heaven ! who and what was that ?" said Mrs. Merrypin, walking over to the window, and drawing aside the curtains.

Through the window she looked out, but saw nothing, or no one—which she might have done had anyone been there, for it was a moonlight night—but on the floor she saw a letter, which she picked up, and brought over to the table to examine it by the light. It was a mere ordinary letter, sealed, and directed in a very good, but perfectly human hand—

" *To Mistress Dorothea Neville,*
    " *At Madame Neville's House,*
        " *On the Bird Cage Walk,*
            " *The Mall,*
                " *London.*"

" Do you think I ought to take it ?" asked Joe, reading the superscription over her shoulder.

" Well—let me think about it," rejoined Mrs. Merrypin, holding her chin in her right hand, and placing her forefinger perpendicularly by the side of her cheek—which was her mode of putting on her considering cap—as she turned the letter in all directions, and scrutinised the seal. " Humph ! I can make nothing of that," said she, " it's neither arms nor crest, only some foreign word, in old English characters, upon the seal. No—I'll tell you what you had best do, Joe : take this letter to master, and ask him whether you shall leave it, or not, at Madam Neville's. He is in, isn't he?"

" Oh yes, he's in," said Joe, turning down his cuffs—which had been turned up the better to execute his carving—and, also, taking off his holland apron, full of chips and splinters.

" Well, then, you take it to him, and see what he says about it when you tell him how it was thrown in at the window, and what the voice said."

Master Hartsfoot was sitting beside the fire reading—at least, he had been reading, for his reading lamp was on the table, and, also, Gascoigne de Turberville's " Book of Hunting," and open at this passage—

"The place should first be high on pleasant gladsome greene,
    Yet under shade of stately trees where little sun is seene ;
    And near some spring, whose crystall running streames
    May help to cool the parching heate yeaught by Phœbus'
    beams."

Somehow this Sylvan picture made him think of The Chestnuts, and, above all, of the Charmille at The Chestnuts; and then—and then—of a tear he had, with very abnormal audacity, kissed off a very white and satiny hand, freely placed in his,—and then the poor man shivered, and placed his own hand tightly over his eyes. Yet, surely, he was not such a Sybarite that the mere remembrance of *one* drop of human rain should chill his very marrow? Be this as it may, he turned from the book, and looked into the fire,— and there he traced a vivid picture, which quite absorbed him, and he was thus lost in the mazes of his own creation, when Barton entered the room with the letter.

Master Hartsfoot started;—what business has innocence often to look so like guilt? really it is a bad and dangerous habit, considering that the world's jurisprudence is made up of circumstantial evidence, otherwise called appearances.

"If you please, sir," said Barton, attributing the deep blush on his master's face entirely to the fire, "Mrs. Merrypin and, I were very much frightened just now by a deep, strange voice, calling out at the window of the housekeeper's room, where we were sitting, and where the window was open a little way at the top, on account of the smoke—

" ' *Joe Barton! Joe Barton! if you are alive,*

look alive; and take this to Mistress Dorothy Neville before you are two minutes older.'

" And whoever it was, he threw in this letter; and, if you please, sir, Mrs. Merrypin thought I had better bring it to you first, and ask if I should take it."

As Master Hartsfoot took the letter off the salver a sudden conviction struck him, that although not familiar with it, he had seen the writing before, which was remarkable in *that* day for its clearness and legibility, and though bold as to character, was yet fine and delicate in its caligraphy; in short, what would in the present day be called an unmistakeably gentlemanlike hand. As Mrs. Merrypin had done before him, he turned and scrutinised the letter in all directions. At length, tapping his forehead—(the writing this letter reminded him of was the note Gilbert Broderick had written to him on the day the latter had called, and found him out, previous to his (Gilbert's) intended departure for Tangiers).

" Barton," said Master Hartsfoot, " have the goodness to go into the Cedar Parlour, open the drawers of the library table there, and in one or other of them you will find a Russian leather blotting-book, which bring here to me."

" It must be his writing," soliloquised Master Hartsfoot; " I pray Heaven I may not be deceived."

Barton returned with the blotting-book.

" Bring me my hat, cloak, and gloves," said his master, " I will take this letter to Mistress Dorothy myself."

And while Barton was gone for the things he carefully examined the contents of the blotting-book, shaking every paper separately. At length *the* note he was in quest of fell out ; he carefully compared the direction of the letter with it ; yes, there could be no doubt about it ; all the experts in Europe would have decided that the note and the superscription were written by one and the same person, for the two writings were identical.

" Oh! jubilate !" cried he, tossing up his hand-kerchief and catching it again with all the *en train* and dexterity of a school boy. And then, thinking that Dorothy would prize even Gilbert's note to him more than to leave it lying *perdu* in a blotting-book, he carefully enveloped the letter in it, and placed them both within his pocket-book. He enquired the hour, and was told it was a quarter past eight, but had it been past twelve he would have gone, thinking with truth, that it is never too late to be the bearer of good news.

The mother and daughter were sitting opposite each other by the drawing-room fire, doing nothing, which was a rare event for them; that is, doing nothing with their hands, but thinking their own thoughts, and occasionally uttering them.   After an unusually long pause in their conversation, Dorothy burst forth with—

" For my part, I think not only ' the times are out of joint,' but that the world is so old and rusty that it is off its hinges, and every one and everything goes wrong.   I'll turn iconoclast, and have no more idols ; their feet of clay, sooner or later, do so mire and spoil what I suppose Jessop would call the Puck's parlour of one's heart. Now what does that Master Hartsfoot mean by scarcely ever coming near us ? I'll go and call him out to-morrow; that is, I'll give him one more chance, and if after that he don't mend his manners, why down he shall go, and never more find pedestal in my estimation."

" Master   Hartsfoot,   madam," announced Jessop, opening wide the drawing-room door.

" How   strange !"   said Dorothy, rising   to receive him. " Your name was hardly out of my mouth when you appear to answer to it ; but you need not look so conceited ; for though I spoke of you it is true, yet it was as you deserve, in the most opprobrious terms I am the mistress of, for as you know, or rather ought to know, for you really are so hardened that you don't seem to be aware of it—*les absens ont toujours tort.*"

" And what you appear to be equally ignorant

of, Mistress Dorothy, is—that talk of the devil, &c., &c., &c."

" Well, you certainly did come at the first mention of your name."

" And what more can your dog—your slave— do than come when he is called ?"

" Well, my slave should be a little oftener at his post, and my dog should fetch and carry."

" Agreed," said Hartsfoot; " but the dog being the nobler animal, let his case be called first. You, of course, are for the prosecution ; but what if I had retained one councillor Gilbert Broderick for the defence ?"

Dorothy became white as ashes, and re-seated herself. Mrs. Neville came over to him, and said—

" Is it possible that you have heard any further tidings of Gilbert ?"

In order not to startle Dorthy, or raise her hopes too high, by the intelligence he had for her, by communicating it too suddenly, he begged of them both to sit down and listen to the details of what he had to tell. He then gave them verbatim the account Barton had given him as to the letter having been thrown in at the window.

" But how do you know ?" asked Dorothy, with a look of unutterable anguish and disappointment, " that the letter is *from* him, or even about him ?"

" I know it, and am quite sure of it, in this way," he replied, " and you shall have the same proofs." Whereupon, he explained to her his having been struck by the similarity of the direction to writing that he had somewhere seen ; his recollection whose it was ; and his subsequent successful search for Gilbert's note in the blotting book. " And now," added he, taking out his pocket book, opening it, and producing the note and the letter, and handing them to her, " compare the two writings yourself."

One glance was sufficient for Dorothy ; but when she saw the well-known seal, with " CHADMEL" on it, she seized Master Hartsfoot's hand, saying—

" Oh, you are, indeed, a guardian angel to me !" and rushed out of the room with her treasure. We shall avail ourselves of our Asmodeous privilege of following her, only staying to mention that no sooner was she gone, than Mrs. Neville, for the second time in her life, held out both her hands to Hartsfoot, saying, " You are, indeed, kind and good ; how can we ever repay you ?"

Perhaps he thought there might be a way found of doing so. However, he said nothing, and was altogether so agitated and confused, that any third person witnessing the scene would

have supposed that *he* had been suddenly called
upon to either pay some enormous debt, or
to repay some heavy obligation, which, in either
case, he had no possible means of doing. So he
stammered out—" You—you will want to hear
about Captain Broderick's letter, and you will
perhaps kindly let me hear about it to-morrow?"

And with that he made as precipitate a retreat
as Dorothy had done two minutes before. While
she had no sooner reached her room, locked the
door, and lit the candles on the toilet, then she
sat down in the large chair by the fire, and kissing it first, she carefully cut the seal round so
as not to break it; and then, hastily took the
letter out of the envelope, her heart beating so
violently the while, that the noise disturbed and
irritated her. After all, it was not a letter—only
a copy of verses. So blank and utter was the
disappointment and revulsion of feeling, as they,
instead of the hoped for—craved for long letter
met her view, that the paper fell out of her hand
on her lap. Whether it is because poets are said
to excel in fiction, or because there is too much
head work in versification, but certain it is, that
no poetry addressed to the particular object in
whose honour it is indited, ever yet succeeded,
either in conveying, and still less in satisfying
affection; and in the present instance Dorothy
felt it almost as a cruel and unpardonable insult!

It was exactly as if, after this long, terrible, and mysterious separation, she had been about to rush into her lover's arms, and he had drawn up with a vapid smile, and began bowing over her hand.

Still, she must not condemn him unheard; the paper was signed with his initials. So, after a few minutes of bitter disappointment and indignation, she took up the lines and read them.

The breeze, which cannot *prison'd be*,
  To thee this longing message brings ;
That my ONE thought, like it, is free,
  And round thee, dearest, ever clings.

For all the rest *thou* best cans't tell,
  How my riven heart is weeping,
Since at our last, too long farewell,
  I left it in thy gentle keeping.

But bid Hope wrest the glass of Time,
  From out his trembling, palsied hands,
And brim it up from life's fresh prime,
  With all of Love's most golden sands.

For, where willows weep full early,
  By a murmuring river's side,
And the lilies, gemm'd and pearly,
  Float fair above the rippling tide ;

Where the violet coy, yet kind,
  Doth trembling meet the summer air,
Whose kisses from her heart unbind,
  The perfumed treasures hoarded there !

We shall meet in happier hours,
  When these dark days have past away,
When the earth, laughs out in flowers,
  And when the air brings home the May.

Doubt there are tides within the sea,
  Doubt there are stars above thee;
Doubt, if thou wilt, that thought is free,
  But—Oh! never doubt I love thee.

More now, I must not—*dare not* say,
  And *all*, what words of earth could tell?
Thoughts only utter'd when we pray,
  Recorded where the Angels dwell.

                             G. B.

Dorothy read and re-read these lines; she weighed and spelt over every word, and then she became fully aware of two facts, viz., that Gilbert was imprisoned somewhere, and that there was some omnipotent restraint upon him to prevent his communicating freely with her, or with anyone, and more especially to inhibit him from explaining his present whereabout and position. Being now convinced of these facts, she became as grateful for, and happy at these lines, as she had before reading them been disappointed and indignant. For lovers always treat the offers of Fate in their behalf as Tarquin treated the books of the Cumæan Sibyl—refuse at first to pay the price she demands, and then end by paying an equally large sum of gratitude for infinitely less. And Dorothy's high expectations had now so come down, that she would have been grateful for the mere envelope, directed in Gilbert's hand, and sealed with his own—own seal; how much more then for the intelligence the inclosure conveyed to her? and above all, for the positive and specific promise in these lines that they should meet by the next summer! Once more she read them, kissed them passionately, and at length put them in her bosom, which she had no sooner done than she burst into a flood of tears, and knelt down to thank God for so great a boon, so vast a lightening of her heavy—heavy load, so silver a lining to her cloud of dark despair!

No one knew better than Mrs. Neville that a great joy, like a great sorrow, has need of solitude at its birth; as they grow older, each craves and requires the nurture of sympathy, with this difference: that joy, in its princely purple, is always sure of finding it to repletion; whereas, the poor pauper sorrow, too often can only obtain as a charity the physic of advice and animadversion, which, like all other bitters, does but increase its hunger for sympathy and help, of which there are none to bestow a single crumb.

Besides, in the present instance, Mrs. Neville had to smooth the ruffled plumage of her own little romance. She would not, for any consideration, have owned it even to herself; yet, nevertheless, it was the fact that she was hurt and disappointed that Master Hartsfoot, under such very favourable and unforseen circumstances, should have bounded off like an antelope, and thus *voluntarily* put the distance of half the Mall

between them, when chance had brought them as
closely together as "twin cherries on one stalk."

We quite agree with her. Silly man! what
could have possessed him ? the room to themselves,
both of her hands in his, and yet he not have the
courage even to ask for one of them; although
she was actually begging the question, by asking
by what means she could possibly repay all his
kindness ? Well, it must be that my grandmother was right, and that we men, clever as we
think ourselves, *never do* take advantage of the
right moment when women are in the YES
humour, but generally obtrude our propositions
at the wrong time and place, when they are in
the NO frame of mind; and my grandmother,
having, besides being a very shrewd, clever
woman, also been a celebrated beauty, must have
been a good authority upon this particular branch
of epicene Ethics, for there was a great deal of
love, and love making, going on in her day—
indeed, there is a great deal too much love
making going on in our day;—but little, or no
LOVE, if we except that ugly changeling SELF-
LOVE.   And this *fait accompli*, at once reminds
me, and confirms, another observation of my
grandmother's upon this " still beginning, never
ending" subject. She used to say, after inquiring
if it was possible that I should have reached the
age of nine-and-twenty without having looked

out for a convert—that is, for a lady to convert
into Mrs. Gordon Scott;—and when she found
that I rather winced, and waived the subject,
she would add, "Ah! George, in my time L,
stood for love, S, for sincerity, and D, for devotion;
but now-a-days £ s. d. never means anything but
pounds, shillings, and pence,—and men's devotion to the modern signification of these three
mystic letters, is so equally divided between them
and themselves, that they have none left for us
women. Indeed, their devotion to the £ s. d. is
so all engrossing, and so undeviatingly constant,
that they are often false to themselves rather than
forsake the former." Very true, my dear grandmother, so far as the mere bare, hideous, and unde-
niable fact goes; but whatever our posterity may
do, certainly our forefathers have not discovered
the meaning, or the mystery, of that seething,
surging maëlstrom of human passions, which, for
want of a wider, broader, deeper, and truer definition, we call LIFE. Speaking of the sea, or,
rather, of navigation, Victor Hugo says, in his
last work " L'Homme qui Rit"—and says it in
his own inimitable and profound manner—
" Quand on naviguera sur de l'instabilité étudiée,
quand le capitaine sera un météorologue, quand
le pilote sera un chimiste, alors bien de catastrophes seront evités. La mer est magnétique,
autant que qu' aquatique; un ocean de force flotte

inconnu, dans l'ocean des flots ; à vau-lau pourrait on dire. Ne voir dans la mer qu'une masse d'eau, c'est ne pas voir la mer ; la mer est un Va-et-Vient de fluide, autant qu'un flux et reflux de liquide ; les attractions, la compliquent, plus encore peut-être que les ouragans."

Now this, slightly paraphrased, would hold good with regard to that still deeper, more uncertain, and more unfathomable sea—human nature—till we learn how to steer through it scientifically, instead of merely mechanically, as we now do ;—that is, till we learn to sound its depths, and know the *causes*, whence come the dangers, and the drifts, of its ceaseless changes ; instead of as now, merely seeking to utilise, or to foil them with a selfish and superficial expediency— we can never, effectually—that is, to a certainty, and on fixed principles—really avoid the shoals, and quicksands, sunken rocks, or storms, and calms of either sea. Above all, till we recognise the truth in the moral world—of what Victor Hugo says of the ocean—that " its attractions perhaps complicate its mysteries more than its antagonistic storms ;" till, in short—instead of contemplating the fates and lives of our fellow-creatures as a mere chain of events and circumstances,—we can acquire the art of knowing what has gone before, and what follows after, each individual's packet of events and circumstances ;—

we must continue, as we do now, always to judge at the wrong end—that of effects, instead of causes. But as the little span that we call "life" is, no doubt, as mere a germ and first stage to our real existence, and complete development in Eternity—as the fragile blossom is to the rich, ripe, perfect fruit—WE are not likely ever to attain to this scientific and accurate knowledge of ourselves, or of our common nature ;—still the greatest, and darkest, mystery to us of the many mysteries of God's creation.   Who can war against the inevitable ?—contend against it they may, but conquer it NEVER ;—and it is because there *is* an inevitable for each and all, that we are especially commanded to "Judge not, lest we be judged."

CHAPTER VIII.

." IT'S ILL WAITING FOR DEAD MEN'S SHOES
OR FOR DEAD KINGS' CROWNS, AS THE CASE MAY BE."

EVER since the July excursion to Hampton Court poor Lady Castlemaine had been sent to Coventry, without quitting London or even her magnificent quarters in Whitehall Gardens. It was to her own and every one else's astonishment, the very longest time she had ever been banished to that over-populated penal county. *Mais à mauvaise fortune, faire bonne face,* being the philosophical maxim on which she acted, her nightly receptions were more brilliant and more crowded than ever. And the Duchess of York, to show that she wished, with her newly-acquired royalty, to shuffle off all the *bourgeois* vulgarities of mere private station, and not enter into family quarrels, while at the same time she had no idea of worshipping a mere sun that had risen, and so in the natural course of things must set, and therefore treated " his most excellent majesty Charles the Second " strictly as a brother-in-law, and not the least as a king. To the Queen, she was a

little more patronising and gracious, as she really
felt grateful to her; that is, grateful to her in
the worldly sense of the term; viz., she conde-
scended to approve her conduct in never having
introduced any barrier to the Duke of York's ac-
cession to the throne. Moreover, Lady Castlemaine's *salons* had many attractions for her, not
only young Jermyn's and young Sidney's society,
which she appreciated quite as much as the fair
Barbara herself; but the play was always high,
and as her Royal Highness had began her career
by playing for a tremendously high stake, with
everything to lose if she *had* lost it, but which,
on the contrary, she had won, she did not see why
she should not continue to pay her court to fortune. It is true, that well as she had played
her own cards, those of Lady Castlemaine were
not always equally propitious to her, and her
tremendous losses did divers times and often,
rouse her obedient husband into asserting his
rights in a marital hurricane, by asking her
" where the d——l she thought he was to find
money to meet such ruinous and mad extravagance, when even his brother could not get his
ever recurring debts paid, and he really thought
that a private gentlewoman by birth, *might* contrive to live on £60,000 a year, and not every
year, and sometimes every six months, add
£20,000, and £30,000 to it, and so bring

the country about his ears, and no wonder, till he was almost ready to hang himself."

Now all these conjugal *tremontanos* she listened to with the silent patience of a Griselda—that is, they went in at one ear and out of the other, and the very same night she would repair to Lady Castlemaine's, and endeavour to retrieve her losses at the Board of Green Cloth, though generally only increasing the terrible amount beyond his income, that the Duke had to lay before the other Board of Green Cloth. But she had certain theories about divide and govern, from which she never swerved. As Mr. Pepys observed, the Duke of York was ruled and fooled in everything by his wife, except in his amours; it was not that she ignored them, but she determined never to interfere with his mistresses, and therefore thought he had no right to interfere with her gambling or other amusements; still, this was not quite a fair partition, as the *rôle* she had assigned to herself was much easier than the one she had imposed upon him, for never having cared for James Stuart, she did not care what the Duke of York did; whereas the tremendous sums that he had to bear the odium of having squandered, owing to her unprincipled and reckless extravagance, made him bankrupt, both in purse and character, and without being over-burdened with any great delicacy of feeling, embittered his life from the sheer worry of his eternal monetary difficulties.

It was a foggy night in November, the carriages were rolling—or rather rumbling—about White Hall, for, having no springs, they did rumble rather than roll.

The Duchess of York was sitting *en péignoir* in her dressing-room, waiting for La Fond, *the* hair-dresser, before she could complete her toilet to go to Lady Castlemaine's, for in all ages the very greatest personages have had to wait for that *head* potentate, the *Coiffeur*. She was getting impatient, and tapping her foot against the floor; all that could be done to advance her dressing had been done, her bracelets clasped, her pearl necklace also, everything but the earrings, with which the hair would interfere.

" I almost think, Natalie," said she, addressing her maid, " that I'll not wait for him, and let you do my hair."

" *Mais pourtant*, that would be a pity; if your Royal Highness pleases, I will let down your hair, that it may be ready when Monsieur la Fond comes ?"

And as her Royal Highness assented, she did so, and the very next moment La Fond arrived. *Et se confondait en excuses;* but the City was in commotion. Had her Royal Highness heard the report, that an attempt had been made to assassinate the King as he was going through the Banqueting Hall to the Green Drawing-room, at White Hall?"

"Good God!" exclaimed the Duchess, starting to her feet and clasping her hands, "you don't say so?"

Now this was one of those expressions resorted to by the diplomacy of the Vicar of Wakefield, in some of the brown or blue bed Cabinet Councils, held by his wife, which, as Doctor Primrose astutely remarked, would do equally well, whichever way the event turned out. And the Duchess of York's exclamation was one that would have done equally well to express consternation and horror, or incredible delight had she been suddenly informed that she had been left a legacy of half a million.

She dismissed La Fond, telling him she could not possibly think of going out, till she had ascertained the truth or falsehood of that terrible report; and seizing a candle, rushed to her husband's dressing-room, with her hair all dishevelled, which is the orthodox thing, for all female heralds of dire events, whether on or off the stage.

The Duke was also dressing—or rather he was dressed—and had dismissed his valet, and was seated before an *escretoire*, not exactly writing, but sealing up a diamond ring which he intended for Wilson, Lady Castlemaine's handsome maid, when his wife rushed into the room, without the ceremony of knocking. He hastily thrust the ring into his pocket, and locked the escretoire.

"Good heavens, James! what do you think?"

She never called him James but on very momentous occasions, of which there were many in those days of plague, pestilence, famine, and plots.

"La Fond has just brought word that there is a report that the King has been assassinated!"

"My God! I hope not," said the Duke, turning very pale, and speaking in the first impulse of a sincere and natural feeling.

"Go!" said his wife, holding out her arm at full length, and pointing to the door, with an air of command, as if she had already a sceptre in her hand, "and see what truth there is in the report."

"Of course I shall go," he replied; "but, my dear Ann, you are not queen yet, therefore you need not order me with so very regal an air."

And although the poor Duke of York was no prophet in his own country, nor even in his own estimation, he added these truly prophetic words —"And goodness knows, you need not be in such a hurry, for plots, assassinations, and an empty exchequer, make but slippery steps to a throne."

She hurled at him a look of ineffable contempt. He saw it, but gave no answering look; all he said was, very quietly, as he took up his hat and hurried out of the room—

"Take care of your hair with that candle, for tow soon ignites."

He ran all across the Court to the other side of the Palace, and neither stopped to interrogate the sentries, the porter, the guards, nor the servants, but hurried straight up to the Queen's apartments, where the King always was of an evening when he was not out; and there he was on this evening, playing Gleek, with his usual set.

"Stole away!" cried the King, when he saw his brother enter the room, looking so scared and out of breath ; "have the hounds mistaken you for a fox?"

"I beg your Majesty ten thousand pardons for rushing into your presence in this unseemly way ; but I was so horrified at an infamous report that they have set about, that your Majesty had been assassinated, that I was almost beside myself with terror and indignation."

The King laid down his cards, looked at his brother from head to foot ; then, holding out his hand to him, said—

"I thank you for your brotherly anxiety ; but make your mind quite easy, for depend upon it, my dear James, no one will ever kill me to make *you* king."

There was a by no means suppressed titter at this; but, if " a soft answer turneth away wrath," the retort courteous, equally disarms ridicule, and the next moment the laughers were on the Duke of York's side, when bowing very low, he replied—

" Quite true, sire; therefore, had I reflected a moment, I should not have given the least credence to such a report; but as is so often the case, my affection got the better of my judgment."

" Ah! my dear James, that is the curse of all our race; we act foolishly first, and think wisely after; or, as Rochester has more tersely put it, we, for it is all of us, and not only I—

' Who never say a foolish thing, and never do a wise one,'

we have all plenty of wit, plenty of brains, only we never use them at the right time, nor in the right place, which is pretty much as if one was to wear one's George and Garter in bed, and one's nightcap in public."

" Your Royal Highness must console yourself with hope," said Silas Titus, " for you know, as Wycherley says, ' Our hopes, though they never happen, yet are some kind of happiness, as trees, while they are still growing, please in the prospect, though they bear no fruit.' "

This was said in scarcely a stage whisper, which the King must have heard. But then, we never were a well-bred people, and it is to be feared never will be; that hideous national selfishness—the root of all social evil—is too deeply rooted in us, and too carefully cultivated by arrogance and self-laudation; while, on the other hand, we laugh what we call "sentiment" to scorn, and with it, have effectually exterminated all good feeling, and even common decency, and this accursed and ever increasing selfishness it is, which makes our commercial dealings so completely dishonest, and our two great national sources of power—politics and literature—rotten to the core. The germ of this selfishness is at once ludicrous and revolting, in the individual Englishman; but it is a national leprosy. We laugh, perhaps, when we read this cool, and matter of course little entry in Evelyn's Diary*— " We arrived that evening at Beveretta; being extremely weary, and complaining of my head,† and finding little accommodation in the house, I caused one of our hostess's daughters to be removed out of her bed, and went into it immediately, while it was yet warm, being so heavy with pain and drowsiness that I would not even stay to have the sheets changed !"—*chacun*

* Vol. 1st, page 238.
† His heart was much more to be complained of

à son gout !—" but shortly after I paid dearly for my impatience"—to say nothing of your brutal selfishness, which you richly deserved to pay for —"for," adds this amiable and well-bred English gentleman, " I caught the small-pox."

Again, we may laugh when Mr. Pepys notes in his diary—no doubt, as a proof of his cleverness and *savoir faire*, despite his *manque de savoir vivre*—" I did see Madam Williams, my Lord Brouncker's miss, at the play, but did make as if I did not see her, for I should have had to offer her my seat, which was a much better one than hers."

Well, laughable these individual instances of the *mal du pays*, with a difference, may be, just as we laugh when we see a drunken man reeling and tumbling about, and ineffectually trying to articulate. But just fancy an entire population of drunkards ! The vice would then be what in reality it ought always to be, truly appalling ! and selfishness, ridiculous, and contemptible in individual instances, *is* perfectly monstrous in a national aggregate. It is this national selfishness, with its *alter ego* apathy, which makes us so utterly regardless of the impression we produce on other countries, and the deference and consideration due either to their courtesies or idiosyncracies. When, for instance, " The Resolute" was abandoned in the ice, during one

of Sir John Franklin's expeditions, and the good
ship, when summer came, drifted all by herself
out of the ice, and once more " walked the waters,
like a thing of life," an American whaler fell in
with her, and comprehending the state of the
case, towed her to New York, where the American Government had her put in thorough repair,
and with great delicacy and good feeling, which
we so much despise under the name of "sentiment," had everything in her decks and cabins
left intact, and in *statu quo*, as her former officers
and crew had left it, even to a stray glove, a
musical snuff box, a pipe, or a sheet of paper,
and after having made a very large outlay in her
repairs, sent the ship to England as a present to
our government.

The poor " Resolute," which so well deserved
her name, arrived off Osborne, where the officers
of the American Navy in charge of her received
the Queen and poor Prince Albert, and their
children, on board of the good ship, which was
dressed in colours, with all her yards manned.
They went all over her, and were much affected,
as any one of human feeling would have been, at
sight of all the little memorials so carefully preserved of all the officers of Sir John Franklin's
crew, just as they had left them on abandoning the
ship.   More especially poor Prince Albert, who
had too nobly well balanced a character not to

have as great and sound a heart as he had a head.
Well, would it be believed, or *could* such a thing
have happened in any country but England?—
the return that was made for the generous and
chivalric kindness and courtesy of the American
Government was, instead of preserving this
miraculously recovered ship as long as her tim-
bers would hold together in common decency, as
a memorial of the kindness of our American
cousins, as even a savage African king would
have done, " my lords," in some fit of farthing
retrenchment and million waste, had the " Resolute" broken up and dismantled the very next
year.   Poor good ship ! better have perished
naturally amid the blockade of less frigid, Polar
ice, than have returned through so many vicissi-
tudes to your native shores to have been " done
to death " by our huge national freezing machine
of selfishness, apathy, and routine.   But " my
lords" always keep the unities, for which reason,
when a French man-of-war, whose name 1 am
ashamed to say I forget, so nobly rescued the
shipwrecked crew of " The Bombay" East India-
man, conveying every single soul, officers and
men, to their respective homes, " my lords," taking a whole year to " screw their courage to the
sticking point," even to perpetuate that insulting *gaûcherie*, sent five hundred pounds to be
divided among the officers ! ! ! and crew of the

French man-of-war that had rescued the crew of
" The Bombay." Now the French, though they
never " eat mutton cold," do always " cut blocks
with a razor ;" so the officers of the French man-
of-war, instantly returned this precious five
hundred pounds, requesting that it might be
divided among the *sailors* of the shipwrecked
crew of " The Bombay." Not a word about the
" officers," mind, grossly insulted as the French
officers must have felt. Oh ! no ; we have no
sentiment, nor need we fear that any one will
ever accuse us of it. No doubt it is this fine,
manly absence of sentiment and intense selfishness and apathy, which makes us leave the graves
of our poor fellows who fell in the Crimea so
desecrated and neglected, while those of the
French and Russians are so carefully secured
and tended. When one reads Dr. Russell's
graphic and Arabian-nights-like descriptions of
the almost fairy-tale splendour and beauty of the
magnificent reception of the Prince and Princess
of Wales in the East and at the Crimea, it is not
even the magical subjugation of nature and the
luxury of a palace conjured up in a desert that
impresses one so forcibly, as the delicate, thought-
ful *prevoyance* of their every want and wish being
ministered to by all—their home comforts and
usages. Now, though undoubtedly it must have
required a vast expenditure to have achieved all

this, money *alone* could never have done it; it
was that careful study of what would be agreeable and commodious, and advantageous to *others*,
no matter at what sacrifice of personal trouble
and inconvenience. Now, how much better we
manage these sort of things in dear, selfish,
apethetic, money-worshipping England; instead
of spending a king's ransom upon our. royal
visitors, and " putting a girdle round the earth"
to bring to a focus for them every possible
luxury, including those of their own particular
homes, as these poor sentimental, semi-barbarians,
are foolish enough to do, we let our royalties
go to an inn and take their ease there, if they
can find it, and when, *mirabili dictu!* the Sultan
was domiciled at Buckingham Palace for a few
days, we took care to animadvert in our newspapers—newspapers of course being strictly
private and confidential—upon the *dirty* state his
majesty's suite had left the Palace in, which was
about as well bred and in as good taste, as if
before he quitted it, some chamberlain had remonstrated with the Sultan in person on the
subject. In like manner, although our volun-
teers were received with princely hospitality in
Belgium, we not only found great difficulty in
collecting the pence to entertain them in return,
but we took care they should not ignore the
fact of all the trouble and expense their visit

put us to, by daily expatiating upon it in the papers, so that had not Baroness Burdett Coutts come to the rescue, the poor Belgians must have had a strange notion of English hospitality.

But all this horrible coarseness and ill-breeding, is caused by the black vein of selfishness, which flaws the whole block of the marble out of which is hewn our national character.   It is self first, self last, self always, and self only !   Ask a French or a Russian man, or woman, to walk ten miles to render you, as a stranger, even a trifling service, and they would not only willingly and gracefully do it; but if they chanced to break their leg in doing it, their only anxiety would be to keep the circumstance from your knowledge, lest you might reproach yourself as being the unwitting cause of the accident.   While, ask an English person to do the slightest thing, they would be sure to inform you of all, so as that you might know and never forgive yourself the immensity of trouble you had occasioned them.

This omnipresence of self it is, which makes English people, in all public places, whether in the House of God, or in its antipodes, the Houses of Parliament, always spread themselves out like split eagles, when they see any of their less fortunate fellow creatures in want of sitting, or even standing room, and which makes them tear the clothes off of each other's backs in a crowd, whether at a court ball or a chartist meeting, in order to practically illustrate Old Rapid's apophthegm of " Push on—keep moving." Nor when we get out of the rolling, surging billows of bustling, tustling, gasping, grasping, work-a-day reality, and soar upward into—what should be the purer and more rarefied atmosphere of the intellectual, are we a bit better off; for all is self, system, cliqueism, and joint stock association there too.   Indeed, within the last quarter of a century the word " genius" has been so profaned, that no one really possessing what the term used to represent, but would repudiate the name with disdain.   Mr. Disraeli, more than forty years ago, in " Vivian Grey," prophetically sounded the key note of modern literature and cliqueism, when he said in that work, *viâ* one of his *dramatis personæ*, speaking of another—

" If ever you know him as well as I do, you will find him vain, superficial, heartless.   His sentiment a system, his genius exaggeration, and his learning merely a clever adaption of the profundity of others."

We are quite aware that in all ages, through contemporary influences, the lesser have been exalted over the greater, leaving it to impartial posterity to adjust the true equilibrium of the balance.   Even Shakspeare in his own day, was thought inferior to Ben Johnson! and though

Milton and Dryden were still living at the time
of Cowley's death, the latter, by his contemporaries, was styled " England's greatest poet !"

When such things could be through mere
tavern *cameraderie*, at a time when even the puff
simple was unknown, what must this sort of
" union is strength" glamour be, in these days of
clubs, cliques, and steam engine puffery? A
modern poet says—

> " What an impostor genius is ;
> How, with the strong mimetic art,
> Which is its life and soul, it takes
> All shapes of thought, all hues of heart,
> Nor feels itself one throb it wakes !"

Then, it is *not* genius in the original and true
meaning of the term, when fiction merely meant
its own wide domain of the ideal; but the above,
is a very accurate description of what is now
called genius, when fiction is no longer pure,
creative, and spiritual, but has grovelled down
into the FALSE, and its only hippocrene is the
sewage of Pactolus.*

But this is a long digression, and we must return to the less sophisticated and more unvar-
nished vice of the seventeenth century.

" Did your Majesty hear that they had spread
a report that you were a widow ?" said the King,

---

* For are not the Newgate calendar, the pothouse, and the
demi monde, the pure sources, from whence modern *popular*
novelists—with some few rare and bright exceptions—derive their
inspirations ?

calling out to the Queen, who was playing at Basset at another table.

" Dat I vas a vindow!" repeated the Queen, in much surprise.

" Well," said the Duke of Buckingham, who was her partner, " windows and widows are so far alike, that both are always on the look out; only a window is much more easily seen through than a widow. *Mais on a fait courir le bruit, Madame, que votre majesté etiez veuve, qu'on avait assassinait le roi.*"

" Ah ! *quel horreur!* tank God he is a lie."

" Since you are here, my dear James, I hope you will stay to supper."

His Royal Highness, not liking to own that he had been bound for Lady Castlemaine's, assented, and seated himself husband-like, not thinking of his *anxious !* wife whom he had left at home in agony to hear of the welfare of her brother-in-law ! It is true, that without waiting for the Duke's return she might easily have assuaged her anxiety by despatching a servant to the Palace to ascertain the real state of the case; but as "conscience makes cowards of us all," she feared that by so doing, her anxiety might be attributed to its real motive.

" It is a wonder," said Killigrew to Lord Rochester, as they were standing at a little distance together behind the Queen's chair, " that the King holds out so long against the fair Barbara."

" Je crois, qu'il aime toujour Sa *Barbe*, mais il n'aime pas *ses favoris!*" said Rochester, and the two laughed imm oderately.

"Very true," rejoined Killigrew, "and her newly fledged Royal Highness of York, seems quite as *entichée* with Jermyn and Sydney, as the Castlemaine is. I can't conceive what the deuce the women can see in those two gossamers."

" Very true, my dear fellow ; we men never can understand what it is that women see in any man, when their vision is not exclusively directed to our irresistible selves."

" Have you yet been able to discover," asked Killigrew, " who the happy individual was, who picked up Broderick the night he frightened the fish, by falling into the Thames ?"

" No ;—what a mystery he makes of it. Now, if the man who saved him was ashamed of the transaction, no one would be surprised, but that Sir Allen should make such a dead secret of it is absurd."

"Oh! depend upon it," said Killigrew, " he either gave the man sixpence—which was more in proportion to the value of the person saved than to the trouble of saving him, and so is afraid the poor man should find out 'his style and title,' as the Heralds say—or there is some other

crooked twist of his at the bottom of it; so I'm
determined I *will* find it out, as there is no such
fun as working that beast Broderick."

Just as he ceased speaking they heard the
Queen exclaim—

" Oh! you pretty fellow! I do admire you
great, big, much !"

".Was your Majesty speaking of me ?" said
Rochester, advancing, and bowing in a most cox-
comical manner, which caused a general roar,
led by the King.

" You! Oh! no," replied the Queen; " for
you, milord, are vat de Inglish call de ugly
dog."

At which the laughter was renewed double
tides ; and when it had in some degree subsided,
the Queen explained, by saying—

" No, I vos speak to dis bootiful pup Penderel,
who come and put his paws on me ; to look at his
bootiful ears and eyes, he de finest of fine
fellows."

" Well, Penderil has certainly grown the handsomest dog in England, as I foretold he would,"
said the King. "I should like to convene all
the judges to award him the palm for canine
beauty."

" Ah ! sire," said Rochester, with mock gravity,
" where find even *one* judge competent to the

onerous task? for I fear we cannot boast of a
Bramstone* now !"

"By-the-bye," said the King, he did not say
àpropos, which would have been a bad compliment to his Majesty's judges—"I hope, Killigrew, you did not forget to tell Casanove that I
preferred the Ardennes boar's head that the
King of France sent to me for supper, instead
of dinner?"

"Not only that, your Majesty, but I myself
told him that it was to be dressed in that peculiar
way that you had the boar's head at Breda dressed,
so that since little Jeffrey Hudson was served in
a pie, and naturally looked very crusty at being
so treated, I don't think so 'dainty a dish' will
ever have been 'set before the King.'"

"At all events, as the boar can't begin to sing,
I hope he won't begin to roar," said the King,
"when he finds himslf in his new *tusculum*."

Least the reader should exclaim with Mr.
Pepys—"Lord! to hear how common those
great people do talk, just like ordinary men, and
very ordinary even for them," we will not inflict any more of this brilliant conversation on
him by following his Majesty into supper, where

* John Bramstone, of Charles the First's time, of whom it was
said " popularity could never flatter into anything unsafe, nor
favour bribe to anything unjust." Alas! that he should have
died, "and left the world no copy."

the boar's head was duly discussed, and done ample justice to, not only by the biped puppies, but by Penderel and his fellow spaniels. When the Duke of York returned home, he found his affectionate wife sitting up for him, and anxiously awaiting him.

The vigil, the suspense, and the annoyance of having missed *all* her *partis* at Lady Castle-maine's. had not improved her looks; but so much the contrary, that her royal spouse began to do what all the rest of the world had done from the first, viz.—wonder what on earth he could ever have seen in her so to flout his royal race.

" Well !" said her Royal Highness.

" Well," responded the Duke, " I hope your Royal Highness"—and he emphasised the words —" won't take cold sitting up so late. I have just left *both* their majesty's quite well ; *elles soupaient, on ne pouvait mieux.*"

" I think, sir, you might have let me know that a little sooner."

" Oh ! my dear, no news, you know, is good news," and he added, as she took up her hand-candlestick, and sailed, with rather more sulk than majesty, out of the room ; " you also know—

" ' Uneasy sleeps the head that wears a Crown.' "

CHAPTER IX

T was the beginning of the month of February, 1671, and as each day passed, and the violets became more plentiful, Dorothy became more cheerful. So thoroughly convinced was she, that even under shelter of poetical license, Gilbert would *not* have held out a false hope to her, and therefore that they really should meet again in the now fast approaching summer. Not so, her mother and Master Hartsfoot, they thought the time that had elapsed since Gilbert Broderick's *most* extraordinary and mysterious disappearance without any tangible and *bonâ fide* explanation of its cause from himself, was becoming quite too long. This desponding view of the matter, however, arose, perhaps, entirely from their own frame of mind, for our minds are always either a Claude glass, steeping every prospect in its own enchanting hue, or else a piece of common dismal black-smoked glass, enabling us to see all our eclipses the more distinctly—but nothing else.

Joseph Barton had that morning made his offering of his really exquisitely carved frame and looking-glass after Hollar's design, for Dorothy's *boudoir,* or, as it was called in those days, "closet." His master had accompanied him to give him courage, and Dorothy had not only accepted the gift most graciously, but really with genuine pleasure and admiration, and told him he must keep out of Mr. Grindling Gibbons' way, not only because two of a trade can never agree, but because artistic rivalry sometimes produced dire consequences. And having dismissed Joseph Barton in the seventh heaven at her praises, and the success of his labours, she playfully caught Master Hartsfoot by the cloak, as he was also beating a retreat.

"Not so fast, and it please you sir, for there is other carving to be done, and you must do it."

And so Master Hartsfoot was springed and kept to dinner.

"Good Lord! as Mr. Pepys says," cried Dorothy, as she held up Barton's glass with both hands admiringly against the wall, "to see how soon one do make and break one's vows. There have I been for the last six months vowing that I'd have no more idols, those provoking and disappointing pieces of sham perfection do behave *so* badly," and she cast a meaning and reproachful look at Hartsfoot, which first made his face wear the Lancastrian roses, and then the snowy

ones of York, which Dorothy pitying him for, yet
provoked, added, " yet, despite all my vows, here
am I now going to set up an idol of wood, for Mr.
Joseph Barton's carving is really beautiful ; and
what a good glass, too."

" There is a hackneyed, and for that reason
somewhat vulgar toast, always given at club and
tavern suppers, which I really think might be
paraphrased with great truth as a motto for
your looking glass, and had I known what he
was about I would have made Barton carve it
round his handy work," said Hartsfoot.

" What may it be ?" asked Dorothy.

" Why, the toast runs, ' May the evening's
amusement always bear the morning's reflection.' But I would have had on the frame of
your mirror, ' Here the evening's amusement
always bears the morning's reflection.' "

" Ah ! Mr. Flatterer, and what if the evening's amusement has been—as I assure you it
very often is—to reflect upon one Master Oliver
Hartsfoot, the most churlish and keep aloof and
unneighbourly of neighbours, who is such a
heathen that he does not know it is written, ' Thou
shalt love thy neighbour as thyself.' Well, poor
pagan, I forgive you, from being perfectly aware
that you *do* that after an inverse fashion, inasmuch as that you do not love yourself at all."

And having hurled this last javelin, she hur-

ried off to tell her mother that she had made
Master Hartsfoot stay to dinner.   And for the
rest of the day she was very good and merciful
to him, sparing all 'jibes and jests, and every
other blush-trap that she usually set for him.
They were sitting all three by the firelight, talking of the most indifferent persons and things,
and of everybody's business, which is proverbially
nobody's business, till they all felt perfectly at
their ease, and Master Hartsfoot so brave, that I
really don't think that *now*, he would have ran
away had he been left in such imminent danger
as to be alone with Mrs. Neville; but Fate was
not at that time of day going to make any devia-
tions in his favour, and it is one of her most
Mede and Persian laws, that those who have
neglected to profit by the THENS, shall have no
opportunity of doing so by the " NOWS."

"My dear child," sighed Mrs. Neville, "it is
so long since I heard you sing, that I almost
forget the sound of your voice.   Those who have
kept you silent so long have angel choirs to listen
to now; so do let me hear once more what I
used to think must be very like them."

"I will, dear mother, if you will let me sing
to the polythore,* and not ask me to go to the
harpsichord, away from your faces and the fire."

"With all my heart ; indeed, I prefer the ac-

* An instrument that Evelyn describes as being between the
harp, lute, and theorbo, and very harmonious.

companiment of the polythore—it is so much
more melodious, and, as the French say, marries
so much better with the voice."

The instrument required some little tuning,
from not having been played upon for more than
a year; but in Dorothy's skilful hands—she being
musicienne jusqu 'au bout des doigts—that was
not a very long operation.   She then sang that
most charming song of James the First, " Come,
summer come ;" though I don't think the music
could have been so exquisite, as that to which Sir
Henry Bishop set it in our time.   Be this as it
may, her very small, but most appreciative audi-
ence were so enchanted with it, that they encored
it twice, and would have done so a third time only
that Dorothy laughed outright, and said—

" Nay, good people, you would make me repeat
the invocation till summer actually *did* come ;
and find us, like a trio of superannuated crickets,
sitting round the embers of our winter's hearth."

Here Jessop brought in the lights, and with
them a letter.

" It's astonishing," said Mrs. Neville, as she
broke the seal, " ever since the year before last,
when all our evil tidings came to us by letter,
how the very sight of one agitates me, especially
if it is in a strange hand."

She was not the only one, for both her companions became red, and pale alternately.   This
letter, however, could not be said to convey any

especially—that is, any new, bad tidings, though
the contents, naturally, opened the scarcely closed
floodgates of both the mother and daughter's
hearts again.   The letter was from Tom Killigrew, and ran as follows :—

" DEAR MADAM—
           " I am commanded by his Majesty to
desire your presence, and that of Mistress Dorothy
Neville, at White Hall, on the evening of 14th
proximo, at 8 p.m., for the purpose of hearing
officially read, the Will of Mistress Phillida
Broderick, late of Clumber Chase, in the County
of Suffolk, a few days more than thirteen months
since her demise having now expired. His Majesty
would not, on any account, wish to do your feelings the violence of constraining you to quit your
mourning; but all white, being equally mourning,
his Majesty makes it a request that you would be
pleased both to wear that, instead of black."
       " With my respectful homage to yourself
           " And your fair daughter,
               " I have the honour to be, madam,
                   " Your devoted servant,
                       " THOMAS KILLIGREW.
                   "Palace of White Hall,
                       " February the 10th, 1671.
       "To Mistress Neville,
           " On the Mall."

Dorothy sobbed aloud—

" I do think it shocking and shameful !" said
she, " that his poor aunt's Will should be read
before Gilbert returns, for of course it concerns
him more than anyone else; indeed, I don't see
what we can possibly have to do with it, that we
should be there like a family conclave, at the
reading of it; for even with her usual never-
failing kindness, if she has left us any little
memento of her—a work of great supererogation
on the part of one, whom all that ever knew her
can never forget.   Surely it could have been
transmitted or announced to us by the lawyer or
executor, or whoever the proper person is, and
we need not have been dragged into this very
painful public exhibition."

" My dear," said her mother, " the King being
poor dear Phillida's chief executor, I suppose
there *is* some reason for it ; at all events, we
cannot disobey his commands, and by far the
most painful thing that I see in the business,
next to poor Gilbert's absence, is that that horrible man, Sir Allen will be there—of course under
the plea of brotherly interest—for he has always,
if not some pompous high sounding virtue, at
least a respectability or a plausibility, or some
other smooth varnished hypocrisy—ready to
label all his vials of wrath with, so as those who
run may read.   But of course his real object in

being there will be to try his uttermost to set aside and invalidate his poor dead sister's wishes."

" Mother," said Dorothy, rocking herself to and fro in her chair, as she kept her hands before her face, " I really *cannot* go through such an ordeal; you must say I am ill. I wonder at the King; I should have thought, from his manner, he would have had a little more kindness and consideration, but words and manner cost nothing and buy everything, especially with princes, they are *l'eau bénite de la cour.*"

" My dear child, you must nerve yourself and sacrifice yourself this once, for I cannot disobey the King's orders, neither can *I* possibly face such an ordeal by myself."

" Depend upon it," said Hartsfoot, now speaking for the first time since Killigrew's letter had been read, " things will turn out much better and less painfully than you expect; I feel quite certain that it is neither from thoughtlessness nor want of kindness, that the King has commanded your presence at the reading of the Will, but quite the reverse; and that on the contrary he has some kind and considerate motive in so doing. And as for Sir Allen, I know that *he* is no favourite with the King, and the whole Court detest him, more especially Tom Killigrew; so you may be very certain that you will be the figures and he the cipher there."

" Ah ! Master Hartsfoot," said Dorothy, holding out her hand to him, " you are always my *en cas de malheur*, and have a never failing supply of oil and wine for every wound, or you'd be no good Samaritan if you had not ; but—but—I do so dread it ; we have suffered so terribly this last year, that I feel like one great raw wound, which even a chill air can goad to torture."

" I quite understand that," sighed he, " and that is the worst of all great moral blows ; the pain may cease, and the wound cicatrise in time, but they leave us confirmed cowards, and ever after we tremble at every shadow and wince at every echo. We forget, too, that Fate, like sin, has no holidays ; spin ! spin ! spin ! day and night, night and day, our destiny is being eternally woven, and nothing we can do or not do, will either hasten or retard the completion of the tissue, or alter its warp or weft by half a hair's breadth. For all that, we are like children, who sow seeds to-day and dig them up to-morrow, to see whether they are growing ! I once read in an old Spanish author that it was a mistake to say that we met our fate, for that, on the contrary, it followed and overtook us. Now, I perfectly understand the sequence of this idea ; for what we *meet* we must see coming, and so have the option of avoiding it, but what overtakes us comes upon us unawares, and leaves us no means of escaping. Now, in this instance, Mistress Dorothy, your fate is to obey the King, and kings are the Dragon flys of our world, and that you may understand my simile, I will read you the fragment of a poem, entitled 'The Insect World,' by Captain Broderick, that Ferrol rescued from some torn up papers, and I'm sorry to say that both the commencement and the ending were torn off, for I much like what there is of it," said Hartsfoot, taking the fragment out of his pocket book, and reading it out to them.

> There a Dragon fly, girt with green,
> And all be-prank'd with orient gold,
> Did his bright spear of purple sheen,
> And long shadowy wings unfold.
>
> Athwart the noon day's sultry haze,
> He listless flings him down to rest,
> Like to a victor tired of praise,
> And e'en with Fame's bright gauds oppress'd.
>
> Tho' of new conquests he still dreams,
> Fierce wars to wage 'gainst moth and moat,
> To prove by " right divine," Sol's beams
> Were only made for *him* to float,
>
> Within their bright, exclusive sphere,
> And not for vulgar insect life;
> Tho' from their myriad's 'twould appear,
> The world with, such is much more rife.
>
> What, then ? they're *only* made 'tis plain,
> For Satellites to gem *his* way,
> Mere living links to bind the chain,
> Of his hereditary sway !
>
> "For lo !" thinks he, " from Eden's birth,
> Each Caitiff insect life's been ours,
> Since first on the primeval earth,
> The Angels traced God's laws in flowers."

" May I ?" said Dorothy, holding out her hand
for the lines.

" Certainly you may," said he, rising to wish
them good night.   " I'm sorry it's only a fragment, but when summer comes, he'll be able to
give you the rest.   And now farewell, till after
the fourteenth, when I shall be very anxious to
see you, as I have a *presentiment* that you will
have good tidings of some sort to tell me."

" Not merely to tell you, dear Master Hartsfoot," said Dorothy, " but to share with you ; for
they will be no good tidings to me, unless I *can*
share them with you."

" No, that I'm quite sure they would not," said
Mrs. Neville.

But I am not quite sure whether he heard her,
for he was already at the head of the stairs, with
his foot on the first step.

CHAPTER X.

GREAT EVENTS ALWAYS HAPPEN SUDDENLY.

THE morning of the fourteenth of February, 1671, dawned one of the fairest days that heaven ever gave to earth; the birds seemed to feel its influence, and sang out their valentines even more blithely than usual. When Dorothy opened her window, and saw how bright and joyous all things looked above, beneath, and around her, she almost shut to the casement impatiently, as if hurt at all Nature's want of sympathy in looking so joyous, when she was so sad. The day wore heavily on, both for mother and daughter, who, dreading the trial before them, could only console themselves by saying —

"Well, by this time to-morrow, it will be over."

"Yes," said Dorothy, "neither executions nor martyrdoms, however dreadful, can last beyond a certain time; only the worst of it is, that what are merely chronological minutes in the ordinary course of time, always appear like separate eternities to those who suffer."

Seven o'clock in the evening at length came, they had to dress—the doffing their black garments for what Dorothy called " those glaring whited sepulchres," seemed like the first stretch on the rack to them.   There was no muslin in those days, except fabulously dear Indian muslin —fine as woven air, it is true—but very little of that even ; but there was a much prettier thing, so far as the soft—without being flat and limp— graceful folds, and draperies in which it fell, and that was *crêpe lisse*.   It was in vain that the two victims had cried the whole day ; when they were dressed the elder looked a queen, the younger a goddess ; the simple unadorned, dazzling white at once tried, tested, and proved their beauty indisputably, for there was no " foreign aid of ornament," either to share it or confer any additional charm.   The perfect harmony and blending of snow-white of Dorothy's dress, and the blush-rose white of her skin and complexion was heightened and relieved by a large bouquet of dark double violets in her bosom, the only ornament she wore.   But being dressed, we must leave them to rest for a short time to try and get rid of the traces of their tears before they set out for White Hall, and precede them there, to see what preparations were making for their advent.

The long gallery at White Hall, or as it was then called the matted gallery, was partitioned off for that occasion only, by a large green velvet curtain, trimmed with broad gold lace and a deep bullion fringe. In the one half the gallery, visible to all comers, was a long oval or oblong table, also covered with a tight-fitting green velvet cloth, fringed with bullion ; on this table were placed, at equal distances, divers quires of paper, blotting paper, pens, and ink, in silver standishes, as at a Council table. While round the table, were cushioned low-backed chairs also covered with green velvet and large nasturtium headed gilt nails and gold fringe round them. Presently, from the private apartments, their Majesties entered ; the Queen leaning on the King's arm, followed by their lords and ladies in waiting, all *en grande tenue.* Lady Castlemaine, had she not been still under ban, would not have been there, for the King had had the good taste on this occasion to weed his court of all objectionables in order to confer honour where honour was due. He led the Queen to the upper end of the table, and seated himself beside her, while upon another chair, at his left hand, were two of his dogs, the Blenheim Penderel, and Beauty, the King Charles, who always attended him at all meetings of the Privy Council, the P.C.'s woefully complaining that, no matter how important the affair, it was impossible to get the King's ear, he was so taken up with his dogs' ears. Their Majesties seated, the suite remained standing. Presently Killigrew came into the gallery from the green drawing-room, cramming his handkerchief into his mouth, and evidently much amused at something.

"What is it?" asked the King, as he approached. "Not Sir Allen Broderick pretending to be ill, I hope, in order to escape the pleasure in store for him?"

"No, no, your Majesty, he's come safe enough, but in such a gorgeous parade of woe, that it was too much for my risible muscles. Hamlet, Prince of Denmark, actually wears the motley in comparison to him, he positively glitters like a firmament—such a moving mass of black bugles is he."

"Oddsfish! Kil; you, a dramatist! and not understand keeping the unities, which Sir Allen apparently does; for when a man is his own trumpeter, he surely cannot have too many bugles."

Of course, they all laughed, as in duty bound, at this sally, all the more, that the *mot* was at Sir Allen's expense.

"But," added the King, "'pon my life, I begin to have qualms, and fear we may have carried the jest too far; for when he finds himself springed and circumvented on all sides, what if he should go raving mad upon our hands?"

" I've thought of that too, your Majesty, and so have the remedy all ready at hand; for I sent for Doctor Erasmus Everhard, the mad doctor—a *conditional* appointment as Court Leech Extraordinary—in *case* his services should be required. So he's safe under lock and key, in Titus's room, *till* we want him, for ' 'Tis a mad world, my masters.' "

At this the King actually roared.

" Oh! Kil! Kil! you are too bad; *tu ne perde jamais la carte.*"

" Never; at least, when your Majesty gives me *carte blanche,* as you did on this occasion, for the better and more perfect enactment of my little ' morality.' "

" Why, it's so little morality that any of us have," said Rochester, " that a *carte blanche* is almost a work of supererogation."

" The lawyer had better come in and take his seat," said the King; " but don't let loose Sir Allen upon us, for the world, till Mistress Neville and the fair Dorothea have arrived."

And as Killigrew left the gallery to go for the lawyer, two pages entered, with a very large gilt basket, filled with flowers, and placed bouquets all round the table before each seat. Before they had finished doing so, Killigrew returned, accompanied by Mr. Jambres Fairbrace, with a portfolio under his arm, and a blue bag in his hand, and was duly presented to the King, who graciously said to him, as he desired him to take his seat opposite to him at the foot of the table—

" As joint executors to Mrs. Phillida Broderick's will, you and I, Mr. Fairbrace, are colleagues ; therefore, it is a sort of antithesis *en action* that we should be in opposition."

" I hope not, sire,'' bowed Fairbrace. " Your Majesty will only be in your proper place, administering justice under the eyes of the law."

While they were speaking, Killigrew had removed the bouquet that had been placed before Sir Allen Broderick's seat, and put some sort of green herb in its stead.

" What on earth are you doing, Kil?" asked the King.

" Quite the right thing to do, sire ; for, as Mr. Fairbrace will tell you, it is always customary to place rue for the prisoner in the dock."

" No, no. *C'est par trop fort !*" laughed the King ; " let the poor devil ' wear his rue with a difference.' "

" Oh ! very well," said Killigrew, hiding the rue by placing the bouquet on the top of it ; " so goes the world—sweets first and bitters after."

Here, a servant informed Killigrew that Madam Neville and Mistress Dorothy Neville were in the red drawing-room. And he again left the gallery to conduct them in, and soon returned with them, when Mrs. Neville advanced to kiss the Queen's hand, which her Majesty prevented, by graciously rising and kissing both mother and daughter upon both cheeks, for in vain are those poor foreigners born, even monarchs, they cannot divest themselves of their natural grace and amiability; no, not even when they have had the of course great advantage of living for years amongst us, can they succeed in acquiring the great Anglo-Saxon art of substituting disagreeability for dignity, and repulsion for attraction. The King gallantly kissed their hands, and seating Mrs. Neville next the Queen, and Dorothy next to himself, the very next moment Master Penderel did her the honour of jumping into her lap, for there is a freemasonry between dogs and dog-lovers, which fully proves Fourrier's doctrine of affinities, or *atoms crochus.*

"Now," said the King, turning to Killigrew, "we are all assembled; so, I think Kil, you may sound the bugles, and let loose Sir Allen."

Killigrew bowed and withdrew, and shortly after, re-entered from the green drawing-room with Sir Allen Broderick, who was, as the former had described, really a glittering firmament of radiant darkness, from the mass of black bugles with which his black velvet suit was studded.

He saluted the King and Queen most obsequi-
ously ; then, perceiving Mrs. Neville and Dorothy,
but not choosing to let them see that he had
honoured them so far, he fell into his usual atti-
tude of his left hand on his hip, and his head
thrown haughtily back, as he strutted past them
and took the seat the King had indicated to him
at the opposite side of the table.   Meanwhile,
Mr. Jambres Fairbrace had emptied the contents
of his bag and his portfolio, and arranged all his
papers in business order before him on the table.
All things being now ready, the King rose, and
turning to Sir Allen, said—while Killigrew,
standing behind his Majesty's chair, emphasised,
in dumb show, every word he uttered, just as
finaticos at an opera or concert beat time with
head and hand to the music—

   " Sir Allen Broderick, you perhaps remember
that one morning, now rather more than two
years ago, a country woman accosted us on the
Mall, presenting a letter, which we read, and
promised on the same evening to send an answer
to it by a special messenger, whereupon you were
good enough to offer us your services as the messenger in question.   You will now understand
our necessity for declining your loyal zeal, when
we tell you that that letter was from your late
highly esteemed and lamented sister, Mistress
Phillida Broderick, requesting us to accept the

trust of chief executor to her will, Mr. Jambres
Fairbrace there, being our colleague and joint
trustee in the executorship. Being so far back
as that time made cognizant of the contents and
bequests of that will, we have, to the best of our
ability, and under legal advice, acted so as to
fulfil the last wishes of the testator, and insure
the interests of the legatees, a line of conduct,
Sir Allen, which we hope will ultimately receive
the sanction of your approval."

The King paused, as if expecting his assent,
and Sir Allen rose accordingly, and with an expression of face that flatly belied his words,
assured his Majesty that whatever *he* did must
always be approved of by his most faithful servant and subject, Allen Broderick, and then he
re-seated himself, hiding his face in his snow-
white cobweb handkerchief, so as that concealed
rage might do duty for either decency or grief;
while Killigrew was enacting such a pantomime
of throwing up his eyes, placing his hand upon
his heart, and sighing profoundly, that all who
saw it—and fortunately, the King was not among
the number, or his gravity would have given way
—were convulsed with suppressed laughter.

"We were quite sure," resumed the King,
"that we could always reckon upon Sir Allen
Broderick's loyalty, devotion, and *implicit obedi-
ence* to our wishes. And now, having so far

opened the business by this short preliminary
statement, it is for our colleague to do his duty
by reading out the will."

So saying, the King resumed his seat, and Mr.
Fairbrace giving a preliminary tap to the parch-
ment, so as to straighten its folds, read out in a
clear, sonorous voice—

"I, Phillida Broderick, spinster, of Clumber
Chase, in the county of Suffolk, being in perfectly
sound mind, on this 14th day of May, in the year
of our Lord One thousand six hundred and sixty-
eight, do hereby will and bequeath my estate of
Clumber Chase, with all its lands, messuages and
tenements, now perfectly free and unencumbered,
to my beloved nephew, Gilbert Broderick, only
son of my brother, Sir Allen Broderick, Bart., of
Broderick Park, Yorkshire, and Whitehall Gardens, London, M.P. for the county of Suffolk,
and Surveyor General of Ireland, to be entailed
upon the heirs male of his body, lawfully begotten,
and, in default of male heirs, on the female heirs
of the said Gilbert Broderick; and should he die
unmarried or without heirs, I then bequeath the
aforesaid estate of Clumber Chase, its lands, messuages, and tenements, to my dear and much beloved Dorothea Neville, spinster, only child of
the late Colonel Algernon Neville, and Dame
Margaret, his wife.   To the said Dame Margaret

Neville, my earliest and dearest friend, I bequeath all my mother's diamonds, including the
carcomet with the large union in the centre, and
besides this union, my long suit of pear-shaped
pearls ; also my ruby and pearl suit, and my
diamond and sapphire stomacher. I further
leave to Dame Margaret Neville my rare old suit
of Queen Eleanor's point lace, and what rare
specimens of Oriental, French, Italian, and other
china she may choose to select from the house
at Clumber Chase. To my brother, Sir Allen
Broderick—"

And here Sir Allen allowed his eyes to be
seen above his handkerchief, and looked out at
the corners of them very much like a fox at
bay, not exactly sure in what direction he heard
the hounds.

"To my brother, Sir Allen Broderick," continued Mr. Fairbrace, "I bequeath the object I
know he has always valued most, viz., a full-
length portrait of himself in oils by Vandyke.
To my dear friend, Dame Margaret Neville, I
also bequeath the full-length portrait in oils, by
the same artist, of her late husband, Colonel
Algernon Neville, and all the other portraits,
pictures, statues, whether in marble or bronze,
absolutely to my dear nephew, the aforesaid

Gilbert Broderick, as well as all the furniture, books, prints, plate, china, glass, linen, and fixtures in the house at Clumber Chase. That is, all the furniture, with ONE exception, which I especially, and under certain conditions which she must agree to fulfil before accepting the bequest, leave to my dear young friend, Dorothea Neville, spinster, and that is MY NOBLE RED WORSTED BED AND ALL THE HANGINGS, as I will on no account consent to have the hangings separated, as is too often done in these days, out of economy, for to cover other furniture with them.* This bed, having been the work of my dear mother's hands, and slept in by his late Majesty King James, when he came to hunt at Clumber Chase; and the splendid effect of the vine leaves, embroidered in green bugles on the scarlet ground, was greatly admired both by his majesty and Queen Anne. Therefore, and as my dear mother's work, my dear Dorothea Neville must promise to take and to keep *all the hangings intact*, or else not accept the behest at all, which would be a great disappointment to me. I

---

* These red worsted beds, as they were called, were thought so valuable from Elizabeth's time down to James the Second's time, that they were generally bequeathed separately by will, being for the most part elaborately embroidered on a ground of red worsted damask. But as the fashion changed for a lighter and a more elegant style of furniture, profane hands were wont to desecrate these ancestral labours by taking some of these too voluminous curtains to cover chairs with, and it is against such *lèse* grandmother, that Miss Phillida Broderick provides so stringently in her will.

further bequeath an annuity of £20 a year to my own woman Alice Arden ; also £20 a year to my housekeeper, Joan Daventry ; also £20 a year to my trusty dairy-woman, Eldrid Marsh, who so faithfully conveyed my letter to his Majesty respecting my Will in 1668. To my butler, Ambrose Trueman, I also bequeath an annuity of £20 a year, and to my steward, Frank Standish, an annuity of £50. To all my servants I bequeath a year's wages and mourning. And I further bequeath to my own woman, Alice Arden, all my wearing apparel and linen, with the exception of my point, Dresden, and Flanders laces, which I leave to my dear Dorothea Neville. It is my wish that my dear nephew, Gilbert Broderick, should retain, in his service, all my old servants (unless he should hereafter find reason to part with them), for as I leave him, besides all the live and dead stock on my farms, all my horses and dogs, the poor things might not like strange faces about them. To his most excellent Majesty King Charles the Second, for so graciously condescending to accept the office of my executor, as a slight token of my gratitude, I bequeath the sum of £5,000 for the purchase of a diamond ring, or any other jewel he may choose, and to my good friend, and legal adviser, Mr. Jambres Fairbrace, of Clifford's Inn, I bequeath the sum of £1,000, and £500 to each

of his sons, Arden Fairbrace and Oliver Fairbrace.

> "PHILLIDA BRODERICK
>   "Witness my hand and seal,
>   "Frank Standish,
>   "Ambrose Trueman.
>   "Clumber Chase, Suffolk,
>   "This fourteenth day of May, 1668."

During the reading of the Will, Mrs. Neville
and Dorothy were in floods of tears, that they
could not suppress, and the Queen kindly pressed
Mrs. Neville's hand and offered her her own
pomander. As for Sir Allen, he had been for the
last ten minutes nervously twitching his fingers,
and when the reading at length ended, he mut-
tered as loud as he dared—

"Infamous! perfectly infamous! The woman
was mad, that's evident."

The King heard him, but did not heed him;
while Killigrew, continuing his pantomime, kept
blowing kisses to him from the tips of his fingers,
and then, with his right hand in the palm of his
left, imitating the turning of a screw, as much
as to say, "We've not done with you yet, my
fine fellow, till we've screwed you a little more."

"Now," said the King, addressing Dorothy,
"we can proceed no farther in our duties till we
know, Mistress Dorothy, whether you consent to

accept Mrs. Phillida Broderick's red worsted bed, with *all* the hangings ?"

" Of course, your Majesty; if you only knew, sire, what my love and veneration for Mrs. Phillida Broderick was, you would be convinced that even one stitch in that bed I would not allow to be touched, much less think of dividing the hangings."

" I am delighted to hear it," said the King ; "but to keep to the very *letter* of the law, and have everthing *en règle*, I believe it is necessary, Mr. Fairbrace, that Mistress Dorothy should see this bed first, and make this affirmation before witnesses, is it not?"

" Quite so, your Majesty, for then there can be no future dispute or misunderstanding upon the matter."

If a man could frown himself to death, Sir Allen would have certainly done it within the last half hour, for the furrow was so deep between his brows, that it looked exactly as if the process of cleaving his skull in two had been commenced, and that already a deep gash had been made ; nor did his murderous brows much relax, when the King, turning to him with a bland, though, albeit, a Judas smile, said—

" Then, Sir Allen Broderick, we must request the favour of your attendance as one of the witnesses, for the red worsted bed is here at hand within yonder green velvet curtain."

And his Majesty led the way, taking Dorothy's right hand in his, and followed by all present. Arrived before the large green velvet curtain, or rather curtains, for it was divided in the centre, Killigrew tapped it with a long white wand that he held, and the curtains instantly separated, and discovered that part of the gallery brilliantly illuminated, and the red worsted bed, with its green bugle embroidery glittering out in bold relief.

"Now, Mistress Dorothy," said the King, leading her close up to the bed, "you must again affirm, before all these witnesses, that you promise to take this bed, with *all* the hangings, and to *keep* them all!"

"I do, sire, solemnly promise to do so."

"You hear?" said the King, looking round on all present.

"We hear, and bear witness, sire."

"And you, Sir Allen Broderick, you heard Mistress Dorothy's solemn promise to accept and to keep *all* the hangings?"

"Of course, sire, everybody heard; and if she parts with *one* of them, she is to forfeit the whole," hissed out Sir Allen, with a degree of emphasised spite that in some degree relieved him, as he fancied—though he could not tell how or where—that he was laying a trap for Dorothy.

"Good," said the King. "Now, Killigrew,

favour us with another touch of your wand, and
separate the hangings, that we may count them,
and Mistress Dorothy perfectly understand what
belongs to her, and what she must on no account
part with."

Killigrew approached, and pushing aside with
his long wand one of the massive curtains of the
ponderous bed, discovered Gilbert Broderick!
suspended, not certainly by the neck, but by a
broad leather belt, round the waist, from which
projected at the back a very large iron ring and
long chain, which being terminated by a hook,
fastened him to the rod along which the curtain
rings ran, while he stood on the bed and leant
against one of its huge and richly carved posts,
so that the "hanging" was a mere "legal fiction," and not a reality; the spectators, led by
the King, clapped their hands in token of their
approval—all, except Sir Allen, who rapped out
an imprecation, and hurried back to his seat in
the other division of the gallery; and Dorothy,
who uttered a piercing cry, and fell fainting into
her mother's arms. While all this was taking
place, and in a far shorter time than it has taken
us to describe it, Killigrew had released Gilbert,
who the next moment was by Dorothy's side.

" I think, Captain Broderick," said the King,
"you will be much better able to support that
lovely burden than Mistress Neville, and when

she has sufficiently recovered your presence, all three will be required at the council table to terminate this business, which has so well begun and so happily progressed."

And as the King ceased speaking all the spectators were dispersed as if by magic, the green velvet curtains that partitioned off the gallery were lowered, and Mrs. Neville and the two lovers were left alone. Gilbert soon contrived by very simple means, without the foreign aid of smelling bottles or even of cold water, to recover Dorothy; when, being so deeply indebted to the law and its quibbles, these silly young people showed their gratitude to it by still preferring deeds to words, for they said nothing, but continued to embrace each other repeatedly, and with such fervour that it must have thoroughly convinced them that they were both there, substantial facts, and not either phantoms or dreams. At length Mrs. Neville said—

" For heaven's sake, my dear Gilbert, do explain all these marvels and mysteries."

" No—no; not now, to-morrow," said Dorothy. ' It is quite happiness enough to see him and to *know* him here ; but what business have you, sir, to look so well, when you were causing such long torments to others ?"

" Those who live in glass houses should not throw stones ; look at home, madam, and see

what your own radiant looks are," retorted he in
the same playful tone.

Here Killigrew put in his head between the
curtains of the *portière*, and then came towards
them, saying—

" Ladies and gentlemen—or rather gentleman,
as there is but one – no, gentlemen is right, as
the man is evidently beside himself, so that
makes two—I am sorry to—to play the marplot,
but his Majesty waits. May I humbly venture
to hope that our little MORALITY of WHERE
THERE'S *a will* THERE'S A WAY has met with
your approbation so far as it has gone ? We are
now about to commence the third and last act,
which requires your presence."

" Oh ! Killigrew, you are the very best fellow
in the whole world," said Gilbert, shaking him
cordially by the hand.

" What! for turning King's evidence, and getting you hanged? Well, I'm glad you are thankful
for small mercies, as it shows a right frame of
mind ; but we must not keep his Majesty waiting,
or we shall have him roaring out like his cousin
of France, ' *Messieurs j'ai failli attendre !'* "

Gilbert gave his arm to Dorothy, but Killigrew took her hand and placed it within his own,
saying to Gilbert—

" *Non pas mon cher, à la cour il faut toujours*

chasser le naturel, mais n'ayez pas peur dans quelques heures d'ici il reviendra au galop.''

So Gilbert, giving his arm to Mrs. Neville instead, they all four returned to what Killigrew called the council table, and the King again seated Dorothy on his right, and flipping down Penderel and Beauty with his handkerchief, made Gilbert and Dorothy take their seat on his left hand.

" Now, Sir Allen Broderick," said his Majesty, as soon as they were all seated, " I think it right to explain the mystery of your son's disappearance. His hat, and glove, and broken rapier, found on the Mall, was a mere *ruse*, the better to insure the mystery of his disappearance, and put all conjecture on a false scent. Not choosing him in reality perhaps to lose his life going to Tangiers, it was I who issued the *ne exeat regno*, so that he has never been farther than Theobald's, where, as you may perceive, he has not been too badly cared for, as indeed every blessing was provided for him—dogs, books, musical instruments, everything, with the trifling little exceptions of his personal liberty, and the liberty of communicating with his friends, and above all with Mistress Dorothy Neville, for which little preliminary imprisonment I hope she will forgive me by allowing me on this day month, in the Chapel Royal, to make him over to her, so as to

insure his loss of liberty for life, and then she
will have no right to cast any blame upon me
for my comparatively short and trifling cruelty;
though I hope she will find some one else to give
her away—as it is called—upon that occasion,
as such a gift would really be a stretch of
generosity quite beyond me. And now, Sir Allen,
I hope you will let byegones be byegones, and
be a witness to your son's happiness this day
month."

Sir Allen said, or rather hissed out—

" Of course your majesty has a right to amuse
yourself as you please, and as a loyal and dutiful
subject, I hope I have at all times and in all
places, and under all circumstances, no matter at
what cost of personal inconvenience, endeavoured
to promote your majesty's pleasure; but I must
be permitted to remark, that it argues a great
want of self-respect, and, indeed, I may say a
total want of delicacy upon the part of Mistress
Neville and her daughter, to meanly take advantage of your majesty's condescending kindness, to
smuggle themselves into a family of which the
head and chief, so strenuously objects to their al-
liance."

And Sir Allen fanned himself with his handkerchief, and darted looks between fork light-
ning and red hot knitting needles at Mrs. Neville,
who quietly took from her pocket a little gold

filigree pocket-book, which she opened, and took out two sheets of thin, but closely written paper, which she handed to the King, as she said—

"It would indeed argue great want of self-respect to act as you have described, Sir Allen Broderick, but you surely must remember that scarcely fourteen months ago you came down to The Chestnuts to inquire after your son's disappearance, and on that occasion you volunteered —for the proposition was entirely yours—to give me in writing your full consent to my daughter marrying Captain Broderick, should he re-appear, and—"

"It's false !" thundered Sir Allen, "for I took that—" But suddenly recollecting the disgraceful avowal he was about to make, he stopped short.

"Quite true," continued Mrs. Neville, calmly. "I am well aware that you took away, as you thought, the written promise you had volunteered to give me ; but if you remember, I warned you that you were writing upon embroidery tracing paper, and offered to bring you proper writing paper, but you refused, saying that paper would do very well; the consequence was that instead of one promise you wrote three ; one you took away with you, the other two I have just handed to his majesty."

" *Your writing*, Sir Allen," said the King, "or else the State Paper Office knows it not."

Sir Allen, now desperate, actually foamed at the mouth, as he vociferated in a voice hoarse and nearly inarticulate with rage—

" A lie! an infernal lie! Not content with cajoling my mad sister to cheat me and leave you everything, you work upon a weak king to—"

" Sir Allen! Sir Allen!" said Killigrew, taking him forcibly by the arm and leading him out of the gallery, " recollect that there is such a thing as *lèse majesté*, and there is such a place as the Tower of London, or the Gate House, if you prefer it."

By the time he had got him into the green drawing-room, Sir Allen had become perfectly rabid; he kicked, he cursed, he even attempted to bite Killigrew, as he stuttered out—

" This is some of your infernal buffoonery. I have a mind to thrust your accursed tongue down your idiot throat."

" Hard names break no bones," said Killigrew; " but you must not carry that game too far, Sir Allen, for remember—

" —— What dangers do en-viron,
The man who meddles with cold iron."

" And though associating with *you*, I am a gentleman, and wear a sword."

But Sir Allen became so outrageous that Killigrew could hardly hold him. So making a

signal—before agreed upon—to Silas Titus, who
stood at the outer door, he vanished, and in a
few seconds after, returned with Doctor Erasmus
Everhard, who was greatly taken a-back at seeing who his patient was, and to describe Sir
Allen's demoniacal rage, when he saw *him*, would
be utterly impossible. Nevertheless, the Doctor,
who had not lost his presence of mind on the occasion, but behaved with five hundred pounds
worth of honour, and affected the most perfect
ignorance of Sir Allen's identity, calling him
" the gentleman," while Killigrew spoke to the
Doctor about him, as if he—Sir Allen—had been
in a swoon, or else really mad, and incapable of
comprehending what he heard.

" Poor man, it has come on very suddenly,
Doctor ; he was always saying his poor sister was
mad ; but as she never evinced the least symp-
tom of being so, no one believed it; but it really
would appear that there is insanity in the family,
by its having broken out so awfully suddenly
in him."

Upon hearing this, capped with Doctor Everhard's presence, professionally pouncing upon,
and despite his struggles, retaining his hold of
the Baronet's pulse, it may be supposed how
fearfully Sir Allen's symptoms of lunacy increased; indeed, so thoroughly was Doctor Everhard convinced of their reality, that he felt his

honour and discretion absolved; so, turning to Killigrew, he said, *sotto voce*—

" I think, sir, I had better have Sir Allen Apsley at once conveyed to my house ?"

" Sir Allen Apsley !" repeated Killigrew, " you mistake ; Sir Allen Apsley never had brains enough to go mad—this is Sir Allen Broderick."

" Oh ! indeed, sir," said the Doctor, in a moment perceiving, with great admiration, with what method the mad man had concocted the plot of assuming a false name.

But Sir Allen no sooner heard his real name handed over to Doctor Everhard by Killigrew, than he really did become raving mad for the moment, with rage at being springed in his own trap; and as " the ruling passion" is always strong in madness as in death, he wrung his hands and exclaimed, apparently quite incoherently to all, save Dr. Everhard, who perfectly understood the allusion—

" Five hundred pounds gone, lost, robbed of it, all through a fool's trick."

And here he became so violent in his gesticulations, and flung out so murderously in all directions that Killigrew cried out—

" Have a care, Doctor ; keep your distance, Titus, or we may lose our lives without even having the law to avenge us, for you know, *meus peccat non corpus et unde consilium abefûit*

culpa abest.   By Jove ! it's becoming serious, you
had better get the doctor's man in too."

And Titus went out in quest of him while Sir
Allen continued to foam and rave.

"Anything so infamous I never knew; all
family ties disregarded, all natural affection outraged."

" Perfectly true, Sir Allen, and I am glad you
have a lucid interval to see your conduct in its
proper light; there is some hope for you now,
according to the merciful proverb which says, 'A
sin confessed, is half forgiven.' "

"Ugh! if I could only get at my sword,"
hissed Sir Allen through his set teeth, " I'd lard
your foul words through your vitals, you accursed
popinjay."

" Ah ! well, all fowl is certainly the better for
being larded," rejoined Killigrew.   "*Ainsi vous
voila piqué, beau sire.*"

Here Titus returned with Sampson Golightly.

" Good Lord deliver us !" exclaimed that
worthy, starting back and flinging up both his
hands, when he saw Sir Allen.

" So you also know this gentleman, it would
seem ?" asked Killigrew.

" Know him, your lordship's worship, I should
rather think I did.   Why he is the sir as master
and I, last July, in a terrible thunderstorm one
night on the Thames, saved from dying the death

of a hinfant cat, that is to say, your lordship's worship, from being drownded."

" Whew !" whistled Killigrew. " *J'y—suis !*"

" Will you hold your infernal tongue, you unbottled abortion of a strait waistcoat," roared Sir Allen, looking handcuffs at Sampson.

" Well," said that functionary, forgetting the baronet in the Bedlamite, " them as is born to be hanged won't never be drownded, as the saying is ; so we needn't have troubled ourselves, only praps 'twas as well to make sure as it wasn't a case of *hydreefobee*, which taking to the water in that way proved."

" Have you the bracelets, Sampson ?" whispered the Doctor, which was his courtly euphuism for handcuffs, out of respect to the royal precincts, and not to shock " ears polite."

" All right, sir," responded Sampson, putting his hand into his pocket, and withdrawing a coil of rope, as well as " the bracelets," wherewith he immediately proceeded to pinion and handcuff Sir Allen.

" Ah ! Sir Allen," said Killigrew, " it's dangerous playing with edge tools, or in other words to try and make out our relations mad, even if we *do* want them out of our way, for it may, in God's justice, recoil upon ourselves."

But as Sampson attempted to pinion him, Sir Allen roared with such stentorian strength that

Gilbert, all pale and alarmed, hurriedly entered the room from the gallery.

"Gilbert, my son, my only son!" cried Sir Allen, "you will not, surely you will not, let these miscreants drag your father to a mad-house?"

This pathetic and paternal appeal was the first notice Sir Allen had taken of his son's existence since the re-appearance of the latter.

"Certainly not, sir," said Gilbert, in reply to it, and ordering Sampson not only to desist from his attempts to pinion him, but also to leave the room, an order which he instantly obeyed without any attempt at remonstrance, for there was in Gilbert Broderick's whole bearing, that real dignity and influence, the outward and visible signs of genuine worth and irreproachable integrity, which are never either disputed nor disregarded. Then, turning to Dr. Everhard with an air of unwonted severity, he requested him to accompany him into the next room, which was the white drawing-room, where, closing the door after him, he asked the doctor by whose authority he had acted in so unwarrantable a manner towards his father?

Doctor Everhard stated the simple truth of his having been sent for, or rather gone for by Colonel Titus, and retained in case his services should be required, and that when sent for a quarter of an hour ago by Mr. Killigrew, Sir Allen's language, conduct, and whole demeanour fully justified their opinion that he should be placed under restraint; and then, in order to still more thoroughly exonerate himself, he proceeded to narrate in detail, Sir Allen's having first called upon him more than a year before, to try and bribe him (Dr. Everhard) to give a certificate of the insanity of his sister, Mrs. Phillida Broderick, so as to invalidate her will, which he, Dr. Everhard, never having even seen the lady during her life time, had positively refused to do for any consideration whatever. He then further related the fact of his having rescued Sir Allen Broderick last July, when, being tipsy, he had fallen into the Thames; acknowledging the £500 Sir Allen had given him on that occasion, perhaps not altogether as a remuneration for the service he had rendered him, but chiefly, no doubt, to insure his silence; and then he further detailed the clever expedients Sir Allen had resorted to, to pass himself off for Sir Allen Apsley, whom he, Dr. Everhard, was perfectly convinced he was, till undeceived by Mr. Killigrew a few minutes ago.

Poor Gilbert groaned inwardly; a deadly chill ran through his very marrow; his heart sickened, as if his pure and noble aunt's grave had been impiously desecrated! It *was* terrible to have such a father! for light to be the son of darkness—it was to have been born heir to an hereditary curse! which by no act or thought of his own had he incurred. Altogether, he felt like one of those fabled Athenian kings, lashed from exile to exile by the furies, with no opening for escape, but his dark adamantine, inexorable destiny meeting him at every turn, and barring every egress! He passed his hand tightly over his eyes, as if to shut it, or to pluck it all out—vain endeavour! REALITY is the electric fluid of Fate, and *cannot* be shut out.

" I see, sir," said he, apologetically to Doctor Everhard, " you were not to blame. May I request, however, that you and your assistant will instantly quit the Palace? and if you will call upon me at eleven o'clock to-morrow morning—I am to be found at No. 70, in The Pell Mell—I shall be happy to remunerate you for any trouble or expense you may have been put to in coming here to-night."

So saying, he opened a door in an opposite direction to the one by which they had entered, and telling him what turn he should take so as to find his man in the corridor outside the green drawing-room, he also indicated to him after that another turning to the left, which would lead him to a back staircase, by which he could immediately, and by a much shorter way, leave the Palace.

Dr. Everhard bowed several times nearly to

the ground, and in profound silence, doing exactly as he had been desired, by leaving the room and taking the direction that had been pointed out to him.

Gilbert then went into the long ante room, where the pages and lackeys loitered in charge of the hats and cloaks, and taking his own and his father's hat from one of them, he returned to the green drawing-room, where Sir Allen was sitting in an arm-chair, his feet elongated before him, both hands thrust into his pockets, his shoulders up to his ears, his chin resting on his breast, and his bloodshot eyes, like a tiger at bay, darting unutterable imprecations at Killigrew, who was walking up and down the room, oiling Sir Allen's fire, as he termed it, with every sarcasm and every home thrust he could think of; while Silas Titus was leaning upon his right elbow against a girandole, an infinitely amused auditor and spectator.

"Ha! at last," said Sir Allen, starting to his feet as soon as Gilbert entered.

"I have brought you your hat, sir, if you will allow me to accompany you to your own door; we need not go through the ante-chamber, but can go down the back staircase, which will bring you to your house in two minutes."

"Ugh," growled Sir Allen, by way of assent, as he snatched his hat from his son and pounded it on his own head.

"Ah! Gilbert, my too fine fellow, you are wrong; when a man's habits are so *crooked* as Sir Allen Broderick's, a *strait* waistcoat would have been an improvement ; and the doctor would have tried a hair of the same dog upon him—that is, Dr. Erasmus Everhard's casual close shaving, against Sir Allen Broderick's chronic close shaving ; and depend upon it, it would have done him all the good in the world."

"For heaven's sake! be quiet, Killigrew ; you have pushed the jest quite too far," said Gilbert, as he left the room with his father, who did not so much lean upon him as clutch his arm till he really hurt it, much as a child does its nurse's hand or dress, under the influence of extreme terror.

"Jest!" echoed Killigrew, as the door closed, "nothing of the kind ; I never was more in earnest in my life. Well, they say pearls are produced by a disease in the oyster, and I believe it ; for see what a pearl of a son that dilapidated old oyster, *Père* Broderick has produced."

"How do I know," said Sir Allen, when he had got his foot on the first stone step of the narrow back stairs, stopping suddenly, "but that those infernal scoundrels may be after me?"

"There is not the least fear of that, sir ; I took care to send them away before I returned to you."

" But I hope you told them you'd prosecute
them, and *ruin them* for having dared to offer
such an outrage to a man of *my position !*'" and
here Sir Allen again stood still, and placing his
hand upon his left hip, flung back his head as
far as the wall intervening would permit, evidently wishing to awe his son, by conveying to
him a due sense of his own illimitable greatness!
so far as it would reach in the circumscribed precincts of the very narrow pointed staircase.

" Why, sir, you see these men were really not
to blame; they had been sent for by others, and
the quieter these sort of *mauvaises plaisanteries*
are kept the better, for then they go out, like a
spark, instantly; whereas, a prosecution would
fan the affair into a flame, and excite a
dreadful s candal."

Sir Allen, of course, felt the truth of this, but
relieved himself by throwing up his eyes and his
right hand, as he remonstrated with heaven, by
exclaiming—

" What a fate to have a son devoid of all
filial affection, and regardless of all family ties !"

Poor family ties ! when they require them to
serve their own particular turn, it is astonishing
what hard and gordian knots they are twisted into
by those persons, who, when the said family ties,
only relate to *their* debts to others, are in the
habit of relentlessly severing them with two-
edged razors !

Arrived at the great man's door, Gilbert asked his father if he should see him up to his room? To which that fond parent and affectionate stickler for the sacredness of " family ties," curtly, but specifically, replied—

" Go to the devil !"

We are sorry to have to record so flagrant an act of disobedience on the part of Gilbert—another lamentable instance of his disregard for family ties,—but instead of doing as his father had ordered him, he did the very reverse, and went back to Dorothy, who was only waiting for his return to take leave of their Majesties.

When Gilbert rejoined them, the King was still laughing at Killigrew's description, or rather en-actment, of Sir Allen's passage of arms, or rather of feet and of teeth, against the mad doctor—

" And I assure your Majesty," concluded he, " the doctor's man would have given Sir Allen quite rope enough to hang himself with, if that Phœnix of a son of his had not come to the rescue at such a very *mal-à-propos* moment. Ah ! talk of the devil—*le voici !*"

Mrs. Neville and Dorothy rose, took leave of the Queen, respectfully expressing their deep sense of her Majesty's great kindness.

When Dorothy approached the King, she attempted to kiss his hand, which he would not allow, but kissed hers instead. She then faltered out, with the tears in her eyes—

" If I do not thank you, sire, it is your own fault : your Majesty has laid such a life long debt of gratitude upon me, that it has made me a bankrupt in thanks."

" Fore George ! Mistress Dorothy," smiled the King, " if all debtors were only half as fair, there would be no such thing as dishonesty in the world."

" And," said Killigrew, aside, " what a saturnalia it would be for the accursed race of creditors !"

Could it be possible, that Dorothy, who had arrived at the palace a few hours before with such a heavy, heavy heart, was now returning from it with all she loved best in the world—her lover beside her, her mother opposite to her, and she so supremely happy, that she could hardly persuade herself of her own identity ; but Gilbert being perfectly sure of it, at last contrived to convince her too.

It was half-past eleven when they arrived at their own door, where they found Hartsfoot walking up and down like a sentry, for he was, in truth, so anxious to hear the result of the summons to Whitehall, that he could not wait till the morrow. Dorothy was the first to perceive him.

" Lean back, Gilbert," she cried, " while we get out, and let me have the pleasure of surprising dear Master Hartsfoot, for whom, I may as well tell you at once, I have had divers times and often—serious thoughts of jilting you."

CHAPTER XI.

EXPLANATIONS.

RS. NEVILLE, entering into Dorothy's plan of surprising Hartsfoot, said, as soon as Jessop had answered the door, and Lancelot had put down the carriage steps—

"Jessop, go and tell Appleby to let us have the best supper she can immediately. And, Lancelet, go and ask Ruffle to give you a velvet cardinal for me, for I am very chilly."

And having thus got rid of the servants, Dorothy was free to act; and leaning forward so as to completely hide her mother and Gilbert, she held out one hand to Hartsfoot, and with the other hid her face in her handkerchief.

"Well!" said Hartsfoot, his heart failing him at seeing that.

"Well!" echoed Dorothy, in a lachrymose voice, "I was not aware before that we lived under an absolute monarchy; but it seems that a King of England can do just as he pleases with his subjects, and move them about at will, like a set of chess men. He might well order

us to be dressed like victims, all in white, for the
sacrifice ; for his next autocratic command is,
that I am to be married this day month. Oh!
it is incredible ! positively incredible ! No one
would believe the things we have seen and heard
to-night."

And she sighed deeply.

" But—but," said Hartsfoot, in a sort of blank
and bewildered despair, not knowing exactly
what to say, and not liking to own even to himself his utter disappointment, for he had hoped
so much from this summons to Whitehall, and
the reading of Mrs. Phillida Broderick's Will,
" but are there then *no* tidings of Captain
Broderick ?"

" Why, yes, there are ; but I am really too
tired to say more now, and here is one who can
tell you a great deal more about him than I
can."

And so saying, she leant back, and Gilbert
came forward, holding out both his hands to
Hartsfoot, who could scarcely believe his eyes,
as the full flood of moon-light revealed the graceful figure and handsome face of Gilbert Broderick, so radiant with happiness.

" Good heaven !" exclaimed Hartsfoot, shaking him by both hands, cordially, " this *is* a delightful surprise !"

And Gilbert sprang out of the carriage.

"Well, dear Master Hartsfoot," said Dorothy, following him, while he held out his hand to help Mrs. Neville out, "I owed it to you, for the more than one, you have brought to me," and then clasping his arm by passing both her hands through it, she led him into the house, leaving Gilbert to escort her mother.

Jessop had by this time returned to the door ; his surprise and delight at seeing Gilbert were unbounded, and although there was no election going on, and Captain Broderick was not a candidate, and Jessop had no vote if he had been, Gilbert cordially shook hands with the old man. They then all went into the dining-room, where the table was ready laid for supper, and where there was a blazing pine fire, which seemed to do its very best and brightest to welcome them.

"I declare," said Dorothy, "by the way the fire crackles and sparkles, one would think the very wood knew all about it, and was glad."

"I often fancy," replied Hartsfoot, "that inanimate things *do* sympathise with us, and reflect our moods of joy or sorrow. At least, to poor anchorites who live alone, their *Lares* and *Penates* stand in lieu of kith and kin, and so are bound to do so."

Jessop, after placing chairs for them, hurried out of the room, not only on account of certain arrangements he had to make of his own, towards doing honour to Captain Broderick's return, but because he naturally thought they would have a great deal to say to each other, and to tell Master Hartsfoot. No sooner had he closed the door, than Dorothy, having seated the latter next her mother and herself beside Gilbert, than she said—

" I know Master Hartsfoot is dying to hear everything that has happened to us since we left this house at eight o'clock this evening. So I'll begin at the beginning, and we'll keep Gilbert's history as a *bonne bouche* till after supper; for I could not patiently brook any interruption to *that* when once commenced."

So, accordingly she narrated most graphically and minutely every incident, Hartsfoot's ears appearing to have stolen into his eyes, so intently did they seem to listen to, as well as look at her, while she spoke. She had just got as far as where Gilbert, hearing his father's vociferation, had gone to him to see what was the matter, when the door opened, and the servants appeared with the supper ; she rose and said, *sotto voce* to Hartsfoot—

" I'll tell you the rest of that scene to-morrow ; it will keep, and I daresay Gilbert would rather not hear it told."

Upton placed the first dish on the table—a dish of stewed red mullet; while Jessop and

Lancelot followed, dragging in between them an
enormous jar, or bottle, cased in wicker work,
that might originally have been white, but was
now as black as the bottle or jar it enclosed,
which had two handles, something like the Port-
land vase, and held about six gallons ; the mouth
of this huge bottle, or jar, was sealed at the top
with a large lead seal, to which was appended
two pieces of thick watered black ribbon, four
inches broad and a quarter of a yard long, which
were also sealed at the end on the basket
work.

" What on earth have you got there, Jessop ?"
asked Mrs. Neville, as he and Lancelot, not
without a considerable final strain upon their
strength, succeeded in standing it down before
the sideboard.

" Well, madam, it's one of the greatest curi-
osities you have in your house ; at least, you have
two of them, but one I always keep at the Chestnuts, and the other here.   They are sherries,
madam— *Vino Puro de Xeres*—out of the cellars
of King Phillip the Second of Spain, of the vin-
tage of 1460, with the royal arms of Spain, and
the king's private seal plombed on them in three
places.   There were six of them in all originally,
taken out of the Admiral's ship in the Spanish
Armada.   Queen Elizabeth got two of them, and
Sir Francis Drake the other four, three of which

he gave to Colonel Neville's great grandfather, and one of them was opened and drank in the old gentleman's time, when he used to go a hunting with King James. These two came to the late Colonel untouched, and so they have remained, for I wouldn't have opened or bottled them for the world ; but I thought they never could be broached on a better occasion than to drink Captain Broderick's health on his safe return. So I've brought this one up to-night, and I only hope the wine may be as good as it is curious, for it was more than eighty years old when taken out of the Armada."

" Oh ! open it by all means, Jessop," said his mistress. " And, as you say, Master Hartsfoot, that there is some latent good even in the worst things, I hope we may get this much good out of Phillip the Second."

They all rose to look at the curious old seals and ribbons before Jessop cut the latter.

" Take care, Jessop, not to injure the top seal, if you can help it, that we may each have one, for the ones attached to the ribbons are intact," said Mrs. Neville.

" The top one will slip off easily enough, like a leaden cap," said Jessop, " when I have loosened the edges round with a knife ; and bring me the wine-strainer and that large Venice glass decanter, Lancelot, which holds two bottles, for if the wine is good, that won't be too much, and I can seal it up again till another more joyous occasion;" and the old servitor bowed respectfully to his young mistress.

When the lead was removed, their labours were by no means ended; such a quantity of rosin, and what appeared like mortar, was there round the mouth of the bottle, for it was made of glass and not of stone.

At length this wall was chipped off, and the wooden plug—for such it was—duly extracted. The mouth of the bottle carefully wiped, Jessop twisting the napkin so as to get it well down round the inside; he then held the decanter under it, while Upton and Lancelot, on either side, bent the jar forward.

" Gently! gently!" said Jessop ; " remember he's a very old gentleman, and must not be hurried." And then as the amber fluid gradually filled the decanter, he exclaimed, with the irripressible ecstacy of a connoisseur, as the aroma of the wine was diffused, " Capital nose! never in all my life met such a one—perfectly delicious !"

" Rather high-coloured for sherry, is it not?" asked Mrs. Neville.

" Oh! that's the age, madam ; but wine, with such a nose as that, must be silky and sound to perfection ; however, the gentlemen will soon be able to tell—the glasses, Upton."

And he filled out four glasses, handing the first to his mistress and Dorothy, and the others to Hartsfoot and Gilbert.

"To the health of Captain Broderick," said Hartsfoot, holding up his glass.

"Nay!" rejoined Gilbert, "you would be pledging an ingrate, if I let you do so, before we have drank—

"To the King; God Bless Him!"

And, as may be supposed, Gilbert's amendment was echoed, and drunk with far more than mere loyalty, for it was drunk with what—alas! it had so rarely reason to be—with sincere gratitude and affection.

"And the wine, gentlemen?" anxiously interrogated Jessop.

"The wine," said Hartsfoot," is too good for mortals! I wonder Jupiter ever let it leave Olympus."

"It is like drinking liquid velvet," said Gilbert. "If rare old Ben had ever tasted it, he would never have written, 'Drink to me *only* with thine eyes, and I'll not ask for wine.'"

Yet, as he spoke, and looked into Dorothy's eyes, his looks belied his words.

"Give me a large glass of King Phillip's sherry," said Mrs. Neville, and as soon as it was brought, she added—"There, Jessop, you must drink that, for you will appreciate it; and you may give all the servants plenty of sack, to drink Captain Broderick's health; but none of that, as I quite agree with Master Hartsfoot, that it is too good for mortals."

"I humbly thank you, madam; for ordinary mortals it may be, but that would only make it just fit to drink your and Mistress Dorothy's, Master Hartsfoot's, and Captain Broderick's health," said Jessop, as he drained the glass, after which, clicking his tongue against the roof of his mouth, he was speechless with admiration for a few seconds, till his mistress asked him what he thought of the wine.

"Well, madam, all I can say is,—let Phillip the Second of Spain have been next best to the devil in badness, if he made it a practice to drink such wine as *that*, I'd rather have been his chief butler than King Pharaoh's."

They all laughed at Jessop's very technical appreciation of this marvellous sherry, and Hartsfoot said to him—

"Your judgment is so clear, Jessop, that it is very evident you never came in contact with any of the darkness that overspread the land of Egypt."

Despite the blazing fire, the night was intensely cold, and Gilbert, thinking Hartsfoot would be warmer on the side where he was, wanted him to change places with him, but he put up his hand and shook his head, as he said—

> " ' Take the goods the gods provide thee,
> Lovely Thea;'

far better than

> " ' Lovely Thais, sits beside thee.'

And on no account let us derange the economy of the table, for when people think of entering upon the onerous duties of housekeeping, they should study economy, for which reason, I'll take another glass of that sherry, Jessop, which I should think was worth about a Jacobus a drop."

"Ah! Master Hartsfoot," laughed Dorothy, " I'm so glad, for when you are a cup too low, I shall know now how to give you a *fillip !*"

Dish succeeded dish, as was the sensible fashion of the time, so as to have everything hot; and they eat their supper—at least, the two elders did, for, for all the appetite they had Dorothy and Gilbert might have eaten a dozen suppers. But at last, this interminable supper, as it seemed to those two, came to an end; the servants had withdrawn, and the little *partie carée* gathered round the fire.

" Now, Gilbert, for Heaven's sake," said Mrs. Neville, " do explain this horrible mystery of the last fourteen months, which has nearly broken the hearts of everyone that knew you."

" Terrible ! indeed," echoed Gilbert, "and yet not half so terrible as if I had gone to Tangiers ; for at *best*, that would have been for three long years, but in all probability I should have caught the fever that kills so many of our fellows out there, and never have returned at all, and so the King thought, and the whole affair was a good natured plot of his and Killigrew's ; though, till within the last month, it was all as great, if not quite as terrible a mystery, to me as to you. Ferrol told me this evening, when I was making *ma toilette de Potence*, that he had told Master Hartsfoot of those two rough looking men who followed and insulted me one morning on the Exchange. Well, all this was only leading up to the *coup d'état*, for they had even got that right good fellow, Jambres Fairbrace, into the plot, as my poor dear aunt's lawyer, which I did not know he was at the time, as he kept even that fact hermetically sealed from me, though I entrusted him with a packet to take into Suffolk to her, but, thank God, he eased *her* mind about my going to Tangiers, though binding her over not to tell me. Well, as Killigrew has since told me, in order to give me my liberty up to the last minute, the plot did not culminate till the night before the day I was to have sailed for Tangiers, when coming through the Mall, having Monk and Charlie with me, I was set upon by

the same two rough looking bravos who had insulted me on the Exchange, while a third man
took a muzzle out of his pocket and slipped it on
Monk before the dog could make any resistance,
after which, he caught up Charlie and hid him
under his cloak. Just as I was about to protest
against this capture of my dogs, up marched a
file of soldiers, headed by Colonel Titus, who
arrested me in the name of the King, and ordered
me to deliver up my sword. I felt so perfectly
guiltless of having said or done, or left undone
anything that could subject me to such treat-
ment, that I told Titus I thought there must be
some mistake? 'No mistake at all,' said he,
curtly; 'the King can do no wrong,' and walked
me off to the other end of the Mall, where a coach
with six post horses was in waiting, into which
I was ordered to get, while Monk and Charlie
were let to follow me. Well, *that* is kind at all
events, thought I. Next, in got Colonel Titus,
and seated himself upon the opposite side, with
his drawn sword, and as soon as the coach door
was closed, he put his head out of the window
and gave the order ' FORWARD !' not saying
where. I fully expected we should go Tower-
ward, and began consoling myself by thinking of
the divers equitable incarcerations, sham trials,
but *real* executions, of many equally innocent,
but far greater personages than myself. But my

chief agony was thinking what you would think and feel, when you came to hear of my arrest, and I then began to fear that poor Ferrol, with his usual zeal to be ready for me, might perhaps sleep on board 'The Surprise,' and sail without me! In short, there was no torture in the way of conjecture, and a broad side of if's and but's, that I did not inflict upon myself, for we are such apes, that whenever fate does her worst towards us, we must always follow suit, and do our worst to ourselves by giving her credit for more evil designs than she contemplates. However, I soon found that I had been mistaken upon one point, for we were soon off the stones, and upon a high road; consequently, it was evident we were *not* going to the Tower. At length we arrived at a large country house, which I afterwards learnt was Theobald's ; I was shown into a fine suite of rooms, comfortably, or rather luxuriously, furnished. I begged hard for pen, ink, and paper to write, in the first instance to you, Dorothy, and to poor Ferrol, whom I knew would be in a fever at my unaccountable absence. I felt also that my father ought to be informed of the reason of my not sailing for Tangiers. But Colonel Titus's answer to his request was—

" No, you are strictly interdicted from communicating with *any* one."

" Well, if I may not do that, or even know

what my offence is, may I at least be made acquainted with the duration of my imprisonment?"
I pleaded.

" ' During his Majesty's pleasure,' was the
vague and unsatisfactory reply.

" ' But for how long will that be ?' I re-urged.

" ' Who can tell ?' said Titus, taking up a lute,
and thrumming on it, for he cannot play, ' when
a man, and more especially a king, lives for pleasure, when it will end."

" The next morning, and each succeeding day, I
was allowed with my dogs to take exercise in the
grounds, but under surveillance, and to keep up
the farce of imprisoment, the windows of the suite
of rooms I occupied had iron bars and spikes
before them, and two sentries were stationed, day
and night, outside each of the chamber doors.
At first, as you may suppose, I chafed horribly
against this, as it appeared to me iniquitously
unjust incarceration, or rather, the being prevented from communicating with any of my
friends.   But I ended by doing what it would be
wiser always to begin by doing—only, when
suddenly called upon, human nature is not equal
to the effort—I mean to submit wholly and passively to God's will.   Months rolled on in this
monotonous, and incomprehensible existence,
for though I knew where I was, I knew no more
why, or for what I was there, than you did.   At

length Killigrew came to see me; he was very
kind, but ultra mysterious as to enlightening me
touching the why and wherefore of my imprisonment. I should know it all in time was his only
answer. ' Yes,' I said, 'we shall know everything
in time, or at least, in eternity !' At length, as
a great concession, he promised that Mrs. Swinburne, under the vague form of an anonymous
letter, should be informed of my existence and
safety, and my ultimate return to her house. But
any communication to you, dear, or to my father,
he would not hear of. Some months after this,
Mr. Jambres Fairbrace paid me a visit; he was
also very kind, but equally mysterious and im-
penetrable. He brought me the dreadful news
of my dear Aunt Phillida's death, and seeing me
so terribly afflicted, I suppose excited his compassion, for he said, although he could not and
dare not be the bearer of any letter, he would so
far infringe his orders, that he would return and
see me in a week, and that if I would promise
faithfully not to give my address, and not to
write you a letter, but merely a few stanzas, and
seal the packet with my own ring, which would
be sufficient to convince you of my safety, he
would undertake to get the packet conveyed to
you."

"Ah !" interrupted Dorothy, "and I was very
nearly tearing your verses without reading them,

sir, so angry was I at being put off with such a
meagre and miserable piece of flimsy fatuity, as
I deemed it, after months that seemed ages of
silence and suspense, and all their long train of
tortures."

" Instead of feeling, as you ought to have done
by intuition," said Gilbert, " that we were both
drowning, and that I pushed you over the only
straw within my reach."

" All very fine," said Dorothy, " but you can
swim, and I can't. Now, go on."

" I have little more to add, except that Killigrew broke into my room early this morning
before I was up, and said, with that imperturb-
able face of his, which can play not only many
parts, but any part—

" ' Well, my dear fellow, it's all over, and you
are to be hanged this evening.'

" ' What !' said I, ' without judge or jury ?'
rather objecting, as people are apt to do, to that
exalted ceremony.

" ' No,' he said, ' you will have a *fair* trial, and
I'll be hanged if I would not gladly change places
with you.'

" He then told me of the clause in my Aunt
Phillida's will, about not separating the hangings of the red worsted bed, and for the better
carrying out of this legal quibble, I was to form
part of those hangings ! which was the *dénoue-*

ment of the King's kind plot of imprisoning me, in order to prevent my being sent to Tangiers. You know all the rest, for I need not tell you how eager and willing I was to be held still further in *suspense,* according to his Majesty's and Killigrew's charming *embroglio.*"

"Bravo! Killigrew," exclaimed Hartsfoot; "the very best plot you ever constructed, and far better than any of Dryden's or Wycherley's."

"There is one thing that I don't understand," said Dorothy; "the King said something about your hat, and sword, and glove being left on the Mall as a *ruse.* What did that mean? for I never heard anything about them."

"No," said Mrs. Neville, "for we took good care you should not hear about them; for every-one else heard of Gilbert's hat, broken sword, and glove being found on the Mall, and concluded from them—as the King intended they should—that poor Gilbert had been killed in a duel. And after your dream that you told me about his hat, sword, and glove being found on the Mall, would you not have been doubly sure of this?"

"Strange!" murmured Dorothy, as she buried her face on Gilbert's shoulder and kissed his sleeve.

"I shall *now,*" said Hartsfoot, "be only too happy to show you that heartrending relic of poor Captain Broderick!—his broken sword, which poor Ferrol parted with to me as such a favour."

" Yes, I insist upon having it," said Dorothy, " and I'll have ' Nil Desperandum' engraved upon it. But you have now four more healths to drink —the King's again, and ever! the Queen's, Mr. Killigrew's, and Mr. Jambres Fairbrace."

" With all our hearts !"

" And now, gentlemen," said Dorothy, standing up with a glass in her hand, into which she had poured some claret, placing her left hand on her hip, and speaking with a lisping affected voice, like the " Court Gallants," as they were called, " I am about to propose an especial toast of my own, which must be drank with all the honours, for it deserves every honour. I give you the health of the best man in the world, and one whom I love and respect with all my heart," and then turning suddenly round upon Gilbert, she said, " Hey day ! most noble Captain, why those blushes and that confusion ? Keep your modesty in check, pray, till your vanity is attacked; it is not *your* health I am about to propose ; I should never dream of being guilty of such a piece of fatuity, as to propose *my own* health. But, as I have told you, that it was the health of the best man in the world that I asked you to drink ; perhaps it is superflous to name— MASTER OLIVER HARTSFOOT !"

Gilbert applauded loudly. Mrs. Neville said nothing, but drank the health in silence—as "the glorious and immortal memory" is drunk in modern times; while the tears came into Hartsfoot's eyes, and he blushed like a girl, Dorothy adding to his confusion by exclaiming—

"Nay, Master Hartsfoot, heaven knows *you* have no reason to be ashamed of yourself, therefore never waste such pretty blushes, but lend them to me for my wedding paraphernalia."

As she was still speaking, the heavy Louis Quatorze *pendule* struck two.

"Already!" said Hartsfoot, rising.

"I hope, Gilbert," said Mrs. Neville, while shaking hands with him, "you will dine, and at all events sup, with us every day, till the *fatal* fourteenth of March arrives."

"I should not think he wanted much pressing," said Hartsfoot.

"I hope you will not, either, Master Hartsfoot," put in Dorothy, "for we shall not feel complete without you."

He stammered out something about their having had rather too much of his company lately, which no one appeared to hear, or to heed if they did hear. At last, all the "good-nights and God bless yous" were spoken, and the two guests departed, though I never heard it clearly explained how it was, that while Mrs. Neville re-

mained in the dining-room, and Master Hartsfoot was at least twenty yards on his way to his
own   house,   Mistress   Dorothy   and   Captain
Broderick lingered for several minutes in the hall
by themselves.

CHAPTER XI.

AS anyone yet ever thoroughly satisfied? thoroughly content? let echo, or any other *propos en l'air* answer, if they can, for the solution of so wide a question is quite beyond any latent spark of sphinx or œdipus that may lurk in my composition. All I can definitely vouch for, is that Dorothy Neville was not; the very next day, after she had so unexpectedly and so triumphantly had Gilbert Broderick restored to her, by an exceptionably indulgent Fate, that unconscionable and *exigeante* young damsel wanted something more! But we shall come to that presently. I know I am not satisfied, for I have just closed the fourth volume of " L'Homme qui Rit," only to find that I have lived to be disappointed, even in Victor Hugo! not in the man himself, for he has lived a good and noble life, making all belonging to him happy; first practising in fact, and in living realities, all the fine feelings and great thoughts, which enrich the

glorious regalia of his fictions ; and his Midas-
like genius having converted all he touched to
gold—in his turn he has transmuted that gold
into a still more precious wealth—the power of
helping and relieving his fellow creatures. But it
is only (unlike most authors) to read his works
to know the man ; in reading them, you read
him ; all is true, real, great, and priceless, and
yet I don't know why I should say, that unlike
other authors, his books are Him, for the true
reflex of most writer's mind *is* to be seen in their
writings.   The false glitter of the sham and the
meretricious, it is true, attracts and imposes upon
the shallow ignorance of the mass ; but real
feeling and true taste in the reader, will always
act as experts to detect the Bristol stones and
paste of sham sentimentality and assumption in
an author, from the diamonds of genuine feeling
and the brilliants of real genius.   If there is
nothing bright or beautiful, or good, or true in
men's lives, we may be very certain that the fine
sentiments scattered through their writings,
however ornate and finished in the style of their
mounting, and however puffed " by the trade,"
are nothing more than glass set in brass.

   But Victor Hugo, being a brilliant of the
first water and of the greatest magnitude,
one's despair over " *L'Homme Qui Rit,*" is
all the greater.   Was there ever such a pro-

digal waste of genius to achieve such a *tour de
force* of absurdity ? Of course, however well-
informed, and even profound a Frenchman may
be on any other subject, the moment he touches
upon England, we are prepared for startling
revelations of things and *facts*, that we never
heard of, or even suspected the existence of
before ; and so far as history goes, this does not
much matter, as at best we know, that what is
received as " history"—*par excellence* is the very
falsest of all fiction. Still, one is astounded
that Victor Hugo should have fallen into such
an extraordinary misconception, touching the
political bias of the non-jurors ! Poor Queen
Anne, too ! it was too bad to " complicate" her
with Bolingbroke, as it never was even hinted
that she had any complications, except Sarah,
Duchess of Marlborough, Mrs. Masham, Doctor
Sacheverell, cherry brandy and the gout; the first
three being quite sufficient to inflame her blood
to gout point, without the cherry brandy. Then,
considering those were the days of stiff-ribbed
whale-bone hoops, rigid brocades, and voluminous Indian screens, the description of " Cor-
leane-lodge" is simply exquisitely ridiculous.
As for that, let us hope impossible monster the
Duchess Josiane, she would have been an ex-
aggerated calumny, had the scene been laid at
the *Parc aux cerfs*, or at one of the *petites maisons*

of *Louis Quinze.* As for the trinue compliment to English pronunciation, in *Maître* " Nikless," " Fibi," and " Vinos," we should take off our hats for that, as we are not sufficiently intimate with them to recognise them more familiarly.

" Lord David Dirry-Moir !"—I thank thee, Hugo, for teaching me that name—is really the outline of a fine character; but take Jupiter, Agamemnon, Cæsar, and Alexander, roll them into one, and cover by way of *physique*, with such a *synonyme* as " Lord David Dirry-Moir, and Tom ! Jim ! Jack !" and what would or could remain either of the god or of the demi-god. Barkilphedro is another scion of a chimera and a night-mare, which forms a suitable *pendant* to the Duchess Josiane. But for the crowning absurdity, Gwinplain's speech in the House of Lords—to say nothing of *the children's bench* in that " august assembly "—" must give us pause." The description of the ugliness of the peers is truly graphic, or, rather, photographic, and would be more so, had M. Victor Hugo been describing the Upper House in the present day, when that " august assembly " is recruited from all that is most hideous in the moral and the physical. Yet why are the terrible but indisputable truths propounded by Gwinplaine in the House of Lords, so overwhelmingly ludicrous? Simply because they are spoken by the wrong person in the wrong place. And the thing would have been, if possible (?) even more ridiculous had he taken the most sublime sermon that ever was written, and delivered it with all the spirit-stirring eloquence and sacred fire of a Bossnet in *that* place, and addressed his auditors as "my brethren," instead of the time-honoured fiction of "my noble friend," however ig-noble the personage addressed may be. This was a terrible artistic blunder on the part of Victor Hugo, for though "*le vrai n'est pas toujours vraisemblable,*" it should always be made to appear so in fiction. The author's conception and intention is clear as crystal; he means poor Gwinplaine as the type and incarnation of the oppressed, and all these hideous, cruel, irresponsible, pampered profligates, as the type of the oppressors. Nothing can be plainer, and unfortunately nothing can be truer; but the fitness of things violated, gives the devil a triumph which he never could have achieved by his own dexterity. A queen might sit by the bed-side of a sick beggar to nurse and attend the poor soul, and would only be the greater for so doing ; but were she to put on her coronation robes and all the crown jewels for the purpose, an otherwise great and good action would then become not only ridiculous, but revolting. Had M. Hugo made either an Epic or an Idyll of his book he would have achieved a great

work, but making it a quasi historical (!) novel,
crammed with the most excruciating absurdities,
such as great ladies going *en grande tenue* to
penny shows in Southwark, and dressed in men's
clothes to boxing matches! though Monsieur
Victor Hugo is kind enough to give us another
little historical sugar-plum, by telling us that
it was the general custom for ladies in Anne's
time *always to travel* in male attire, all this
makes one exclaim—

> *Hélas l'est clair, que l'homme qui rit,*
> *À coup sûr, serait l'homme qui lit!*

From beginning to end the book is an uncomfortable book, and grossly improbable—I don't
say impossible, for nothing is that. About the
most loveable and satisfactory person in it being
poor Homo. Yet, of course, like all Victor Hugo's
books, it abounds in apopthegms that deserve to
be written in letters of gold; such, for instance,
as—

" *Que la misère se cache, et ce taise, sinon, elle
est lèse majesté. Et ces hommes qui avaient traîné,
Gwynplaine sur la claie du sarcasme, étaient-ils
méchants? Non, mais ils avaient, eux aussi, leur
fatalité; ils étaient heureux, ils étaient bourreaux
sans le savoir.*"

Oh! why does not Victor Hugo, like Molière,
keep an old woman—only an English one—to

whom he could read his works, when he lays his
scenes in England, and who could set him right
in these little matters ? He could not well ex-
aggerate the vice or the vulgarity of what is
called " Society " in England, nor the extent of
political profligacy, nor the jobbery, cliqueism,
and unprincipled close borough *camaraderie* of
our literature ; only the mistake he has made is,
he has not gone the right way to work to expose
all this. Yet who knows ? Perhaps he is prouder
of all these mistakes, and more especially of his
Lord *William* Cowper, the Lord Chancellor, Lord
Lineous Clancharlie, and of Richardson, the
novelist, " having profited by the extinction of
the title of Lord Lovelace to introduce him (!)
into Clarissa Harlove, and make a type of him !"
Who knows ? It is recorded of Mazurier, when
having to play the part of a monkey, in order to
be perfect in his *rôle,* he used, day after day, to
don his monkey skin, and repairing to the *Jardins
des Plantes,* stand outside the monkeys' cage.
For a long time, to his great despair, they took
no notice of him, till one day an old monkey,
eyeing him, snatched an apple out of his hand,
whereupon he exclaimed in an ecstacy—

" *Enfin ! je suis singe.*"

So, who knows ? Perhaps even Victor Hugo,
regardless of all the real *chef d'œuvres* which he

has achieved, may, upon writing for the last time the unsurpassable name of

Tom—Jim—Jack !

have flung down his pen and exclaimed, in a paroxysm of pre-Adamite pride, for before Adam there *may* have been such " Britishers " as he describes, but never *since*—

" *Enfin ! je suis Anglais !*"

CHAPTER XII.

IKE all the good old race of servants to which he belonged, Jessop had implicitly obeyed his mistress's orders about letting the servants have plenty of sack to drink Captain Broderick's health; and to do them justice, they would have done so *con amore*, had they had nothing but water to drink it in; how much more joyfully then did they do so in sack. Lancelot, upon that occasion, was the hero of the servants' hall, for he was fresh from Whitehall, and had heard, *viâ* the royal *valetaille*, the whole history of Gilbert's imprisonment at Theobalds, and his re-appearance in the red worsted bed scene, down to that of Sir Allen's narrow escape of sharing the hospitality of Dr. Everhard, which was the episode that the said *valetaille*, from Podgers downward, enjoyed the most. For long before electric telegraphs

were invented, or even dreamt of, except perhaps
by Lord Worcester, people's affairs travelled quite
as rapidly through their servants as they do now
by the electric wires.

" I tell you," said Lancelot, laying down his
hard worked glass, after having drank " the
Cappen's health, and the Cappen's safe return"
for the sixth time—" I tell you as the finding of
Moses among the bulrushes warnt to compare to
the finding of the Cappen among the hangings of
the red worsted bed ; it war tremenjus ! just tremenjus ! that's what it war."

" Well," said Mrs. Ruffle, crossing her hands
upon her wrists, in her usual dignified and dicta-
torial manner, not a little scandalised at what
she considered Lancelot's profane allusion to
Moses—" Well, I may be wrong, and perhaps
it's very wrong of me to say so, but I should think
that most women would prefer having their husbands hanged *after* they'd been married some
time to before."

"I don't doubt but they might, Mrs. Ruffle,"
laughed Jessop.

" Lor, Mrs. Ruffle !" said Lancelot, " considering as you haven't never been troubled with a
husband, what should you know about 'em ?"

" I know this about them—you parti-coloured
Popingay," retorted Ruffle, her eyes flaming—
" that hanging is too good for one half of them !"

" Well," said Lancelot, again filling his glass,
"here's to you, Mrs. Ruffle, wishing you the
hanged half, and I've no doubt you'll find 'em a
deal tenderer nor hung beef."

" The worst of it is," said Ruffle, not condescending to notice either Lancelot or his speech,
at which all the other servants were tittering—
more especially the maids—but fanning herself
with her handkerchief, and turning to Jessop—
" The worst of it is that marriage, like every
other misfortune, when once it gets into a family,
there's no knowing where it may end."

" Not with you, that's sartin sure," said
Lancelot, upon whom the sack was now beginning
to take effect.

" I don't think," said Mrs. Ruffle, rising to
leave the table, which was fortunate, as at that
moment her mistresses dressing-room bell rang
—" I don't think a prudent woman ought to
sit and witness such scenes of riot and drunken-
ness ; but I pity you, you poor contemptible
mortal," added she, as she flung out of the hall,
hurling a look of ferocity, sufficient to excite
anybody else's pity, at Lancelot, who certainly
had began to look more like a Silenas than a
Servitor.   However, it might have been pity—
Mrs. Ruffle's way of showing pity—for it is
astonishing, one way or another, how much pity
is wasted in this world of cross purposes, which

is no doubt the reason why there is so seldom any pity left for those persons and situations that most need and best deserve it; while those who do neither the one nor the other, are sure to have it lavished upon them, like the old lady, who hearing Tacitus spoken of as 'such a nervous writer,' exclaimed, ' Ah ! poor dear gentleman, how I pity him !' ''

But to return to another poor dear gentleman, whom there is no longer any necessity for pitying. It is perhaps needless to say that he passed the greater part of every day at the house on the Mall ; not that we are going to be such bores as to obtrude ourselves upon his and Dorothy's *têtes-à-têtes,* for what is there more utterly uninteresting, not to say ridiculous, than those tautological *niaiserie,* and nothings of lovers, who have at length got into smooth waters, which nothings are yet all the world to *them.* Gilbert had to hear over and over again, and yet was never tired of hearing it—the daily disgrace poor Peveril had indured for bringing no tidings of him. Then she heard " many a time and oft," of all his paroxysms of despair, and his ineffectual attempts to bribe the people about him, at Theobald's, to post a letter.

Then their mutual dreams had to be narrated, and their catalogue of hopes and fears, and their fourteen months' diary of sighs and tears to be

collated.   At length they became a little rational,
and spoke of their affairs and discussed matters
of business, the most important of which was
that, like geniuses as they were, they stepped out
two centuries in advance of their times, and resolved to go down to Clumber Chase on their
wedding-day, and immediately after the execution, or, as it is more commonly called, the ceremony, which was by no means a customary thing
to do in those days, as the *grande mode* was for
people to dance themselves lame at their own
weddings, and submit to divers hymeneal saturnalia after.   But if Mr. Pepys even found that
"pulling Mrs. Bride's ribbons," with other rites
then in vogue, quite too coarse, it may be supposed that both Dorothy and Gilbert had a still
greater aversion to them.   The King had offered
the Archbishop of Canterbury to tie the knot, but
Dorothy felt as if no blessing could rest on a
marriage the celebration of which was performed
by so unholy and profligate a man, and therefore
begged to have Dr. Fairbrace in his stead, to
which the King, only anxious to please her,
readily acceded.   But Dorothy's wishes and as-
pirations did not end there.   She had other designs in her head, which she duly communicated
to Gilbert, and into which he cordially entered
and highly approved ; but, indeed, that was no
great compliment to her judgment, as I fear, had

it been the silliest and most chimerical thing in
the world, that *she* had propounded, *he*, in the
particular phase of lover-like *lèse* common sense
that he was then, would equally have approved
it.   One morning, about four days after Gilbert's
happy and unexpected return, he had an important piece of business to transact, which would
keep him all day away from the Mall till the
evening ; it was nothing less than seeing the red
worsted bed packed and safely sent back to
Clumber Chase, a much more onerous undertak-
ing in those non-Pickford, non-Pantechnicon, and
non-railway days, than it would be now, and it is
needless to say that both he and Dorothy, valued
" my Aunt Phillida's red worsted bed" far more
than any heir-loom they had, and more, even,
than the broad lands she had left them.   So having on this particular morning taken leave of
each other as if they were not to meet for years,
Dorothy having watched him out of sight, and
with great rationality wished that seven in the
evening were come, went and knocked at the
door of her mother's morning room.

" Come in."

Mrs. Neville was sitting before an *escretoire*
strewed with papers, making up her accounts,
an occupation which—punning apart—makes
everyone look bil-ious, and which perhaps was
the reason of her looking so *triste.*

" Where is Gilbert?" was her first question, as she turned round, for she wondered at seeing Dorothy *now*. That chill, blank time, which comes to all mothers when they know that they must step back into the shade, and make way for another, had come to her.

" He's gone to see that dear red worsted bed safely packed and sent back to Clumber Chase, and he won't be here till the evening; but, mother dear," added she, putting her arm round her neck and kissing her, " leave those nasty bills and things, they always be-devil one, and come and talk to me, for I *know* you are beginning to fret and fume, and to fancy that you'll be cold, and will get cold when I'm taken off your shoulders, but you've *not* got rid of me, for all that; for you know you *promised* to come with us into Suffolk, and to let us come backwards and forwards to you, so as we shall *always* be together, only one more instead of one less."

" Yes, dear," sighed Mrs. Neville, as the tears which were in her eyes now flowed over down her cheeks. " Still it *is* a break up; that ' change ' which is so attractive, and always so full of hope to the young, is ever dreaded and full of fear to the old. We are cat-like too, in our love of place, and love the very chairs, and tables, and walls we are used to."

" At that rate," said Dorothy, " I am as old as

you, for if I thought I should never see my dear
old household gods here and at the Chestnuts,
I am certain I should break my heart, despite all
Gilbert could do to keep it in repair.   Then just
consider, if instead of our having come in for the
reversion of a fairy tale, we had *all* had, *really* to
go out to Tangiers, and Gilbert had had nothing
but his pay, and you had had to leave, as you
would have done, all your comforts to keep life
and soul in the poor young fools, ah! then,
mother mine, you would have had cause for tears
and heart quakes; but now, oh verily, it is ungrateful to the good God that has so blest us."

" You are right, darling, and I *am* an ingrate
to murmur at anything, when I have so much to
be thankful for."

" I know how you would have much more to
be thankful for, only people never do see, or
know what is for their real good."

" My dear child, what *do* you mean ?"

" I mean what I say."

" Well, so far as that has gone, it leaves me no
wiser than I was."

" It's not a case of mere wisdom ; it's a matter
of common justice and good feeling."

" I cannot say that I see the incompatability
of wisdom with justice and good feeling, for I
think justice and good feeling the very highest
wisdom."

" I'm glad to hear you say so."

" You really puzzle me ; I cannot see the drift of all this ?"

" I'm afraid it's a snow drift, and one that will never melt."

" My dear Thea, do speak intelligibly, for I positively don't understand you."

" Then, in plain English, mother, I wish you would marry Master Hartsfoot; I think it's the least you could do, and that you ought to do it."

Mrs. Neville did not laugh ; but she opened her eyes very wide at her daughter, as she said slowly—

" My dear, I cannot marry a man who does not ask me."

" Oh! it depends upon that, does it ?"

" I suppose it generally does depend upon that."

" Not always, *vide* Sir Angus Tullibardin. Humph! why cannot offers of marriage, once made, be like leases, renewable? You know he *did* ask you once."

" Sir Angus seemed quite of your opinion, that proposals of this nature *were* renewable, or he would not have renewed his so often," smiled Mrs. Neville.

" Yes, the demmed vairlet!" said Dorothy, imitating him, till she actually looked like him, and her mother was obliged to laugh, in spite of herself. " As he was so anxious to be at my wedding, I think it would be only a pretty attention to ask him to it; so I'll go and consider about it," added she, leaving the room, and going to her own, where, without ringing for Phœbe, she managed to get out her whisk and gloves, and to equip herself for a walk—not, I suppose, despite all the strange liberty that unmarried women have always had in England, with the intention of calling upon Sir Angus Tullibardin.

CHAPTER XIII.

"*Miserum istuc verbum et pessimum est,
Habuisse et nihil habere.*"

PLAUTUS.

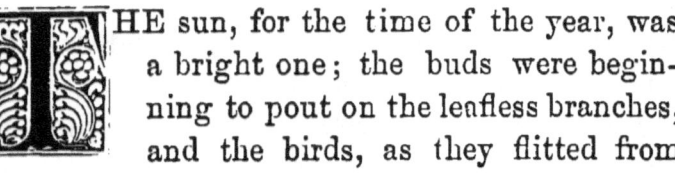THE sun, for the time of the year, was a bright one; the buds were beginning to pout on the leafless branches, and the birds, as they flitted from tree to tree, chirruped so loudly, and seemed as busy as if they were trying to get all their building done before summer came, that then they might have nothing to do but enjoy themselves. So that all above was bright enough, but the earth was still strewed with withered leaves, as the winter wind had blown them there. True types, both of them ; who wants brightness must always look above, for Earth ever has, is, and ever will be, cumbered with tokens of neglect, death, and decay.

Master Hartsfoot was sitting at the glass door window of his dining-room that looked out upon the Mall. Although he had a book in his hand, he was not reading; no, he was watching the withered leaves, some blown hither, some thither, and others whirled up into the air, where, after a few rapid gyrations, as if struggling desperately against the aërial aggression, fell flat on the ground, and were trampled on by the next passer. Hartsfoot watched these contests as if they had been human ones, and then occasionally he'd turn from the window, and give a long, purposeless look round the room; it was astonishing what a strangeness of desolation had fallen upon his home of late. All seemed so cold, so still, so lifeless—such a mere husk, without an animating spirit. Was he sorry that Dorothy's happiness had returned so fully and unexpectedly, and that consequently *his* part in the drama of her life was over? Oh! no; he rejoiced with all his heart, with all his soul. He knew he would always be welcome at *her* house; but still, she no longer wanted him. He could be now of no use to her; he could no longer mingle in the current of her and her mother's life. Once more he must shun the house on the Mall, for he could have no possible pretext for going near it, much less of haunting it.

Yet it was hard; he had been uprooted, as it were, from a sort of isolated rock, where he had, at least, calmly vegetated, to be transplanted amongst the most lovely and luxuriant exotics, which had caressingly twined around his rugged solitary life, and now that he had grown to feel the necessity of their warmth and their perfume, he must go back to his rock and again take root, or perish, as fate might decide. And tears came into his eyes, if they did not come out of them.

Then he wandered back far away into the not shadowy, but adamantine past; and he lingered separately over all the torture epochs—the day Margaret had refused him—the day he heard of her marriage with Algernon Neville. Well, he had lived through that! and why should he not again continue to "linger piecemale on the rock?" Then came the *remembered* gradual diminishing of that great agony! and he recollected the sort of soothing sensation of coolness to his fevered, tortured heart, when he heard that the marriage was not a happy one. Was he revengeful?—did he really wish the woman he had so madly loved to be miserable? No; still, his misery would have been too great if any other man had made her completely happy. Then, he lowered the curtain over that part of his life, and stagnated till the day—long years after—when she was a widow, and he heard that she had come to live on the Mall, whereupon he had tried hard to get rid of the lease of his house, but not being able to do so, had made up his mind to stay and bear it, as he *should never see her!*—never see her! And the day she had taken him by storm,

and of her own accord walked into *his* house !
Poor Master Hartsfoot grew sick and faint ; he
passed his hand over his eyes, relieved his heart
with a deep sigh, or rather groan, and then
shaking himself, as if that could shake off everything—memory included—he began to read, or
pretended to do so, lest any of the servants should
come into the room.

He had for about five minutes performed a
sort of literary goose step ; that is, he had read
the same line twenty times over without getting
any further, when presently a great shadow fell
upon his book as if to greet the one that had
fallen upon his heart. He looked up, and there
stood Dorothy, her face against the door, tapping
for admission.

" Ha ! robins I have admitted before now, but
birds of paradise never," said he, opening the
door, and trying to rally his spirits to receive
her, though indeed seeing her, and that so unexpectedly, and for the first time paying him a
visit, effectually did that.

" As usual, dear Master Hartsfoot," said she,
entering ; " I have come to ask you a favour—a
great favour."

" Nay, not as usual, for this is the very first
time you have honoured me with a visit; but
' ask, and you shall have.' "

" Remember *that*," laughed Dorothy, pushing
over the pen, and ink, and blotting book, that

was on the table between them. " Have you any objection to put it down in black and white, that I shall have what I ask for ? For I have a great fancy for springing you in your own snare, as my mother did Sir Allen Broderick, for by the high flights of the birds of paradise with which you received me, I fear that, like all your hollow, deceitful sex, your intention is to put me off with compliments and *façons de parler*, whereas, like those very practical wiseacres, the robins, I have come for the substantial crumbs of reality, and all the compliments in the world, either to my plumage or my *rammage*, will not do me instead."

" I don't at all plead to the indictment; indeed, as to the general charge of hollowness and deceit, as idiosyncracies of our superior sex, I don't attempt to deny it. I merely wish to state that they have been so thoroughly monopolised by the said superior sex, from the creation downward, that I don't think there was any of either left for me by the time I came into the world."

" Well, I must say, from my own experience of you, I believe it; so, despite your flummery, I *think* I may trust to your sincerity—that is, to the sincerity of your friendship and regard for me, and put you to the test."

" I should hope so; at all events you can but try."

" Well, then, dear Master Hartsfoot, I have

set my heart upon your acting as—as—my father, and giving me away on the fourteenth of next month; will you ?"

" But I thought the King was to do that ?"

" No ; the King in the kindest manner, as he has done everything throughout, left that to my choice, and who could I, or should I, choose but you, you dear, ever kind, unselfish friend ? Who have been *so* more than kind and *prevenant* to me during the whole time of my misery and despair, when often I really think I must have died of utter hopelessness, but for you. It seems so natural to me that you, and only you, should befriend me on this supreme occasion, that I frankly tell you it will break my heart if you refuse me."

And she fairly burst into tears.

" Refuse you ; why should I ? In asking me, you flatter not my vanity, but my sincere friendship for you too much not to leave me your grateful debtor."

" Thanks, ten thousand thanks, Master Hartsfoot," said Dorothy, stretching out her hand to him across the table.

And then, as soon as he had pressed it and relinquished it, casting down her eyes while her cheeks became crimson, and a poor innocent bunch of violets that she held in her hand, was flower by flower cruelly decapitated and strewed about the table, she stammered out—

" But—but—I should not like—that is, it—it would not be at all what I mean—that is, what I wish—and—and—indeed—what ought to be; unless you—you—were to act *as* my father, and give me away legally."

" Surely I could not do otherwise; it is quite legal, or rather it has nothing whatever to do with the law. Anyone has a perfect right to give a bride away, whom the bride or the bride's parents may select to do so."

" Oh! yes, the bride's *parents*; there it is, and unless you were really my parent I should not like it—that is, unless—unless—you were my—my—father-in-law—in—in fact—my mother's husband."

There ! *le grand mot était lâché;* there was not another violet left to immolate, so the fingers of her *peau d'Espagne* gloves had to suffer in their stead, and have each finger stretched on the rack. She was pale enough now; had she committed some terrible crime she could not well be paler, as she seemed to stand, as it were, on the extreme edge of a great gulf, awaiting " The hazard of the die." Not so Master Hartsfoot, all the blushes had flown to his face; he rose from his chair, paced the room, with his right hand plunged into his bosom as if to act as a sort of slave-owner to keep down his heart. At length he stammered out—

" But—but—Mistress Dorothy, I should not even then—be your father-in-law, I—I should only be your step-father."

" Even so, that is the legal step I want you to take ; for loving you as I do, Master Hartsfoot, I feel that I ought to have a legitimate right to do so—that is, that you *ought* to belong to me."

" Oh! Dorothy! Dorothy! why so tempt and torture me?—others—that is—the—the chief person to be consulted, might not think so ?"

" You remember what you said to me just now, when I spoke of putting your friendship for me to the test ?"

" No, I remember nothing," said he, passing his hand over his forehead.

" I'll repeat the words as my strenuous advice," and looking up at him, the tears still trembling in her eyes, though a very wicked smile played round her mouth, and stumbled into the pit-falls of innumerable dimples, as she said very slowly, and in a solemly impressive tone, like that of warning—

" YOU CAN BUT TRY."

" Oh! but the world! what *will* people say? What will they think ?"

" That I should live to hear my Solomon, my Socrates, my Wisdom of all ages in one great living concrete! talk such utter, such puerile, such servile nonsense ! And pray, in the name of

all that's good, and just, and honest, does it
matter half a moat in a sun-beam, *what* that
brainless, heartless, superannuated old echo, the
world says or thinks about anyone or anything ?
Did it ever yet think or say, or even *know* the
truth about any human being, or of the events
and circumstances which, with their iron circles,
bind round the lives of human beings ? Does not
the world still go on calling that very worst and
vilest of all old women, Queen Elizabeth, " good
Queen Bess ?" I'm afraid poor Mary Stuart was
no better than she should be ; but then, her
horrible old Cousin Elizabeth was undeniably a
great deal worse than she ought to have been.
And poor Mary, whatever her sins, look at
her sufferings—the Holyrood tragedies, and
Lochlieven episodes, all pale before the long ages
of pin-sticking she must have endured from that
terrible termagant Bess, of Hardwick ; and I've
no doubt Mary Queen of Scots being guilty of
the unpardonable sin of great beauty, this old
virago, like her royal name-sake, and of course
champion, was jealous of Mary with her henpecked old noodle of a husband, Lord Shrews-
bury, and so meanly made the quantity of wine
used for Queen Mary's baths a stalking horse for
her fury. The world, indeed !—and from you,
Master Hartsfoot ! were *you* one of those sentimental *vaurien*, who must varnish their oblique

actions by fine phrases, which cost nothing, and
being everything in that great SHAM, the world,
I should have expected neither more nor less
from you than to make the said world your arbi-
trator. But though sentiment and principle are
generally confounded into a synonyme, by the
undiscerning mass, they are wide as the poles
asunder—you *have both*, but you properly keep
each in its own sphere. Sentiment is the virtue
of ideas, and principle the virtue of action;
sentiment has its seat in the head, principle in
the heart; sentiment suggests fine harangues
and subtile distinctions. Principle conceives
just notions, and performs good actions in
consequence of them. Sentiment refines away the
simplicity of truth, and the plainness and genuineness of religious convictions. Sentiment may
be called the Athenian, who knows what is right,
and principle the Lacidemonian that practises it,
and in doing so, must fling the world and what
it will say over his shoulder, and cast them behind him. Still, the world being a potentate,
should—like all other potentates, however bad,
or little to be respected—be treated with due
deference; that is, in self respect, we should
never wantonly violate any of its established
rules or customs, or even prejudices; but when
it comes to a case of right and wrong between
the great triune Omniscience, God, our con-

science, and ourselves, we should put the world
out of court, from its utter incapacity to judge.
Oh! Master Hartsfoot, that you of all men,
knowing it so well, should talk of what the
world would say or think, more especially in
time-serving, mammon-worshipping England,
where you are well aware, that no matter how
infamous the man, or the woman either, for that
matter, so long as they have sufficient money to
give them sufficient position and power—and
money is *both*—they will not only be tolerated,
but adulated; their very infamy being apparently their patent for influence and impunity.
I am not invidious enough to be thinking only
of our own times, for it has always been so with
us, and always must be so in any country where
there is a rich, profligate, arrogant, irresponsible legislative oligarchy, and where the magnifi-
cence of the few, glares out like an inverted
funeral torch upon the squalid, abject, famished
misery of the many."*

Dorothy had gone on speaking and lashing

---

* Dorothy was pretty right, and yet in the teeth of such chronic
and damning facts to the contrary, we have the *aplomb* to call
England a moral country. Of course it would be libellous to give
any "modern instances" of the male and female *notorious* in-
famies that lead society in the present day; but we can, without
any scandal against Queen Elizabeth, take a look into our *moral*
past, which makes an admirable pendant to our equally *moral*
present. The Archbishop of Canterbury of that day preached the
funeral sermon of Nell Gwynne; and, indeed, poor pretty Nelly,
looking to what the Americans would call her "braughtens up,"
seemed to have had every virtue but the one, the want of which
à *l'Anglaise* made her famous instead of infamous. The really

herself into a sort of spurious vehemence, to give
Hartsfoot time to regain his composure, and also
to make the one subject she had at heart less
formidable when she resumed it.

"All you say is quite true," said he, ab-
stractedly, and then added, which showed that
he was still pondering the original topic, "but
would it not do if I were Captain Broderick's
best man ?"

"No, Mr. Killigrew is to be that.   I wonder,"
continued she, abruptly, "why they are called
the bridegroom's best men?   But I suppose the
real reason is that at so many weddings the bridegroom turns out to be the worst man."

Her companion smiled.   Dorothy fastened her
hood under her chin, put on her tortured gloves,
and feeling that desperate cases required desperate
remedies, got up, walked across the room, and
taking both his hands, said—

"Dear Master Hartsfoot, I won't plague you
any more now, but I shall be so very, very

infamous Anne Catley, at the close of her public life, married a
general officer, and as so often happens in *moral* England, was
not only received, but *fêtée* in what is called "the very best
society," alias the highest. Mrs. Oldfield, who was alternately the
mistress of Mainwaring and General Churchill, and intrigued
with dozens beside, "lived respected!" to quote her contemporaries, and was borne to her grave by Lords Harvey and Delawar,
and Babb Doddington, and Westminster Abbey was the place of
the virtuous matron's rest, while our morality is such that these
sacred precincts were refused to the ashes of Byron, while we
bepuff and beplaster the living corruption of men, compared to
whom, in point of morals, he was pure as an angel, and as virtuous as an anchorite, and at the blaze of whose genius they could
not light their farthing vesuvians.

miserable if we are to be broken up and separated after having been so united, so happy even when I was miserable ; and then my mother, my dear, good mother, she *ought* to have some *alter ego* when I go to mine ; some one to watch over, take care of her, and anticipate her wishes. The kindest, gentlest, best, most unselfish woman, could not do that as well as you; and, on the other hand, I know you still love her, for who could help doing so ?   And *don't*, dear, dear Master Hartsfoot, throw away your own happiness for a quibble, for a punctilio—for—for—well yes then, 'tell truth and shame the devil,' for an old grudge."

"Oh ! no, no ; there is no grudge.   There, indeed, you wrong me ; but—but—when the fresh young heart, flowing over with devotion, was rejected, will the poor withered one fare better, think you ?"

"Ah ! Master Hartsfoot, some withered things that tell of deep, undying love, have a priceless value.   I have a pansy that Gilbert gave me three long years ago ; it is all faded and discoloured now.   I think I must have kissed it to death, poor thing ; yet, I would not give it for all the fresh bright flowers that ever bloomed in Eden, or all the gems that ever sparkled out of Golconda.   Dear Master Hartsfoot," and she laid her hand upon his arm, and looked up be-

seechingly and wistfully into his face, as a dog
does who has no guile, and whose whole heart is
in its eyes, while the tears streamed down her
cheeks, "Dear Master Hartsfoot, try my mother
with *your* withered Heartsease? I will give you
a whole week before I see you again; but it is
my own selfish cause I am pleading. I never
yet found you fail in your truth; and remember
your promise—'*Ask, and you shall have.*'"

And before he could stop her, she had glided
through the glass door and was hurrying home
through the Mall. Hartsfoot stood like a man
in a dream; was it—could it be, that it depended
upon him to ask and have? All these years he
had never been anything but a human Hecla—
all ice without and fire within, and now the lava
came gushing out through his eyes, and he sobbed
aloud. This saved him; for no one can continue
at that weird high pressure of heart and brain,
without one or both giving way. He then dried
his eyes, gathered up all the *débris* of the poor
mutilated violets with which Dorothy had strewed
the table, sealed them up in a sheet of paper,
wrote something on the back of it, adding the
day, the hour, and the year, and locked it up in
a bureau, and had scarcely done so, before Pump
came in to lay the cloth for dinner.

"You need not do that, Pump; I don't want
any dinner. I am not well, and shall go and lie
down for an hour."

CHAPTER XIV.

IT was about five days after Dorothy's visit to Master Hartsfoot; she had not said a word to her mother on the subject, but occupied as she was with Gilbert, as the "week" she had allowed the former for "screwing his courage to the sticking point," was within three days of expiring, she became feverishly anxious about the result. She could not hear that he (Hartsfoot) had been at the house; she did not like to ask the servants point blank whether he had or not, and between her mother and herself, his name had been tabood, by tacit consent. On this fifth morning in question, Gilbert had been sent for by the King, and so Dorothy, being at liberty, was as usual anxious to look after her mother. She had sought, and not found her, in her own morning room, and was on her way to the drawing-room when she met Jessop in the corridor with a letter.

"For me, Jessop?" she asked, putting out her hand.

"No, Mistress Dorothy; it's for Madam. Master Hartsfoot is in the drawing-room; he and Madam came in together about ten minutes ago."

" Oh! give me the letter, Jessop, and I'll take it to her, as I am going to the drawing-room."

And she took the letter off the salver and pursued her way, while Jessop retraced his steps downstairs. Dorothy's heart beat so violently as to be quite audible by the time she reached the door, where she stood some seconds, not certainly with the intention of eaves-dropping, but because she was literally too nervous to open the door. If her intention had been to listen she would not have been rewarded in the proverbial way of listeners, that of hearing ill of herself, for she heard nothing. The silence was so profound that she began to think that Jessop had been mistaken, and that there was no one there; but not liking to remain listening outside the door, she at length turned the handle and entered. Was she mistaken, or in her confusion did she fancy that she had seen her mother's head lying upon Hartsfoot's shoulder? Be that as it might, they both started up on her entrance, Hartsfoot very pale, her mother very red; but affecting the most perfect *nonchalance,* and indeed blindness to all this, she held out her hand to Hartsfoot with an unconcerned—

" Good morning, Master Hartsfoot."

And then turning to her mother, said —

" A letter for you, dear, which I intercepted on the stairs, as Jessop was bringing it."

" Not for me," said Mrs. Neville, looking down upon the missive with considerable embarrassment.

" Yes," said Dorothy, reading the direction over her shoulder—the writing was almost print plainness—

> " To
> " Mistress Neville,
> " On The Mall,
> " St. James's Park,
> " London."

" Yes," said she, putting her arm round Dorothy's neck, and hiding her face on her bosom; " but I am no longer Mrs. Neville—I am now Mrs. Hartsfoot."

" Oh ! mother, now, indeed I am completely, and supremely, and terribly happy !"

And disengaging herself from her mother's embrace she threw her arms round Hartsfoot's neck, and kissing him on both cheeks said—

" My dear, good father, you shall find me the most dutiful, as I am already the most affectionate, of daughters."

" You will wonder at this, Thea," said her

mother; " but Oliver "—here the bridegroom
looked his unutterable thanks, for it was the first
time she had called him Oliver, and he felt that
now indeed she was his—" but Oliver wrote to
me four days ago, and told me his feelings ·to-
wards me were still the same ; mine were not,
for I had learnt to know his worth, and who
could do that without loving him ? And so—
and so—we were quietly married at St. James's
Church, at nine this morning."

" No, I wonder at nothing, except, mother,
that you did not marry him long ago. I am *so*
happy that unless I get the spotted fever, or
Gilbert the plague, or some other dreadful
calamity happens to pull me down, there will be
no bearing me, for unalloyed happiness is the
most insolent, overbearing thing in the world."

" As I firmly believe that the age of miracles
is past," said Hartsfoot, " I have no fear of anything of the kind ; and as I am no lover of
novelty, but rather a devotee of the past—"

" Except where past and present unite," interrupted Dorothy.

" As you say, except where the past and present unite," and he looked fondly at his wife.
" I am no lover of novelty, and therefore hope
never to see such a terrible change as that would
be."

" Well," said Dorothy, taking the unopened

letter out of her mother's hand, " as there is no Mrs. Neville to read this letter, I suppose Mistress Dorothy Neville will be the best substitute for her, and as there will soon be no such personage as Mistress Dorothy Neville, either, I had better make haste and do so, shall I?" she asked, looking at her mother, while she held the letter in abeyance before breaking the seal.

" By all means, dear."

And Dorothy opened the letter, and not recognising the writing, bold and clear as it was, she turned to the signature for information.

" Only think, mother, a letter from Bridget Barton !"

" Not written by herself, surely?"

" By her own, own self—let us hear what she says."

" MOST HONOURED MADAM,—

" I had hoped and intended to have writ you this at Christmas; but Madam Fairbrace, who in this way, has taken as much pains with me in spite of all my stupidity, as dear Mrs. Dorothy has in every other way—Mrs. Fairbrace, madam, did not think I could write quite plain enough to write to you, honoured madam. If I waited till I could tell plain enough all the gratitute, mother, Joe, and me feels to you, Mrs. Dorothy, and good Master Hartsfoot, I should

have to wait for ever. But having heard of
Captain Broderick's joyful return, and that Mrs.
Dorothy was to be married to him by the King's
command, I cannot wait any longer to tell how
glad mother and me is—' I will repay,' sayth the
Lord, which mother says means He will repay
for good as well as for evil—so what a load of
good He will have to repay you and Mrs. Dorothy,
madam—is my prayer. Mother says this letter
is full of bad grammar and faults, and not fit to
send to a lady like you ; but as I could not read
or write at all, madam, but for your dear Mrs.
Dorothy and Madam Fairbrace's goodness to me,
I think it more honester to show what I can do,
with all my faults, than to let Madam Fairbrace,
or mother, furbish and tidy up my letter, so as
to make it more fit to come into your presence.

" God bless and repay you, and Mrs. Dorothy
and Master Hartsfoot, madam,

> " From your humble,
>> " Most obedient,
>>> " And ever grateful servant,
>>>> " BRIDGET BARTON.

" The Gate Lodge,
> " At The Chestnus,
>> " Richmond, Surrey,
>>> " This 28th of February, 1671."

" Poor girl, it is really well written and put

together for her," said Mrs. Neville—we beg pardon, Mrs. Hartsfoot. While they were still discussing Bridget's letter, Gilbert came in.

"Captain Broderick," said Dorothy, rising with great ceremony, "allow me to have the honour of presenting to you two very dear relations of mine, with whom you are not acquainted; but when I say two relations, that is in a round about and supererogatory way of putting it, for they are in reality ONE. My father, Master Hartsfoot—Captain Broderick. My mother, Mrs. Hartsfoot—Captain Broderick."

"With all my heart and soul, I congratulate you, my dear sir," said Gilbert, shaking him cordially by the hand; and then turning to his mother-in-law elect, he added, "and you too, my dear madam; for though in most marriages there is not much reason for congratulating the wife, yet from all Dorothy has told me of Mr. Hartsfoot's rare and purely unselfish character, and his harmonious chime of high and noble qualities, I do think you are a rare and singularly happy exception."

"*Et moi donc, Monsieur?*" pouted Dorothy.

"Oh ! *you*," cried Gilbert, looking at her, with mingled adoration and veneration, as if his soul was kneeling in his eyes, "the man does not live who is worthy of *you*."

"Clearly," she said, putting her handkerchief

to her eyes and affecting to cry, " since the only man who ever *was* worthy of such—ahem!—perfection, was hanged about a fortnight ago, poor fellow !"

" And yet, strange to say," laughed Gilbert, " the extreme penalty of the law will not be inflicted upon the poor wretch till the fourteenth of next month."

"Ample time between this and then, to run away from such a dreadful fate," said Hartsfoot.

" He had better not attempt it," said Dorothy, " for I'll get another *ne exeat regno* from the King."

" By-the-bye, the King is to be on the Mall at four to-day. He graciously expressed a wish that you and I should be there, Thea, and don't you think it will be a good opportunity of announcing the marriage, and presenting Mr. and Mrs. Hartsfoot to him ?"

" Very good," replied Dorothy, " but there are other matters to be thought of first, and young people *are* so thoughtless," said she, tossing her head and glancing from her mother to Hartsfoot, " so we poor sensible, rational people ; that is, you and I, Captain Broderick, must attend to all the vulgar huckaback, work-a-day matters of fact, such as announcing to their respective households the marriage of Mr. and Mrs. Hartsfoot. You, Gilbert, as befits the superior gallantry and

courage of your superior sex, shall lead the for-
lorn hope, and brave the dangers of announcing
it below stairs, while I will undertake the safer
fatigue duty of confronting Mrs. Merrypin and
Mr. Pump."

"Oh! ten thousand, thousand thanks, dear
Dorothy," said Hartsfoot.

"Dorothy me! No Dorothy's, but give me
my proper and lawful title when you have occasion to address me, sir, and call me dear child,
for how can you expect me to fulfil my filial duties
if you do not set me the example of performing
your parental ones?"

"In reality, dear child, so proud and happy a
parent can never forget them."

"*À la bonneheure.* And now wait here
patiently, like good children, till we return from
publishing the banns."

And she and Gilbert left the room, he, to go and
announce to the servants below that their mistress had a new name, and she to put on her
things to confront, as she called it, Mrs. Merrypin; but she was scarcely outside the drawing-
room door before Hartsfoot called her back.

"You see," smiled he, "I lose no time in exer-
cising my paternal authority; but would you,
dear child, tell Mrs. Merrypin, Pump, and in fact
all of them, that I still retain them in my service; so that they will not have to seek a new

master, they will only have another and a better
home."

" To be sure," replied Dorothy, " and if that
old Tabby Ruffle shows her claws too sharply to
the new comers, why she must only ruffle it else-
where, *voila tout.*"

Gilbert was received with a perfect ovation in
the lower regions, which was rather augmented
when he proclaimed the tidings of which he was
the bearer, for Master Hartsfoot was an universal
favourite with the whole household; even Ruffle
had not a single valid objection to make to him,
with the exception of an *àrrière pensée* to the
effect that perhaps that now there was a real
master to the house she could not hope to continue to be her mistress's master quite so much
as she had been.   But all she said was, with her
hands crossed over her wrists as usual, after having echoed the other servants' congratulations—

" It would seem, Captain, as if I really spoke
prophetically, for on the night that your and Mistress Dorothy's approaching nuptials were announced "—she would not have used such a common, vulgar word as marriage for the world—
" I observed to Jessop that when once matrimony
got into a family there was no knowing where it
would stop."

" So, perhaps you'll be a changing of your
name from Mrs. Ruffle to Mrs. Smooth ; but I'm

sadly afeared it will be only the name and not the natur," put in Lancelot.

And Gilbert being also " sadly afeared" that he should laugh out loud, made good his retreat.

Dorothy meanwhile, was " doing her spiriting" as gently as might be ; she did not now steal in at the back door like a thief in the night, but went openly and respectably to the front door, and knocked clearly and authoritatively, as if she was " somebody," which Mr. Pump being deceived into thinking, by the tone, and altogether the style of the knock, put down his cuffs, himself hurried up stairs to answer it, and ordered Barton to fall back, so as only to let his buttons twinkle like stars in the distance, while he—Noah, the great aqueous luminary, shone out in the fore ground. When he saw who the visitor was, he could scarcely believe his eyes ; he was, if possible, even more taken aback than he had been when her mother had invaded that door more than two years and a half before.

"Is it possible! I have the honour of seeing Mistress Dorothy Neville? Well, madam, you must *ex*-cuse the liberty, but I never was so glad in all my born days as when I heerd as the Cappen was found, and the King had settled it all as you and he was to be married. I'm not one—as my name might tell—as is given to 'toxication, but when I heered it, I says—says I, if so be as sack was a guinea a drop—which it's not, for the country would not stand *that*, whatsomever else it stands. Yes, I says, if sack was a guinea a drop, I'll have a whole pottle to drink the Cappen and Mistress Dorothy's health."

"Well, I hope you'll do so again, Pump," said Dorothy, laughing, and taking the hint by putting a couple of Jacobuses into his hand ; "more especially since I have come to tell you of another wedding. But first let me come in, and have the goodness to·ask Mrs. Merrypin to come to me."

"Aye—sure, ma'am," said he, opening wide the door of the state apartments, alias "the Cedar parlour," and having placed a chair for her, he went for Mrs. Merrypin, having told Dorothy his master was out.

"You are to come up immejet, Mrs. Merrypin, to speak to Mistress Dorothy Neville, who says she's got another wedding—that's another beside her own—to tell us on. Master's been out pretty well the whole morning ; sure-ly, it can't be none of them ere *saveons* as is married ? though who knows ? the devil has always plenty of unmarried daughters on hand."

"Do hold your tongue, Pump," said Mrs. Merrypin, as she put on a clean muslin apron with even a more elaborate tambour parterre than usual. "You ought to be ashamed of yourself, if you had any shame in you, to speak of your master's friends in that disrespectful manner."

And she hurried past him up the stairs, not to keep Mistress Dorothy waiting, though they both entered the room together, she curtseying, and he bowing down to the ground.

"How do you do, Mrs. Merrypin? I'm glad to see you looking so well. I suppose neither you nor Pump have any wish to leave Master Hartsfoot's service?"

"Leave his service!" echoed Mrs. Merrypin, looking quite frightened, "Heaven forbid! ma'am, for where should we ever find so good a master?"

"Where, indeed? He has no wish to part with any of you, I assure you; and you, I suppose, will have no objection to live with him in a larger house?"

"Oh! dear no, ma'am; nor in a smaller one either; anywhere he goes, I'm sure all of us will be content to go."

"Well, I have a great piece of news for you; Mr. Hartsfoot was married this morning."

"Married, ma'am?" almost shrieked Mrs. Merrypin.

"Married! Master Hartsfoot married! Well,

that *is* the greatest curosity of all; howsomedever it's a natrel curosity that, and not one of them there *saveon* devilries," echoed Pump.

" Yes," said Dorothy ; . " he was married to my mother this morning. You are no doubt aware that it is a very old attachment?"

" Oh! I *am* so glad," said Mrs. Merrypin, the tears gushing out of her eyes. " Poor, dear gentleman ; he who has passed his life in trying to make others happy, will now be happy at last. I don't say, ma'am, but what Madam Neville richly deserves the best of husbands, but this I *do* say, that she has got *the* very best man in all the world."

" I quite agree with you, Mrs. Merrypin," said Dorothy.

" Well, I am main glad, too," said Pump. " Master had always a hankering after everything old, and now he's got his old love ; and best of all, now he's got a missus, I'm in hopes she'll rid the premises of them there *saveons,* as a ferrit drives away rats."

" You ought to be ashamed of yourself, Noah Pump, comparing Madam Hartsfoot to a ferrit."

" I didn't do no such think, Alice Merrypin ; I only compared the *saveons* to rats, drat 'em."

" I must go now," said Dorothy ; " but have the goodness to tell Barton, Mrs. Merrypin, and the maids."

And when Barton was told, he was in the seventh heaven to think that he should pass so much time with his mother and sister, and at that beautiful place The Chestnuts, so that altogether this was a happy day for everyone, and the bride and bridegroom felt considerably happier when the ice had been broken for them, and their marriage had been duly announced. But in the midst of his new found happiness Master Hartsfoot did not change his nature and forget his less happy friends. After dinner, before they went on the Mall he went to his old house, and wrote the following note, sending with it £200 by Barton—

"My dear Hollar,

"I know you will rejoice with me and be glad, when I tell you that I am now the happiest man in the world, having married this morning a lady whom I have loved all my life. I do not send you any bride cake, because there is none, everything having been done in such a hurry. I have a vague idea that I am in your debt for sundry etchings ; the accompanying instalment may suffice till you can come and see me at Richmond in the summer, when we can regulate our accounts. Till then *vale*.

"And believe me,

"Ever your faithful friend,

"Oliver Hartsfoot."

He had of course to go through the ordeal of his servants' congratulations. Mrs. Merrypin's he received cordially, as they were given, but Mr. Pump's were, as might be expected, very trying. However, Master Hartsfoot was now so happy that he felt equal to far severer ordeals, a conclusion which he came to as he dressed for the Mall, in all the bravery befitting his new *rôle* of benedict, though he only exchanged his chronic black for a rich, grave, murray coloured velvet, all the display being in the richness and rareness of his point lace. The magnificent "beaver" of Holden's, which used to set Mr. Pump groaning and prophesying destruction every time it ventured under a cloud, was also discarded for a black velvet hat and a plain white ostrich feather. Altogether, not only upon the "fine feathers making fine birds" principle, but because happiness *is* such a beautifier, and the real and only *eau de Jouvence.* Hartsfoot in his dainty attire looked at least ten years younger, and so handsome, which Dorothy did not scruple to tell him. His wife said nothing, but a strange diorama of bygone years came crowding the whole arena of her memory, and she wondered where her eyes, her judgment, or her taste had been, when Hartsfoot had *been* what he looked so strangely *like* now ? She may have told him something of all this afterwards, but we have no business to go prying into private conversations of this nature, and if she said nothing to him now, still there was not a prouder or happier woman in England as she walked up the Mall leaning upon her husband, and looking at her daughter, who walked before with her handsome and *distingué* looking *fiancé*. The King and his suite were at the other end of the walk, as usual, laughing and talking. Ah! could a country only be ruled by laughing, and talking, and *jeux d'esprit*, how well England would have been governed at the restoration. However, to this day, it appears to be considered that the chief art ·of legislation consists in *talking*.

"How came it," said the King, to Rochester, "that the Duke of York failed us at the play last night, when we had promised Dryden to muster in full force?"

"Why, a man can't be ubiquitous; and did not your Majesty hear that 'Thomas Otter' had his own private theatricals at home?—rather trenching upon tragedy, for Mrs. Otter* actually saw a pair of green stockings, with feet in them, and shoes on them, coming out of Thomas's dressing-room! and it is the town talk to-day."

---

* So the Courtiers called the Duchess of York, imitating the King, in his *sobriquet* of Thomas Otter, for his brother, that being the name of the henpecked husband in the play of "Epicine; or, the silent woman."

" In short," laughed the King, " *les bas verts ont fait parler les bavards.*"

" *Le mot, sire, et plus joli, que le cancan,*" said Killigrew.

" By-the-bye," asked the King, " has any one heard how Albemarle is to-day ?"

" Ah ! I thought he must have been ill, by his being at early prayers this morning, for, as we all know,

' When the devil was ill, the devil a saint would be,'

&c., &c., &c. But what's been the matter with him ?" asked Rochester.

" He's not been ill, but he was, as usual, so drunk at his own house after supper last night," said the King, " that he rolled under the table, and was very nearly choked before they could loosen his bands,* and fore George ! it was too bad of you, Kil, for I heard you walked off and refused to help them to carry him up to bed."

" There were plenty of them to do it without me," replied Killigrew. " And, does your Majesty think that I have no fear of all the ' No Popery Acts' before my eyes, that I should run the risk of being found assisting at the elevation of the host ?"

" Ha ! ha ! ha !" laughed the King. " Well, at all events, you deserve absolution for that ! But, oddsfish ! here comes my dainty little Mis-

* Cravat, then called lace bands.

tress Dorothy, like a whole parterre of blush
roses, with her *beau pendu* of a *fiancé*, young
Broderick.   But who is the good-looking gallant
Mistress Neville is leaning upon ?—a marvellous
proper gentleman, upon my word ; but I don't
know him."

  " He is a right good fellow, too, in his way,
though that is not exactly in *ours*," said Killigrew.   " He is one, Master Oliver Hartsfoot—
all books and science—a great friend of my Lord
Worcester, Mr. Locke, Mr. Evelyn, and all that
set of retired respectabilities.   But I never saw
him in anything like such brave attire before ;
he is quite *point de vice*, and a lady leaning on
his arm.   Why, Worcester must have added another century of inventions to his original one,
to have brought *that* about ; for, as regards the
sex, he was thought to be a perfect Monk of
Mount Athos—*not* a Monk of the Albemarle
order.   But, *zito ! zito !* here they come."

  The King raised his hat, hoped they were quite
well, and had not suffered from witnessing the
execution the other night?   " They say," added
his Majesty, with all the florid complimentary
hyperbole then in vogue, " that two suns cannot
shine in one hemisphere ; but astronomers
should be set right on this point, by being
allowed to see Mistress Neville and Mistress
Dorothy together."

" Your Majesty," bowed Gilbert, " has made one little error in your astronomical calculations from the Royal Observatory ; there is no longer a Mistress Neville ; this is Mistress Hartsfoot, the wife of this gentleman, Master Hartsfoot."

" I thank you, my young friend, for setting me right," and after shaking hands with the newly married pair and congratulating them, he turned to Mrs. Hartsfoot and said—

" Mistress Dorothy is much beholden to you, madam ; for one good example is worth a hundred good precepts."

" Ah ! poor man," said Rochester, aside to Killigrew, " how fortunate that *he* is the spokesman ; for had anyone else uttered such a piece of satirical high treason in the presence, he would not have been long before he had seen the inside of the Tower."

While the bipeds were saying their say, the dogs also had their parley. Penderel and Beauty took the initiative, as it was only fit that royal dogs should do. Penderel running with great alacrity to meet Diamond, till within ten yards of each other, when prudence, like " the Queen's Proctor," intervening in the modern Divorce Court, each gentleman stood still, raising his right front paw, which each held in abeyance, pricking up their ears and wagging their tails tremendously ; while the two young ladies, *Mesdemoi-*

selles Beauty and Finette, true to the *one* privilege of their sex, announced their advent by their
tongues, and barked most shrilly.   At last, Penderel having approached, and had a most satisfactory conversation with Diamond, suddenly
perceived Dorothy, and remembering the evening
he had passed so comfortably in her lap, he
immediately ran, with bounding fore-paws, and
paid his respects to her.

" I declare," said she, pulling his beautiful
long ears and kissing his head, " that darling
dog remembers me."

" Do you suppose, Mistress Dorothy," said the
King, " that any lucky dog in England, who had
once seen you, could ever forget you ?"

" More especially," said Rochester, " when it
is a case of like master like man—whew ! whew !
whew !" added he, whistling the dog. " Penderel,
my man, come here."

If Dorothy had been like a blush rose on her
arrival, she was now much more like a damask
rose, and felt exceedingly uncomfortable, which
Gilbert perceiving, he raised his hat, and bowing
low to the King, said—

" I fear we have detained your Majesty too long
under these damp trees."

" Never mind," said the King, as he, with a
very graceful sort of circular bow, returned all
their parting salutations at once ; " on the four-

teenth, my fine fellow, we shall be double and quits, for I shall detain *you* for life."

"My gratitude, at all events, sire," rejoined Gilbert, again bowing low, as they turned away, and retraced their steps homeward.

CONCLUSION.

ND what conclusion can we come to, when four persons, who loved each other so very dearly, and respected one another equally, were about to pass the remainder of their lives together, but that they had entered upon a term of happiness, which only death could change for a still more blissful eternity? As for Hartsfoot, without putting it into words, he every day in thought anticipated Merivale's verdict, and asked his full contented soul, " What is a home without a wife? She is the lamp that destroys darkness, the angel putting loneliness to flight, and is, or may be, the dispenser of every blessing that the mind of man can conceive or the soul sigh for. Home without a wife is ' a strange land,' a head without a brain, a heart without conscience, a ship without sails, an ocean without waves, a world without religion, a heaven without God !''

He said all this, or something tantamount to it, to Dorothy, on the eventful morning of the fourteenth of March, just before the carriage was announced to take them to the Chapel Royal, when she, in her snowy bridal attire, and her almost equally white pure face, looked really very like what he always called her, his " guardian angel."

" Then," said she, after this outbreak, " what a heathen you must have been all your life, and what a mercy you did not die in your sins."

" A mercy indeed! and but for you, my guardian angel, I should."

" Ah! well, then, mind," said she, looking fondly at her mother, " that now I am for a short time going to give up my garrison, you act as if I were always at my post."

" Being now in heaven, I *can't* go wrong," said he.

" Have you no flowers, darling ?" asked her mother.

" As no one has sent me any I shall not wear any ; but I am not without a posey, for all that, though some fastidious mortals want their flowers to be like news, always fresh, I'm not so nice," said she, looking at Hartsfoot and taking a little gold heart locket out of her bosom, she opened it and showed them, with its colours still wonderfully preserved, being pressed flat between two pieces of tissue paper, a faded pansey. " Here is *my* withered heartsease," she added, showing it to Hartsfoot.

" Yes," said he, the tears in his eyes, while he

put his arm round his wife's waist and kissed her, " and like mine you are now going to exchange it for some that can never wither."

As he spoke, Jessop came into the room to say the coach was at the door, and with two bouquets of white flowers and a largish packet tied with white and silver ribbons.

" This package from her majesty, ma'am," said Jessop ; " this bouquet," pointing to one entirely composed of jessamine, with a diamond dove, the wings of which fluttered in the centre of the flowers, as if just about to fly, " this bouquet is from Captain Broderick ; this one," pointing to the other, which was composed of flowering myrtle and orange blossoms, with four large bees in brilliants hovering round it, " this one is from the King, ma'am."

" *L'embarras des richesses, du moins, l'embarras du choix,*" said Hartsfoot.

" *Du tout,*" rejoined Dorothy, placing Gilbert's bouquet in her bosom, " I shall carry his majesty's splendid one in my hand."

Mrs. Hartsfoot untied the package. It was a jewel case, covered with perfect velvet, with a bordering of gold *passemantrie* round it. Upon opening it, there sparkled before them a sort of coronal, to be worn at the back of the head round the plait; it was composed of large brilliant stars of alternate stars of sapphires and stars of dia-

monds, which, being set loose to swing like a
toiletglass, were excessively brilliant and meteoric
in their scintillations; each star was divided by
white lilies, formed of fine large pearls. From
one of the stars was appended a paper, upon
which was written, in the Queen's hand—

" *Vous êtes la plus belle. Avec bien de bons
voeux, pour chère Mistress Broderick, de la part
de son dévouée.*

" KATHERINE R."

" Oh, how lovely!" they all exclaimed. " You
must wear it, Thea."

" Of course," said she, seating herself, for her
mother to fasten it round her hair.

" Now, indeed, you do look a complete guardian angel!" said Hartsfoot, " and as if, in rushing through a starry hedge, as you flew through
the spheres, you had carried off some of the stars
in your hair. The illusion would be quite perfect
if you did not keep your wings so closely folded
out of sight."

" *Andiamo, Padre Mio,*" said she, holding out
her hand to him, " for I shall fall in love with
myself if I keep star-gazing any longer."

And they all descended the stairs; a crowd as
usual—even in those days—round the door to see
the bride depart.

" Good luck, Mistress Dorothy! May as many

blessings attend you as there are minutes in the year," shouted many voices as the carriage drove off. "That all?" cried one man. "As many as there are in a hundred years, which is the age I hope you'll live to."

Their Majesties, and all the invited guests, were assembled in the gallery next to the Chapel Royal, including Dr. Fairbrace, who was to tie the knot, which one clergyman managed to do in those days, without being "assisted" by anyone. Also his brother James, who was speaking to the bridegroom when the bride arrived. She, of course, first paid her respects to the King and Queen, and endeavoured to thank them for their magnificent gifts.

"Ah!" said the King, parrying her thanks, and looking at her coronal of stars, "*La reine avait raison, car on voit souvant des etoiles qui filent, mais jamais auparavent, une fille qui devient etoile!*"

The King then gave the signal to proceed to the Chapel, and for the ceremony to begin. Doctor Fairbrace read, or rather pronounced the service solemnly and impressively ; the bride and bridegroom spoke the responses audibly and firmly. Hartsfoot also did his part well, and gave away the bride resolutely, and not the least grudgingly. Dorothy had determined that there should be no tears shed ; but still there were, for are there not tears of joy as well as of sorrow? only the former are so seldom required, that it is no wonder there are few experts who can distinguish them from the latter. At length the irrevocable words were spoken, and they twain rose up one.

The King upbraided Mistress Broderick for her singularly shabby trick of running away down to Clumber Chase on that very day, and leaving them all to get through the bridal festivities as they could—in short, as he said, leaving them the system, but taking away the sun.

"And you, you poor wretch," said he, turning to Gilbert, "it's too late now to bid you—beware the ides of March!"

"With such brides of March, he may defy all the ides in the world," said Killigrew.

The latter, who never could resist either fun or mischief, much less both combined, having heard of the wooing of Sir Augus Tullibardin—for, indeed, the latter had been so sure of his ultimate success, that he himself, by sound of his French-horn, had been the first to proclaim it everywhere, or otherwise the secret would never have been divulged to this day.

So Killigrew, having heard of it, with the rest of the town, sent him, as Master of the Revels, a polite invitation to Mistress Dorothy Neville's wedding.

Sir Angus raved, foamed, and stormed, and swore that he would take an early opportunity of *chase*-tising that imp*ear*tinent *Jacke*-anapes *Kee*lligrew; and as veracious historians we are bound to confess, that all the " demmed vairlets " in his establishment led a terrible life of it for several weeks after.

It is a trick people have of always accounting for events, and more especially for catastrophes and *contretems*, upon some pet hypothesis of their own, and whenever the end of the world does take place, each individual who happens to be in it at the time, will attribute the immediate occurrence of that long pending event, to some special theory of his, or her, own. Consequently Mrs. Alice Throckmorton, to her dying day, persisted in laying the failure of her nephew's suit, upon his unpardonable oversight in having left his violin in Scotland, for, as she was wont to observe—

"The theorbo and the French horn were all very well, but a beau was nothing without a fiddle, any more than a fiddle was without a bow."

When people are thoroughly and completely happy, there is nothing more to be said about them, except that we are glad to be able to state, that both Mistress Hartsfoot and Mistress Broderick, went on as they began, and continued so;

while their two chosen life-companions never got quite up in their *rôle* of husband, as they stumbled at the threshold, and continued lovers all their lives, the elder couple being no wiser in this respect, than the poor young fools. As for Gilbert, he never looked at his wife for years and years, after, but he seemed to be saying, in that ocular language in which lovers are so proficient—

> " Oh ! that voice of music, and the tender
> Light of fond thought upon her peerless face !
> Oh ! wondrous curls, burnish'd with deeper splendour !
> Oh ! motions harmonis'd with subtlest grace !"

But then he was a poet, so there is every allowance to be made for his deficiency in common sense. Yet despite his being a poet—he continued to serve, and to do credit to the REAL ; and so fully deserved his Saxon name of GILBERT, which means bright as gold. And if Master Hartsfoot's happiness came to him only towards the evening of life, we have the consolation of Martial's assertion—

> " *Ampliat ætatis spatium sibi vir bonus : hoc est*
> *Vivere bis, vitâ posse priore frui.*"

One more circumstance we may as well note, which was, that every year of their lives, whether they were with Master and Mistress Hartsfoot in the house on the Mall, or at The Chestnuts, or that Master and Mistress Hartsfoot were with them at Clumber Chase—for it was always either the one or the other—regularly on the fourteenth of February, there was a great feast, when the King's health was the first toast, invariably followed by that of—

"MY AUNT PHILLIDA'S RED WORSTED BED AND ALL THE HANGINGS !"

And it is very certain that both Dorothy and Gilbert, in their henceforward happy journey through life, took a leaf out of Killigrew's book, and where their less fortunate fellow-creatures were to be served, never forgot that, even without a friend at Court—

WHERE THERE'S A WILL THERE'S A WAY ;

AND FAIR PLAY IS ALWAYS BEST AGAINST FOUL.

THE END.